The Lady Godiva Murder

The Lady Godiva Murder

Laurie Moore

Five Star • Waterville, Maine

This novel is a work of fiction. Names, characters, places and incidents are either the product of the author's imagination, or, if real, used fictitiously.

Five Star First Edition Mystery Series.
First Printing

Published in 2002 in conjunction with Tekno Books and Ed Gorman.

Set in 11 pt. Plantin.

Printed in the United States on permanent paper.

Library of Congress Cataloging-in-Publication Data

Moore, Laurie.
    The Lady Godiva murder / Laurie Moore.
        p. cm.—(Five Star first edition mystery series)
        ISBN 0-7862-4827-0 (hc : alk. paper)
        1. Police—Texas—Fort Worth—Fiction. 2. Fort Worth (Tex.)—Fiction. 3. Policewomen—Fiction. I. Title. II. Series.
    PS3613.O564 L3 2002
    813′.6—dc21   2002029967

For my daughter, Laura Katherine, the light of my life.

Acknowledgements

I want to thank Hazel Rumney and Mary Smith of Five Star, my editor Kristi Holl and all of the wonderful people at Tekno Books for their interest in my law enforcement series. Without them, you would not be reading this. To Jim Varnon, the finest crime scene detective in Fort Worth and the Great State of Texas, your friendship is priceless. To Judge Pat Ferchill and Judge Steve M. King, for appointing me to represent mental patients, you gave me the opportunity to acquire invaluable insight into the world of mental illness. To my mother, who had the wisdom to let me experience college life in a Jewish dorm. And, finally, to my loyal following of friends and colleagues at the DFW Writers Workshop who, for ten years, listened to me read from my novels, thank you for making me a better storyteller.

Prologue

A practical joke.

At least that's how it sounded to rookie patrol officer Cézanne Martin when the dispatcher put the call out over the radio, it being April first. Some deal about gang bangers at the laundromat.

But when she ended up being the first squad car to roll around the corner, the juvenile delinquents looked to be more in their twenties. And their colors, red-laced track shoes and red and black T-shirts identified them as River Bottom Kings. A bit odd since everybody on Northside knew Miami staked a claim to this turf with graffiti. And the RBKs didn't scatter as soon as the patrol car bounced up the incline and into the parking lot.

They stayed put.

False bravado, maybe.

The rookie nudged her elbow against the holster snap until she felt it give. With neck hair prickling, she waited a few anxious seconds for her "assist"—a new dispatcher dishing out calls assigned that sot, Roby Tyson, to back her up. Tyson wasn't even on her Sector, for God's sake. He worked deep East.

Son of a bitch was probably sneaking moonshine out of that flask everybody but The Brass knew he stashed down one boot. Or knocking a piece off some streetwalker in a back alley behind East Lancaster instead of busting-up dice games. The troops knew about that, too, but nobody had

7

the cods to squeal on the rat-bastard.

A by-product of membership in *The Brotherhood.*

A reflected haze of orangy-purple shrouded the Fort Worth sky while gangster-eyes bulged in their sockets like partial eclipses. When Sorry-Roby-Tyson didn't screech up in a respectable amount of seconds she did what any rookie would do.

Barge through the crowd like somebody bulletproof.

"Officer Martin, Fort Worth Police," she announced to a group of five. "Everybody back."

She strutted into the washateria and they let her. Followed her inside, even. They flashed gang signs with their hands and muttered insults in Spanish, names she'd heard veteran hotheads called just before pulling their blackjacks.

She tried to keep her voice even and metered.

Show no fear.

Cops got their tickets canceled all the time over less provocation than this.

"Who called the police?" She glanced at three more Hispanics seated on top of the washers.

Nobody answered.

She cleared her throat and tried out her pigeon Spanish—"*¿Policía? ¿Quién?*"—and still drew blank looks.

One thing for sure, no illegal alien reached twenty-some-odd years old in Cowtown without learning a smattering of English. And the only other attention-getters she knew were *la migra* and *el cárcel.* Wetbacks tended to flee at the mention of Immigration and jail. The rest of her Spanish was enough to start a fight.

"Who called the cops?"

Without a word, their eyes moved in a collective shift to the only industrial clothes dryer running.

Thunk-swish-thunk-swish-thunk-swish.

She'd see about this shit. And where the hell was Tyson, anyway? Ten-to-one, rumor was true—there was only one reason Roby Tyson was still on the force. He'd either caught some headhunter in Internal Affairs in bed with a dead girl or a live boy. Well who needed the bastard?

Okay, she did.

Safety in numbers and all that tommy-rot. No wonder somebody coined the phrase, "One riot, one Ranger." Poor schmuck had an invisible backup like Roby Tyson.

She quit fuming long enough to check out what had stirred up the ant bed.

Thunk-swish-thunk-swish-thunk-swish.

Colors twisted beyond the glass portal of the stainless steel dryer like wedges inside a kaleidoscope—shades of blue, shocking whites and that telltale Hershey bar brown —the mysterious hue that could only come from dried blood.

The rookie stared in horror.

Swiveled her head.

Vectored everyone's location in a glance.

"Nobody leaves this room." She keyed the hand-held radio. "Three-Oh-Three, what's your location?"

"I'm coming." A roguish inflection in his gravelly voice.

Stinking sex fiend. He better mean en route.

A few River Bottom Kings slipped in and draped themselves across empty washing machines. Propped themselves against dirty walls. Plopped into beat-up plastic chairs, looking bored and contemptuous.

"I seen you before," said one gangly puke through a smirk.

"I doubt it. What do you know about this deal?"

"*Sí.* You look familiar." He snapped his fingers as if to shift the mind into low gear more easily. "You hang out at *Bandito Tejáno?*"

How revolting.

The baddest pachuco she'd ever slapped cuffs on wouldn't enter that hellhole. According to street rumor, when customers got stabbed, the proprietor, a swarthy, marble-toothed man with graveyard breath and a nasty Fu-Manchu drooping over his upper lip, rolled them out the back door into the ditch across the county line.

Her heart picked up its pace. She pointed to the dryer.

"Who's going to tell me about this?" She turned her back long enough to study the mesmerizing spin.

The mouthy one pulled at the fine, sparse growth on the point of his chin. "Not Bandito Tejáno," he said, "but I seen you before."

"Whaddya think, Duchess?"

The abrupt presence of Roby Tyson swarmed over her, his words vibrating like a thousand angry bees. Sniffing the essence of a backwoodsy Arkansas still on his breath, she ignored the sarcasm.

She hadn't even noticed him enter the building.

Which meant she'd gotten sloppy.

Otherwise, she'd have seen him swagger in puffing on that nasty cigar like he'd just had the best sex in his life, the son of a bitch. And her attending law school part-time, living like a Trappist Monk. Jesus H. No wonder the guys razzed her about being cranky, not getting any.

Thunk-swish-thunk-swish-thunk-swish.

A severed human hand tumbled against the glass.

A mousey squeak escaped her lips. A mass of black curls fell into the natural orbit and disappeared into the swirling vortex. She blinked, realized her mouth hung open and clamped it shut. When the unmistakable flash of a foot streaked the glass and vanished, she collected her wits and croaked out her conclusion.

"There's a body in there."

" 'Pears so."

Roby Tyson took a deep, unfazed breath, rocked on his heels and belched out an invisible fireball. He stuck his thumbs in the Sam Browne belt bunching the police gear around his doughy middle, and his rheumy gray eyes narrowed into slits.

"You waitin' for the cycle to run down, Duchess?" He stood tall, cocky and jaded, as if he had seen it all.

She twisted enough to permit him a clear view of her name tag.

C. R. MARTIN.

Officer Martin, to him. Maybe even Cézanne, if he ever drew himself up out of the primordial ooze long enough to evolve into a civilized man. With him and his ilk, she'd settle for, "Hey-you."

"What we need is a Crime Scene detective," she snapped. Even a rookie didn't have to take shit off a boozer. "To print the button and door handle. And the Medical Examiner. And Homicide."

She reached for the microphone clipped to one shirt pocket. Roby clasped a meaty hand over hers and held it.

"Well, now, that's a mighty fine idea. They teach you that in rookie-school?"

" 'Preserve the crime scene,' that's what the instructors said. That's all I'm saying."

Thunk-swish-thunk-swish-thunk-swish.

He stared, grim-faced. "According to the little red numbers lit up, we got about fifteen minutes if you want to

11

make sure she's dry."

Enough.

Obviously, opinions differed. He'd win anyway, he'd been on the force longer. Let him take over the damned call, territorial mongrel. Jesus. Couldn't even do the job without some asshole always interfering.

"Fine. You're senior, you handle it. I'll take the *assist*."

"Nope. You were first on-scene. It's yours. I don't do paperwork."

She wanted to ask if that was because he was illiterate, but somewhere during the bickering, River Bottom Kings had gathered behind them in a crescent. Roby whipped around, unsnapped his holster and brandished a .45.

"Get back, *Chingaderos*. *Manos arríba*."

Eight pairs of hands reached for the sky.

Cézanne leaned in closer than she wanted. "What the heck did you just say?"

"I dunno," Roby growled out of the side of his mouth. "I saw it in a Butch Cassidy movie."

"You're psycho," she hissed. "Are you trying to get us killed or do you have a plan?"

Sixteen eyeballs sparked hatred.

"You're the one itchin' to get wasted. Didn't those ya-hoos at the police academy tell you never to turn your back on thugs? Christ-in-a-sidecar. I reckon I need a transfer out to the academy. Teach you rookies survival tactics."

"They wouldn't take you."

Roby squared his shoulders, accepted the challenge.

"You want the fucker printed before you open the door, fine, print it," he snarled, "but we're not hassling the Crime Scene boys 'til we see exactly what we've got."

Thunk-swish-thunk-swish-thunk-swish.

"What I see is a head and a hand and a foot flopping

around in a dryer," she said. "You don't see too many amputees running around—"

"That's profound. A non sequitur. And people call you *The Brain?*"

"I just meant somebody could lose a hand and foot and still be alive. But a head? No way." She quickly backtracked. "Except maybe you. I see one sticking out of your neck but I'm not sure there's anything in it. So let's talk department policy. Standard operating procedure dictates we—"

"Fine." Roby whisked his hands through the air in mock surrender. "Go get your print kit, dust the little red dot, dust the handle, dust the whole goddam thing if you want, but hoof it. I got plans and I'm not sittin' out the rest of the night up to my gonads in paperwork. And you're taggin' the evidence." He sliced a finger through the air. "Git."

She trotted to the car and snatched up the fingerprint kit, certain that even seasoned officers didn't want Tyson around mucking up calls. One damned thing for sure, she'd never ever work with the unreliable skunk once she put in her time on the street and made Detective. No way. Son of a bitch could pickle his liver, screw everything between here and the Trinity River 'til his dick dropped off, far as she was concerned. But no way would anybody ever partner her up with the likes of him.

She returned to find Roby bee-essing with the River Bottom Kings, having a back-slapping, good time. Matter of fact, in her short absence, they'd become asshole buddies.

"You still window peepin', Julio?" he asked the mouthy one.

Roby called all Latinos "Julio". A little pejorative to establish *¿quién es mas macho?*—who's boss.

"Let's see." He licked his thumb before flipping through a pocket spiral notebook. "Didn't I bust you a couple of years ago window peepin' in Rosen Heights? Yep, says here I did. And I told you to get outta Dodge 'cause that's my beat, didn't I?"

"*Sí.*"

"Well, where-ya doing your window peepin' now? Or are you in the big league, pulling rape offenses?"

Cézanne shuddered beneath the heat of the bulletproof vest. She hoisted the kit onto the nearest table, popped open the fingerprint powder canister and touched the feather brush to the dust. With the flair of an orchestra conductor, she whisked it over the glass portal. Dozens of latent prints surfaced.

Nearby, Roby persisted. "You graduate to diddlin' women without their consent, or are you still just peepin'?"

"Just peeping. I don't have to force nothin'. They give it up free." Julio thumbed his armpits with pride.

Cézanne glanced at Roby in time to see him touch the tip of a ballpoint pen to his tongue. She rolled her eyes in disgust and swiped the metal door handle, then, the thumb button.

Bingo.

Prints appeared like Banquo's ghost. Slapping pieces of transparent tape over them, she peeled back the strips and transferred the evidence onto blank cards.

"So now that you've taken your act on the road, where is it you're peepin'?"

Chuckles rumbled through the pack.

"Mostly on Westside."

Cézanne pricked up her ears. She lived on the West side.

"Yeah? Whereabouts on Westside?"

She cocked her head to hear better, with her stare focused on the tumble of clothes." 'Round Crestline—"

Her street T-d into Crestline.

"—near Ashland."

She lived one block over.

"You been peepin' on Tremont?"

"*Sí.*"

"Where else?"

"Western Avenue."

For God's sake, not Western.

Cézanne cringed.

"So, you like watchin' ladies strip down to their skivvies?"

"*Sí.*"

Miserable hyenas, yukking it up.

"Get your jollies that way, do ya?"

No answer. Her ears honed in with the intensity of bat radar.

"So, whatcha like lookin' at best?"

"*Cheeches.* You know, Man, tits. There was this one lady on Western I used to watch all the time, used to sit in her magnolia tree over by the bedroom window and watch her put on a show."

"Think she knew you were watchin'?"

"I dunno. Some do. This one wore her hair in a braid. Pinned up."

Cézanne grimaced. She could feel their eyes practically unraveling the French braid loosely gathering her coffee colored hair.

"She'd take it down and shake her head, then pull her shirt off. You know, prance around? And I'd—"

"Let me guess. Nose pressed to the windowpane, foggin' up the glass, whippin' the ol' thoroughbred with the ridin' crop?"

The Boys Club let loose some real knee slappers.

Perverts.

"You got it all wrong. I mean, that was the plan. But then she took off her bra. It was one of them *Miracle Bras,* you know, Man? The kind that scrunches up their cheeches so they look bigger—"

Cézanne whipped around.

"Goddammit, Tyson, are you gonna help me or not?"

"In a minute, Duchess." He turned to Julio. "You were saying she had a braid?"

She snorted in disgust and wrapped up the job.

When she'd carded and labeled each print, she turned to Roby—who happened to be holding a half-eaten Snickers from the vending machine—dispensing sidebar remarks. She wasn't so green she had to take guff off a man whose personnel file was so thick somebody could break their neck falling off it.

"You want to open it, Big Dog?" she said.

"It's your call, Hot Dog. You open it."

Peanut chunks stuck between his teeth. She decided not to tell him.

She took a deep breath and held it. She didn't need to smell the familiar odor of putrefied cabbage if she didn't have to. One good yank and the machine cut off. The drum made a half-revolution and stopped. Stained clothes tumbled out onto the floor.

Along with the severed hand.

Cézanne took a quick step back, experiencing the surreal swoon that came from an unholy combination of fascination and disgust. She dropped to one knee for a closer inspection. Her stomach somersaulted. Fingers poked out from the crotch of yellowed panties, the skin pasty-white and hideous. Nails removed, Lord have mercy. Drained of blood, except at the ragged cut.

It looked—

—it looked like—

—it looked like latex.

The dawning discovery timed perfectly with the guffaws of the River Bottom Kings.

Ha-ha. Gotcha. April fool, Motherfucker.

With the heat of humiliation rising to her cheeks, she stood and faced them. Roby kept munching like a huge square-headed dog with a chew-bone.

"That's cute," she said, fake smile in place. "I like that. That's a real hoot." She paused long enough to cast Roby a voodoo curse with her eyes. "But let me tell you what's even funnier."

They sobered their expressions, all except Roby, who had propped himself against the detergent dispenser with his arms folded across his chest and a hyena grin angling up his sturdy jaw.

"The real stitch-splitter is, I've got fingerprints from the joker who did this. And once I run these through AFIS, I'm filing a false report charge." She beamed victorious, certain every last one of them could be located in the Automated Fingerprint Index System. "And when I graduate law school, pass the bar and hire on with the District Attorney's Office, I hope I'm the one who prosecutes you. So, April Fool to you."

With that, she packed up the kit and tossed a handful of blank cards onto the folding table, adding, "Here, Tyson, earn your keep. Take comparison prints on these jokers."

At the exit, she shot the most worthless officer on the force another wicked glare.

"Say, Duchess, before you go . . ."

"Officer Martin to you, Shithead."

"Officer Martin." He called her name softly, stroking his chin with his free hand, drawing the last of the candy bar through the air in a swashbuckling slice. "I'd like you to meet some of the guys from Vice. This here's Sergeant Herrera, Sergeant De La Fuente, Corporal Ortiz. . . ."

Chapter One

Six months after Detective Cézanne Martin graduated law school and sat for the bar, the ticking time-bomb Friday arrived when the Texas Board of Law Examiners released the test scores.

If she passed the bar and got her law license, she'd tell Captain Crane in Homicide to take the garbage he filed on her with Internal Affairs and choke on it. For that matter, the entire Fort Worth Police Department could butt a stump—except for her best friend and partner of two years, Roby Tyson.

Downtown, in the outlet mall parking lot located at the base of a steep-grade hill several blocks from police headquarters, Cézanne bailed out of her personal vehicle. She grabbed her briefcase, slammed the door of the aging BMW and angled toward an approaching trolley rocking along its rails. With any luck—something that seemed in short supply lately—she'd beat Crane into the office and still have enough time to make the dreaded phone call for the bar results.

With her face to the pine-scented breeze she lifted her wrist barely enough to note the time.

Seven-thirty-seven.

Jesus H, only twenty-three minutes. And Crane, the old goat, with the precision of an atomic clock.

She broke into a trot, clumsily battling the scarf whipping up from her neck. By the time she tucked the tie-ends down the front of her blouse and glanced over at the loading platform, the cable car screeched to a stop. The surly driver peering out from behind tinted glass sounded the warning bell.

Fifty feet away, max. And he wasn't going to wait.

Cézanne caught the glint of wheels as they began the slow revolution forward and did what any of Crane's troops would've done to dodge his fury. With the spirited grind of steel hanging between her ears, she flung herself into the shuttle's path.

She took the stairs to the loading dock in twos. Near the top, only the suck of air into her lungs filled her ears, punctuated by the rip of the kickpleat in her red gabardine skirt. Three more steps and she'd be home free. God only knew how long it would take another shuttle to show up.

Kind of like the men in her life.

A forbidden memory of Doug Driskoll popped into mind, his hair silvering at the temples and dampened against his forehead from a marathon of satisfaction. As she relived the lusty explosion of her final encounter with the Energizer-Bunny-of-Liars, the door of the cable car banged open.

With a fierce blink, she stood in the present, looking into the reptilian eyes of an unfamiliar face. A serpentine scar ran the length of the driver's jawbone, giving him a mug that would jam police radar.

"Thanks a lot." She averted her gaze when she felt herself mesmerized by the iridescent stretch of tissue bubbled up on his chin. "If I'm late again, I'll get days off."

He shifted his eyes to a sign above his head—DO NOT TALK TO DRIVER WHILE CAR IN MOTION—then, flattened his foot against the accelerator. The commuter bucked, sending her spinning onto one of two elongated bench seats running the length of the car. She hit the cushioned back support with a thud. They gathered speed, turning parked cars into a colorful smear. To ward off a bout of carsickness, she spent the rest of the white-knuckled ride studying the maniac's letterman jacket with the "National Rodeo Finals" logo embroidered across the back in dense, fuzzy yarn.

At the outlet mall, the final drop-off point a block and a half from the police station, Cézanne hurried to the intersection and froze. She knew in a glance the blue-and-white easing around the corner belonged to Doug Driskoll; the car had the number of Doug's patrol beat stenciled on the trunk. Ever since Internal Affairs made staying away from each other a condition of continued employment, she reacted the same way she always did when she glimpsed him outside his district, prowling the backroads for a chance encounter—instinctively ducked him. So, when he finally let off the brake lights and disappeared into traffic, she sneaked back to the curb and waited for the first of two signal lamps to cycle.

Her pager vibrated against her waist, and the secretary's phone number flashed on the digital display. Another homicide. Must be a beaut—the woman pounded in 911 after her extension. Better shift into high gear. An ominous cloud bank dogging Downtown from the south seemed to be closing in with alarming speed. Her first call on her first day back from a week's vacation may have occurred outdoors.

Roby lived by the motto: lost evidence, lost conviction. She crossed against the light and picked up her pace.

Across the street from the PD, the orange hand flashing in the traffic signal box hung in place, and she got the bar score jitters all over again. With blood thundering between her ears, she sealed her eyes shut and made a wish.

Every now and again, the roulette wheel falls on my day. Please, God, let this be mine.

Fort Worth Police Department headquarters, a multi-story brownstone located at the intersection of Taylor Street and West Belknap, jutted up from a hilltop too murderous for anyone out of condition to trudge. Detectives lucky enough to have offices with north or west windows could look past the Trinity River at the hardbodied recruits training at the police academy; those with southern exposures saw a steady flow of traffic or the coral-brick and verdigris-accented Justice Center that Tarrant County built catty-cornered to the station; windows to the east provided a bird's-eye view of the west wall of the old Criminal Courts Building, in bricks of a color best described as owl-dropping white.

Cézanne considered herself lucky. Within a fluorescent warehouse of partitioned offices, she and Roby shared a three-sided cubicle constructed of pre-formed frames up-holstered with insulated fabric, and *knew* people who had views of the north and west sides of Fort Worth.

Uniformed troops patrolling out of satellite stations referred to the downtown office as HQ; the detectives working inside called it *Three-fifty* for its address. And even though the glassed-in foyer appeared reasonably inviting from the street, the building had a kind of institutional quality no fresh paint job could cure; despite the interior fluorescents, the entrance remained dim.

Not to mention, it reeked of human misery.

Up the front steps and just inside the quadruple doors, Cézanne side-stepped a vagabond curled in a fetal position. After the local newspaper printed an article about mental illness and the plight of the homeless one Christmas, the

Chief decided to enhance public relations. He called "King's-X" on bitter winter nights, turning the first floor into a human carpet. It was the job of the Day Shift Watch Commander to run those taking advantage of any misplaced generosity out into the bite of dawn. And since other transients were still proned-out near the elevators, Cézanne figured she might not be the only one running late.

On the fourth floor, she hurried down a musky corridor to Homicide, past a chocolate cake the size of a Volkswagen on display outside Captain Crane's door.

A few feet shy of hers and Roby's cubicle, she recognized the western cut of her partner's jacket and his bow legs, even with his back turned. The-Man-Himself stood with one shoulder leaning against the entry near a makeshift cardboard shingle thumbtacked to the facing.

It read, DOGHOUSE; she didn't need to ask.

He presided over a wiry man with a limp moustache and a pack of Luckys rolled up in the sleeve of his frayed T-shirt. The man was seated in one of two chairs and instead of charging on in, Cézanne hung back and listened. Even after two years, she still picked up an occasional trick of the trade from Roby just by watching.

"Now lookie here, Fella," her partner said, "I'm doing you a favor letting you take up my time."

"Howzat?" A caterpillar brow shot up, and she noticed a small mole on the man's eyelid and absentmindedly wondered why he didn't have it removed when it looked so much like a tick. "You drag me outta bed, haul my ass down here and harp on me 'til my ears is buzzin', howzat doin' me a favor?"

Roby played it cool.

"If you did the crime, you definitely don't want to be talking to me. You need to call your lawyer. Get him to

23

come down, start working on your defense. So just tell me, do we need to phone some shyster to try and get you off?"

The man seemed to weigh his options in a styptic blink.

"On the other hand," Roby went on with mild encouragement, "if you didn't do it, it won't hurt you to talk to me. But remember now, only if you didn't do it. You can tell me what happened, and we'll clear this snafu up in a jiffy."

So much for the Fifth Amendment right against self-incrimination.

The rustle of fabric caught her ears, and she knew the man was shifting in his seat, fixing to spill his guts. Someday Roby would get burned. And judging by her own experience with Internal Affairs, if Captain Crane was the one igniting the flame, Roby would go up like a Buddist monk.

The suspect fumbled for his cigarettes. Roby broke the bad news.

"No smoking."

Bony shoulders sagged in defeat. Roby's prey tugged at the V-neck of the "T" as if it would improve his oxygen intake.

"I didn't mean to, you know. It's just—he came at me, Detective Tyson. I had to defend myself."

Roby handed over a blank confession sheet.

"Let's get it down on paper, Slick, just the way it happened so the DA don't go trying to put words in your mouth later. This way they'll know you was just protecting yourself."

She could almost hear the clang of metal doors slamming.

With the last cuff ratcheted on, Roby clapped a hand across the guy's shoulders the way he always did when he hauled people off to the cooler, and she knew it wouldn't be long before she could reach into her desk and pull out the floral air freshener to give the area a liberal misting.

"Hi ya, Zannie," he said marching his *collar* past, his cheeks wizened and flushed from the grin lighting up his face.

Or from last night's Jack Daniels.

"I told you not to call me that."

"What can I tell ya? It's gonna be a great day."

"For you, maybe. For me? I'm still on Captain Crane's 'Kill-With-Prejudice' list. Not to mention, I got a 911 page from Greta and it's fixing to rain, so see if you can't find somebody else to book this guy for you so we can get rolling."

For what seemed like the longest time, Cézanne sat at her desk staring at the phone, inwardly reasoning how delay only prolonged the agony. Seconds turned into minutes. She picked up the receiver, then eased it back down. What if she flunked?

There's a full bottle of Trazadone in the medicine cabinet.

She sure couldn't stay on at the PD, not with Crane always breathing fire and her career on life support ever since the IA investigation.

When Roby returned, he took a long look, let out a wolf whistle and reached for his overcoat. She knew by the leer, he was fixing to razz her about showing up for work in a skirt and blazer instead of the usual slacks and jacket.

"Nice legs." He leaned in for a closer inspection.

She ignored him and grabbed her purse. Thumbed her hand at the plainclothes officers gathering near the mouth of Crane's den and said, "Please tell me he's taking an early pension."

"Crane's sixty-three today," Roby explained, almost giddy. "He's waltzing with the Grim Reaper. Just think; two more birthdays and he's nothing but a picture on the retirement wall. That's what's put a smile on my face."

"Things're so screwed up around here if you *do* see someone smiling, he's bound to be schizophrenic."

Roby slung the coat, a camel hair she had never seen before, over one arm.

Somebody with good taste was picking out his clothes.

"What's the news on your bar card?"

"Line's busy," she said without energy. "I'll try later."

"Now." Steely eyes bore down on her like a double barrel shotgun.

"Let's just go."

"We can spare a couple more seconds. The body's not gonna get up and walk off. Dial."

With chills prickling the undersides of her arms, she took a deep breath and 'fessed up. "I'm scared to death."

Roby's huge, hairy paw cut the air. "You ain't scared of the Devil himself."

"I'll be the laughingstock of this department."

"You Jewish people do believe in the Devil, don't you?"

"No." Her neck muscles corrugated. "I do, though. They gave him a badge and promoted him to Captain, and we work for him."

She reached for the phone. A sharp pain caught behind one eye and held on. She drew her hand back and let it fall, limp, into her lap.

"What's going to happen to me if I failed?"

"You stay here with me and retake the test next time it's offered."

"How can I? Ever since I beat the IA investigation, Crane's been laying in wait. I swear to God I didn't know

26

Doug Driskoll was married. And if I did, I certainly wouldn't have slept with him in his bed, at his house."

"Handle Crane the way you'd treat a Rottweiler chasing you. Don't run."

Roby tossed the coat over the chair back, reached into his desk drawer, pulled out his back-up weapon—a .38 Smith and Wesson Chief's Special, five-shot stainless she would have arm wrestled him to the ground for—and stuffed it down one size-twelve ostrich boot.

"Let's quit doing the Cotton-Eyed Joe and get down to brass knuckles, Zannie. I want to know if you passed."

"Don't call me that." Lightheaded, she dialed the number.

The unexpected appearance of Greta Carr, a pixie-eared civilian employee and self-ordained office manager of Homicide, broke off their conversation when she waddled into the partition dressed in a mock tuxedo. Bearing a remarkable resemblance to a four-feet-eleven-inch penguin, she slid a pair of outdated granny glasses back into the pink dents on her nose and held out a scrap of paper.

Cézanne put down the receiver and took it.

"Homicide on Hemphill," Greta announced in her high-pitched whine. "Sounds like a hot-sheet place to me so you should feel pretty much at home, Tyson. The grunts are calling her *Lady Godiva*. They say it's a nasty one." She prissed out of the cubicle calling, "Nice to have you back, Cézanne. Looks like you caught some rays. Great tan," over her shoulder and grumbling asides of envy that could be heard long after her bouffant "do" bobbed out of sight.

Roby selected one of several throw-down neckties from a brass hook mounted between the sinister beads of an exploded Saddam Hussein bull's eye target. He lifted a tree trunk arm and noosed his neck with such vigor Cézanne had to duck.

"Hubba-hubba, Zan. Looks like that phone call's gonna have to wait. I don't like how the skies are clouding over." He whipped around and worked the rest of his hulk into the camel hair coat. "Seems you got a reprieve, Counselor."

"Try *stay of execution*."

A shadow fell across the desk, and she sensed Crane's unwelcome presence.

"Sue-zanne."

The balding, grizzle-faced Crane, enveloped in nose-tickling vapors of *Brut,* propped himself against the entry. He dusted chocolate crumbs off his moustache with a festive napkin, then smoothed what few white hairs remained above his ears and adjusted the handcuff tie tack holding an outlandish paisley captive against his shirt. For seemingly endless seconds, Crane did what he did best. Stared through shark eyes.

"Isn't today the day?" he asked in a voice made for needling. "Well, how'd you do?"

"Piece of cake," she lied.

"Still riding that high-horse, I see." Marginally relenting, he added, "Speaking of cake, there's some at the front. If there's any left when you get back, feel free."

He took his shadow and stalked off, but before he rounded the corner and disappeared into a new group of well-wishers he turned and started back toward them.

"I'll handle this, Pinocchio," Roby said under his breath.

Crane wilted her with a look. Then he turned the stiletto-eyed glare on Roby and jutted his chin in the direction of their exploding in-basket.

"You ever get that toxicology report back from the ME's office, Tyson? The arson over in Ryan Place? The one

28

you've been dicking around with for a month? A really *good* detective would've wrapped that case up in under two weeks."

"BAC, point-one-eight," Roby answered, referring to the victim's blood alcohol content, ignoring Crane's barb. "Goat drunk."

Crane rubbed his jaw.

"Yep," Roby continued, ducking into the cubicle long enough to grab a case jacket off the desk. He thumbed through the pages until he found what he was looking for and pointed to a line on the autopsy report, highlighted yellow.

"Says here, Mr. Weingarten got up to change the TV channel during the division playoffs and had a heart attack." For a few seconds, he appeared lost in thought. "Seems to me, a rich guy like that would've had a remote control."

Dark humor fell on unappreciative ears.

"So, the ME ruled out foul play?"

Roby nodded.

A batch of eight-by-ten glossies spilled onto the floor. Scorched from fireplace embers, skewered through and through with an andiron, the porcine Mr. Weingarten looked like a pig on a spit. Cézanne's stomach did a back-flip the envy of Olympian gymnasts.

Crane leaned in close and grimaced. "That him?"

"Yep." Roby met the captain's stare with one of his own. "The ME figures Weingarten tried to grab the fire tools for support. I feel sorry for him. Imagine—"

"The pain he must've suffered," Cézanne said.

"—checking out before knowing whether the Rangers won."

Roby bent over enough to collect the pictures, then offered Crane the file. The captain shook his head. Big shakes.

"What about the guy you just booked? Get a confession out of him?"

"Yep."

Crane eyed the veteran officer with contempt. Cézanne's skin prickled under the once-over of their commander's lightning glare and she avoided direct eye contact. The captain was pissed, all right.

He was.

"Roby was pretty awesome, Captain," she said, concentrating on a fresh scuff mark on the toe of her shoe as if it had the power to ward off evil spirits. "I'd hate to have him grilling me if I were guilty."

"I taught him everything he knows. And I'm the one somebody wouldn't want grilling them if they were guilty."

He knows I schlepped in late.

Guilt eroded her resolve not to look straight at him. In the bat of an eyelash, they locked gazes. She no longer peered into ball bearings, more like two turrets ready to blast her to smithereens.

"If you should decide to honor us with your presence for a full day, Sue-zanne, sign in and fill out a time sheet," Crane snapped. Without another word, he swaggered off.

Roby dropped the file on his desk and mashed a black Texas High-Roller down over his receding hairline.

"Don't worry, Pod'nah. Crane's just pissed because all he got for his birthday was a shirt and a piece of ass, and they were both too big."

Taking Cézanne's elbow, he steered her down the hall to the elevator, to a rear door on first that led out to the parking lot. Together, they pounded the pavement to the unmarked cruiser.

Roby sniffed the air. "I think she likes me."

"Who likes you?"

"Greta."

Cézanne offered up some unsolicited advice. "Forget Greta. Find somebody else. You're the wrong type."

"What's the matter? I got some cash saved up. I could show the gal a good time. She's just playing hard to get."

At the driver's door, Cézanne extended an upturned palm in a silent demand for the car keys.

They were not forthcoming.

"Betcha a hunnerd I can wear down her resistance inside of three weeks. And don't be giving me that puppy-dog look, Zannie. You ain't drivin'."

"It's my turn. And stop calling me that." She decided to go for a sure thing. "As for the wager, you're on. I'll spot you a hundred days or a hundred bucks, you can't get a date with Greta Carr."

"Howzabout double or nothing?"

"Whatever you can afford to lose."

In one fluid movement they shook on the deal. He dug in his coat pocket for the keys. When he glanced up, lines of mistrust deepened around his mouth and eyes.

"What's so funny, Miss Laughin' Hyena?"

"Hard to believe, we get kidded how we're so close it takes a crowbar to separate us. Now, I'm thinking you don't know me at all."

"What's that s'posed to mean?"

"I don't have many vices, Roby. Least not as many as you. True, my language sucks from hanging out with degenerates like yourself but I'm mending my ways." She could tell by the way he scrunched his eyebrows he didn't believe her. "And from now on, I'll be a cheap date. Some guy asks me what I want for Christmas, all I want to see is the docket number to his divorce."

She rested a winning hand on his shoulder and continued.

"What I don't do, generally, is gamble. You ought to know if I let you go double or nothing, I've already won."

Roby unlocked the car door. Hulls from three thousand sunflower seeds cascaded out.

"Should've told me earlier, you wanted to drive." He gave her a good-natured swat on the arm and steered the conversation back to Greta. "I'll charm her. Women go ape-shit crazy over a guy in uniform."

"You're plainclothes. Not to mention the way you *schlep* into work dressed like a Brownsville Jaycee."

"This is my uniform." He thumbed his lapels and grinned wider than the Tasmanian Devil churning up dust on his cartoon tie.

She soured his smile with a hearty laugh.

"Gimme one good reason the broad wouldn't give her eye teeth to go out with me."

Cézanne allowed the thought to roll around in her head before kicking the slats out from under him with facts.

"How many commissioned troops are on the force?" she asked.

"Twelve-hunnerd or so. Why?" He stroked his jaw and gazed past the Trinity where academy instructors were running physical agility tests on a new batch of cadets.

"Out of those, how many do you suppose are female?"

"Say . . . twenty percent, maybe. At least a hunnerd."

"Then I can give you a hundred reasons why they have the right attributes and you don't," she said through a grin. "Let me drive, or pay me now."

Roby's face screwed up in confusion. It took a few seconds, but her words finally registered. She didn't get to pluck the dangled keys from his grasp. They hit the asphalt with a clink.

"GRETA'S A RUG MUNCHER?"

Words tumbled out in a mouth-sputtering rush.

"If you even *think* of telling anybody I *considered* hooking up with a woman who digs chicks, I'll gut you like a deer."

Chapter Two

With Cézanne at the wheel and Three-fifty shrinking in the rearview mirror, they threaded their way past a couple of upscale apartment complexes to the seamy underbelly of Fort Worth's Southside. Not until they drove by a string of Mexican food restaurants—the first sign they had entered the *barrio*—did Roby quit sulking. The aroma of fresh tortillas coupled with the low cloud cover encouraged Cézanne to hit the electric window button and lower it enough to catch a sweet whiff of smells in the air. While the radio weatherman reported dime-sized hail five miles to the east, Roby fretted over Mother Goose, his new silver pickup parked on the street just beyond the employees' garage. At the traffic signal, pulsing bass from the stereo of a nearby lowrider vibrated the windows.

They had arrived, smack-dab in the geometric center of Little Mexico.

"Damned noise pollution gives me a headache," she said.

Roby groped in his shirt pocket, slipped a Marlboro out of a half-empty pack and tapped the filter against his thumbnail.

"You can't smoke in here. Smoke gives me a headache."

"Thank you, Miss Know-It-All. I'm giving 'em up when New Year's Day rolls around. I was just practicing to see how it would feel."

He drew the cigarette across flared nostrils and inhaled. A block and a half down the street he put it away, but the lust never left his eyes. "You making any New Year's resolutions?"

"That empty peanut butter jar in my desk? Come January One, I'm putting in a dollar every time I curse."

"Ain't big enough. Getcha a pickle barrel."

"The hell it isn't. I can't expect the District Attorney to make me a prosecutor, cursing like a sailor."

Roby held out his hand in silent demand.

"What?"

"A dollar, a cuss word. That's what you said."

"Goddammit, I'm not starting 'til New Year's Day."

He held up two fingers.

"That's not fair."

"Life ain't fair." He kept his palm outstretched.

"What? You want to start early?" Crazy bastard. "Fine by me, but that goes for you, too."

Roby surprised her by removing the cigarette pack and crushing it into a ball. The wad landed on the floorboard. She glimpsed his insistent stare locking on her profile, demanding accountability.

"All right, in my bag," she said, giving him the go-ahead to rifle through her purse.

Come to think of it, it wouldn't hurt him to pony up a few bits for his own profanity. Trouble was, Roby didn't go make some insane pact with the Devil to kick *his* bad habit. A thousand curse words in a year's time and she vowed to kiss Doug Driskoll's wife's caboose on the courthouse steps.

She said, "While I'm cleaning up my gutterspeak, you ought to start your own self-improvement campaign."

"Such as?"

"You embarrass me at crime scenes. Your insensitivity to the needs of survivors can be quite galling."

Roby stiffened against the seat. "Well, Zannie, I have a notion you're about to enlighten me with your version of etiquette."

There he was, calling her "Zannie" again, after she'd asked him a million times not to. The name was Cézanne, after the artist. Her loony mother once worked as a museum curator, and inspired by the canvas, *Man in a Blue Smock*, Bernice Martin thought Cézanne fit a babe with periwinkle blue eyes.

The light cycled to green and she stomped the accelerator. The lowrider matched speed only a few seconds before disappearing into a cone of blue exhaust. Her eyes flickered to the rearview mirror.

Teach him.

"You were saying, Miss High-Falutin'?"

"That old man's house, remember? The one with the Dachshund penned up inside for three days?"

"What of it?"

" 'It's either gonna be one-a them queer deals, or the dog chewed his pecker off.' " She punctuated the mockery with an imitation of one of his more swashbuckling hand gestures.

"Thank you, Miss Bedside Manner. Like I reckon you're expecting me to forget the time you threw up your guts, your first floater?"

In the distance, smoke from the locomotive pride of Fort Worth, the Tarantula, geysered into the sky. Its plaintive whistle dovetailed her mood.

"At least I'm sympathetic. I actually hurt for these people."

"You?" Roby snorted in disgust. "I seem to recall a cer-

36

tain pregnant gal fixing to pop out a rugrat in the back seat of that taxi cab back when we worked patrol."

He fished in his pants pocket and held a .45 caliber bullet, glinting in a brief patch of sunlight.

"Oh, my goodness—" His words came out in the high-pitched tone of a man with his gonads caught in a bear trap. "Are you in pain? Here. Bite down."

"My mother didn't tolerate whiners."

He gave her cheek an avuncular tweak. "Just remember, Freud said families are nothing but tyrannies ruled by the most neurotic member. How is Bernice, anyway?"

"Nucking futs."

Her melancholy dipped in a downward spiral. The last thing she wanted to factor into the equation was her mother. She didn't want to tell him she didn't spend her vacation soaking up sun at Galveston Beach after all; nor that the bronze glow came from a few hours at *Tan Your Hide*. It wasn't anyone's business she had to admit Bernice to a psychiatric hospital.

She diverted the conversation before Roby could pry.

"I don't understand how Captain Crane ever got so fixated on my personal life," she said, half-expecting to get a cock-eyed expression instead of a verbal response. She did. "Does he even know Doug's wife? Swear to God I never had any idea the lady existed until she barged in and peppered the kitchen with gunfire."

"Crane's from the old school. He's like the wolf; he mates for life. Courtship, marriage to the same woman, sex, kids, and in that order. No flings. Ten Commandments. He expects people to do things the way he did."

"It's been four months. How much longer does he plan to ride me?"

"He's old fashioned, Duchess. The last of the lead-by-

37

example guys. Not such a bad idea when you think about it. Anyway, plan on at least six. That's how long he's been trying to do me in. 'Course there's others he's had it in for longer."

"Such as?"

"Deputy Chief Daniel J. Rosen. He's been out to get that little prick for years."

"Likes repel, opposites attract."

"Maybe, maybe not. Then again, everybody hates Rosen so I s'pose he's not the best example I can come up with of people whose stock took a drop with Crane."

They drove the last few blocks in silence. Finally, Roby wised up.

"What's the matter, Duchess? You don't have to make the highest score on the law exam, just so's you're not dumber than the bottom twenty percent."

"Thanks so much for your confidence. If I can ever do anything to make you feel like shit, please let me know."

He held up a finger and mumbled, "Reckon I should've taken a five when I had the chance."

Melancholy descended into depression. Roby stretched his arm across the seat and gave her shoulder a playful pinch.

"You flunk the test, you take it over. So you're on the force six months longer than you planned—don't make you stupid."

"It's not just about the bar."

She glanced out her window. A handful of truants, gathered at the corner, waited for traffic to thin before darting across the street to the triple-X movie theater. She changed the subject.

"It's been nine months since the last hailstorm, and my

roofer's still taking my house down to the rafters. He's noisy, inefficient, slow, and on a really good day, I can't tell if it's his hammer pounding or my head."

"Getcha one a-them wetback crews. Slap that roof on in a jiffy."

"Can't." A longing twinge in her voice. "The man's got a handicapped son. Brings him along. And if I hound him, he belts out slave songs. Did you ever hear *Nobody Knows The Trouble I've Seen* sung from a chimney? The guilt, Roby, it's awful."

"That's your trouble, Zan. You try to look for the good in folks. I say fire the bastard. He's sloppy," Roby ticked the reasons off on his fingers, "inefficient—"

"I never said 'sloppy.' "

"—slow as Christmas."

She checked the address painted on the curb against Greta's scrap of paper.

Bingo.

"Let's hoof it." She groped for her purse, stretching a leg out of the car so as to take care not to filét the stitching in her skirt more than she already had. Halfway up the side-walk, she called back over one shoulder. "I used to look for the good in people, Roby, but not anymore. I'm now mod-eling my conduct after you. You converted me to your poke-the-dog-with-a-stick mentality."

"Praise be."

He trotted to catch up. With the expression of a sneaky televangelist and flashes of lightning bouncing off his teeth, he forged ahead to part a sea of midnight blue uniforms—officers loitering at the crime scene, cracking sick jokes in a feeble defense mechanism.

A pimply-faced corporal appeared at the door in high-polished boots and pants with knife creases in the legs.

Cézanne gave him the once over.

A rookie.

He raised a hand to bar their entry. "Hold it. You can't go in there."

She checked the shiny chrome name tag.

B. LEWIS.

"Officer Lewis," she said.

"Beat it, Mutt." Roby brushed past him with a gnat-swatting wave.

"Off limits, Mister," Lewis said with a tremble of authority. He latched onto Roby's beefy bicep. "If you need to get to your apartment, use the back stairs."

The senior detective hardened his gaze into a penetrating squint. With a muscular twitch, he flicked off the grip and pushed aside a flap of jacket. The uniform's hand fluttered to his holster, freezing at the unveiling of a panther-topped shield pressed taut against Roby's girth. Gold. Rank.

"Outta my way."

"J-Jesa," stammered the rookie once Roby put some distance between them, "who was that asshole?"

Not Jesus. Jesus worked for the Chief.

"He's the head dick so we call him Dickhead. And I'm Detective Martin." Cézanne brushed by. "Is Crime Scene here?"

"They just radioed. They're still a good half hour away, finishing up on a home invasion. Last night was one killing night. Lady Godiva's inside."

She left B. LEWIS scribbling their names in a pocket spiral, field notebook and encountered more of The Blue posted at the entrance to the living room. At the far end of a long hall, several more uniforms rummaged through kitchen drawers. So much for an untainted crime scene.

Morons, every one of them.

Somewhere down the hall, Roby's voice buzzed loud enough to be heard in a sawmill. Cézanne followed its resonance.

"Suspects?" Roby asked.

"Three," came the answer.

"Victim's name?"

"Sorry, Sir. Lady Godiva wasn't carrying ID."

She rounded the corner in time to see the sentinel shrug. The partners entered the seedy living room together, greeted by the sight of three officers, each interviewing his own witness. The nude body of a female sprawled face down on the circa sixties, harvest gold shag. Only it wasn't harvest gold. Maroon, maybe, where the blood pooled around her head. Almost black in patches. And that smell— that one-of-a-kind, never-forget, odor of hot iron.

Her stomach loopty-looped.

"Where's the weapon?" Roby said to no one in particular.

"Don't know, Sir," the uniform piped up. "According to the neighbors, there's lots of foot traffic in and out of this dump. You guys got your work cut out for you."

Roby dropped to one knee. He pushed aside a handful of Lady Godiva's amber mane. In a blink, the color drained from his face. His features transfixed into a frozen stare. Just as fast, he regained his composure.

He rose, his looming presence emanating menacing calm, his gun-barrel eyes flickering unmitigated hatred. Something told her Roby stood on the cusp of a dynamic preamble.

"Well I'll be a sonovabitch." His top lip formed a sneer. "Hot-diggidy-damn."

She studied him, the way he eyed each witness with cold

scrutiny, and knew that look.

"I've made the acquaintance of this good-for-nothing slut." His nose broadened in contempt. "And I can see she's in fine shape."

Something didn't add up. It smacked of bad form, even for Roby.

Rubbing his eyes, he announced, "I'll be whupped. Who would've figured this whore'd finally get what was comin'?"

His gaze flickered across three shabbily dressed men—parolees, most likely—judging by knuckles dotted with inky, jailhouse tattoos.

"Roby—"

"I have to tell you, Fellas, this bitch's the sorriest excuse I've ever run up against." He gave the corpse a boot-tip nudge. With shoulders squared, he extended a meaty palm and delivered a verbal left hook. "I'd like to shake the hand of the man who did this."

The scraggliest of the three, the one with the salt-'n-pepper beard, stepped forward and pumped it.

In the time it took to snap on a handcuff, Sorry-Roby-Tyson whirled the man attached to it around faster than a Six Flags ride. Two clicks later, the guy went sputtering out the door protesting innocence and demanding rights.

Roby dismissed the two remaining officers with a wave of the hand and a "Meetcha Downtown".

Alone with her partner, Cézanne leaned close.

"Roby, are you nuts?" One of these days, spitting on the Constitution was going to land The-Man-Himself in hot lava. "Roby?"

He didn't seem to be listening.

She stared with a puzzling mixture of horror and rapt adoration, barely conscious of the first splats of rain drumming hard against the roof.

Roby shouted for Officer Lewis. "Junior, you're in charge of the front. Keep the rest of those fuckers outta here. Got that?"

For the second time, Roby dropped to one knee. Only this time he loosened his necktie. Unbuttoned his collar. Stroked a gentle hand across Lady Godiva's alabaster face.

"Roby?"

A quiet sob escaped his fleshy lips. His shoulders heaved shockwaves. A thousand fireants stormed her spine and took up residence in her armpits and behind her earlobes. So this was what Captain Crane meant when she first came to Homicide.

Sooner or later, everybody loses it.

Careful not to plant a knee in the seepage, she knelt beside her partner with the metallic smell of coagulated blood invading her nostrils. She placed a slender arm across his massive shoulders and felt them ripple. And then like a Louisville Slugger upside the head, it sank in.

"Ohmygod. You know this girl."

She forced herself to look at the corpse, colorless and waxy except for the purple hue of lividity, the girl's eyes frozen in mannequin-like indifference. Something about the contour of her nose seemed familiar. As shockingly pale as her skin appeared, nothing could match the grotesqueness of six pints of indigo blood already settled in the lowest parts of Lady Godiva's body.

Post-mortem lividity.

While Cézanne fought off a grimace, Roby swiped his nose with the back of his hand and refused to meet her gaze.

"Shit. You know her."

She leaned in, put her arms around his neck and pulled him close, dislodging the Texas High-Roller. It rolled sev-

43

eral feet beyond the contaminated area, where he made no effort to retrieve it.

"A friend of yours?"

He rewarded her with silence. She smoothed the hat crease in his hair, let her hand drop to his shoulder and felt him shiver.

"Who is she?"

"You owe the cuss-kitty."

"Whatever you say." She didn't like his lifeless stare. "Tell me who she is."

"Carri Crane."

For the second time that day, she sucked wind.

"Captain's daughter?" She was certain she had misunderstood and hoped to God she had. "Graduated from the police academy a few months ago? That Carri Crane? Jesus." A kind of macabre exhilaration that it wasn't herself stiff on the floor sent a charge through her. "We have to notify Captain."

He clutched her arm. His face lined in a formidable mask of desperation. "We don't call nobody. Not yet."

"Are you nuts?"

"You don't get it, do you? He'll think it was me, Zan. On account of that investigation."

"You were cleared."

He shook his head with a vengeance.

"You still don't get it," he said. "It was the best kept secret in the department."

With an upraised hand, she took the stance of a traffic cop.

"I won't listen, dammit. Nobody's gonna think you had any ill will towards this girl just because she got engaged to that firefighter. Nobody figured you were serious, chasing a pretty girl, forty years younger."

"Carri phoned last night . . ."

With fierce determination, Cézanne covered her ears. "Don't say any more. I mean it, Roby. I didn't hear anything."

He covered his eyes. When he should've been covering his big, blabbery mouth.

"I was with her."

"For God's sake, Roby, shut up. I'm your friend, but I'm still an officer. Don't be a dipshit."

He took a raggedy breath and purged his conscience. "We did it."

She hoped she misheard him. In her heart, she knew she hadn't.

"Dammit, Roby," she cried, her voice crescendoing into an eerie shriek, "are you out of your mind? Why don't you just ask me to take out my gun and pull the trigger? It's a goddam sight faster."

Damn.

Ten bucks shot to hell, an inevitable confrontation with Crane looming on the horizon, and the day only a quarter gone. Imagine, all the time she'd spent trying to fly the coop, only to have her wings clipped by the same man who'd shored her up through law school exams and that unfortunate IA witch hunt.

All at once, passing the bar took a back seat.

Double damn.

Chapter Three

For Cézanne, the rest of Friday went by in a blur. It wasn't until the drive home that she tried to put the thoughts orbiting inside her head into some kind of order.

A sister officer cooling on a marble slab. Found dead in a boarded-up rooming house with an address the victim had no known connection to. No firearm. A *hype* booked into jail and a radical Hispanic group well known for their protests, picketing HQ. Most of The Blue pointing the finger at an ace detective and circulating tales of how Crane's anguish rocked three floors. IA unwilling to run for water if Roby's ass was on fire. And with all the dope fiends, Johns and no-accounts parading through a flea-bag surrounded by crack houses, even on the off chance Carri Crane's death turned out to be suicide, how in God's name could she prove it?

Fragmented images glanced off her brain like misplaced blows.

So the last thing on Cézanne's mind when she wheeled the one-eyed BMW into the driveway after sunset, was that she might find Leviticus Devilrow straddling the peak of her roof wearing a pair of low-riding denims, holding a hammer in one hand and a can of cheap beer in the other.

Devilrow, the son of an East Texas sharecropper and self-proclaimed descendent of the Shreveport Devereauxs, never worked past three in the afternoon.

46

Never.

Yet, there he was.

And on the front porch, dressed in camouflage fatigues with a clay potful of her geraniums balanced on his head, sat Devilrow's son, Levi, looking like an FTD Soldier-of-Fortune bouquet.

She ground her molars and vowed not to swear. Apparently, expecting to come home to a quiet house without Thor beating the shit out of her roof was too much to ask.

She forced a smile and saluted Levi's "Hidee", juggled her keys along with the day's mail and locked herself inside the house. A letter from the State Bar of Texas appeared at the top of the pile, but instead of gutting it out for the results, she dumped the entire kit and kaboodle on the bed and slinked to the kitchen sink.

She needed to whip up a *Mind Eraser,* fast.

On second thought, she emptied the club soda and Kahlua down the drain, left the glass on the countertop, grabbed a bottle of whiskey by the throat and carried it to the sanctuary of her bedroom.

She sat in the middle of her bed, yoga-style, staring down at the letter as if it were a beast to slay. With her heart racing, she broke the seal on Roby's throw-down bottle of Jack Black.

A recurring thought echoed with the sound of Leviticus Devilrow's hammer.

Flunked.

Off came the bottlecap, up went the snout. She borrowed some courage with an enthusiastic swallow measuring at least two fingers' worth.

Loser.

If she openly sided with Roby, she'd end up stuck at the

PD pounding a beat on *dogwatch*, checking out the flora and fauna along the Trinity River hike-and-bike trail. Or worse, on foot patrol at the Stockyards, stomping through the wake of Mounted Patrol's horseshit.

She took another swig of cauterizing fire.

Her head began to buzz with the familiar tickle of someone who couldn't hold liquor; her throat burned with the sting of a thousand wasps. *A WASP in her throat.* She cracked a smile at her private joke. Swill down a couple more and she'd grow testicles. Drive straight over to Captain Crane's and tell him Roby couldn't have done it.

She'd drive because she'd be too damned drunk to walk.

Her eyes drooped to half mast. Jesus. Roby the number one suspect. Even in an imperfect world, how in God's name had that happened?

Devilrow's hammering stopped. Silence pulled her back from the spirits. Her gaze riveted on the envelope. The dotted "I" on her surname stared back like a black eye while her own eyes pulsed in her head.

Something about the thickness was different.

This letter wasn't as fat as the last one—the one with the handbook enclosed that told how to reapply—the one that said to fork over another fee to take the son of a bitch all over again. She cut her eyes at her purse and wondered whether she should just break out a ten and get it over with.

Goddam-rat-bastard lucifers of the law, making the effing test so hard a body had to be a Mensa member to pass.

Only Mensa members wouldn't want to be lawyers.

That's how they got into Mensa.

Better make it a twenty.

She took a long draw off the bottle and set it on the nightstand—the one swimming with two lamps, two jars of potpourri, two telephones, two Caller-IDs, two address books. . . .

First things first.

She gathered the handguns and steak knives and staggered out to the trunk of the rusted-out Beamer. Two mercenaries bearing an uncanny resemblance to Levi Devilrow hit the deck with one scream, shattering terra cotta and slinging geraniums all over the porch. She trudged back inside, fell onto the bed, looked out the window and wished, half-heartedly, that she lived in a high rise.

She stared down at twenty fingers clutching the two letters from the State Bar and damned near got a paper cut ripping open the seal. She held the letter up for more light. There in bold print were her scores.

All two of them.

Squinting sharpened her focus. Her eyes swam over the page but the words made no sense. Except for six of them.

DearDear NewNew AttorneyAttorney.

She screamed bloody murder.

A thunderous bump bounced overhead.

What the hell?

Two seconds later, a metallic missile flashed by her rolling eye, followed by Devilrow, himself. He whooshed past the window and crashed into the holly. Cézanne craned her neck enough to peer beyond the window sill. Momentarily, Devilrow's head popped up from the hedge, eyes floating in his head like blistered egg yolks, over easy.

She held the page up for him to see. "See there? Knew I'd pass th' bar."

"Good. You gwine be yo' first client. When I sue."

"Huh?" She leaned closer, straining to hear. "What giant? Who's Sue?"

"Client. Don't be talkin' 'bout giant. You better have a

giant pocketbook, you know what's good for you."

With a limp hand, she reached up, grabbed the rollershade's pull string and Devilrow disappeared from her delighted view.

Around ten o'clock that evening, Roby's call woke her from the whiskey-induced snooze.

"Meet me at the Ancient Mariner," he said in a low voice. "We gotta talk."

The line went dead.

At the Ancient Mariner, a windowless, dimly lit haven for underworked Assistant DAs and overworked cops, she slid into a back booth and clutched Roby's hands while the rest of the sots played pool.

"Drinks are on me, Partner," she said. A weary grin tightened at the corners of her mouth.

He gave her the once-over. "What're you so hot-to-trot about?"

"I passed the bar. Come Monday, I'm going to the DA's office and grovel for a job. Now I can grow my nails, paint them fire-engine red and say 'up your leg' to all the cretins who made my life a living hell the last three years."

Roby's eyes watered in their sockets.

"What's the matter? Aren't you happy for me?"

"Tickled all the way down to my stones." He looked weather-beaten and pissed.

"At least now I can take my guns out of the trunk and put the cutlery back in the drawers."

"Still paying the cuss-kitty for that smut mouth a-yours?"

"Yes, thanks for inquiring, Mr. Clean." She lifted a petulant chin. "It's going so well I decided to save up for a new car."

"Not s'posed to reward yourself. Ought-a give it to someplace that don't agree with your principles. The ACLU, maybe."

A waitress spilling out of a tube top, wearing a pair of tattooed-on jeans, glided through a veil of cigarette smoke with the grace of a dancing Fatima. A wad of neon pink gum oozed between molars, and a shard of light from the overhanging ceiling fixture glanced off her frosted lipstick.

"What-choo two want?"

"Piña colada."

"Sissy drink." Roby held up an empty and suppressed a belch. "Another Guinness Scout." He blinked. "Stout."

Cézanne spied the dead soldiers sloughed off to one side. Roby looked to be well into the seven stages of drunk. Somewhere past sparrow drunk, but not quite pig drunk.

The girl jotted the order on her ticket pad, shoved the pen behind one ear and wiggled off. Roby didn't even watch the show. Just stared at a dog-eared matchbook belly-up in the ashtray—a bad sign considering his attention span had the shelf life of dead fish when it came to big-busted women. Not that Roby had a roving eye; more like a steel ball in an arcade machine.

"How long you been here?" she asked.

"Dunno. Whatza time?"

"Maybe you ought not drink anymore."

"You ain't my mother."

She bowed up, pouting. "That's not the kind of thing you'd say to a friend."

"You ain't much of a friend, Zan."

The heat of shame rose to her cheeks. Her best bud was in trouble and for the last several minutes, all she could think about was the dream-come-true exhilaration of passing the bar and becoming a prosecutor. How shallow.

"I'm sorry. I guess I got so caught up in my own good luck I wasn't thinking."

He leaned in close enough for her to whiff his booze breath.

"I'm glad for you. Never said I wasn't. You worked real hard to get into the lawyerin' bidness."

"Then what's eating you? You act like you've got a beef with me."

"You ducked out on me without so much as a 'kiss my ass'. I paged you bunches of times. You could-a warned me IA grilled you."

That took the starch out of her laundry.

She melted against the seat back and sighed.

"What am I supposed to do, Roby? The headhunters warned me to keep my distance during the investigation. I'm not like you. You've almost got thirty in. You could've told them to kiss your hiney on the HQ steps." The waitress headed over with a tray and she lowered her voice to a hiss. "Until I found out I got my bar card, I needed that job."

They sipped their drinks long enough for the Jell-O Princess to jiggle out of earshot. Roby took a long gulp and fixed Cézanne with a hard stare.

"Don't be looking at me like that," she said. "I'm not the one who went and spilled my guts."

"You were the first one in. How was I to know? They sure knew the right questions."

"You think I railroaded you?"

Silence shrouded their table. For several seconds he refused to meet her gaze.

"They cut the guy loose, Zannie. On account-a they say I fucked up. Vi'lated his cons'tutional rights."

She pushed her drink away and toyed with the sweat

forming on the glass. Nothing she could say would make him feel better.

"What about her rights, Zannie? What about Carri's rights?" He banged an elbow on the formica and shielded his eyes.

"Simmer down. I ducked into the DA's Office before I left this afternoon and did a search using their computerized law library. A Baltimore cop pulled something similar. Supreme Court case out of Maryland. Mount Sinai-on-the-Potomac held the arrest constitutional."

Roby's hand moved from his face.

"Tell that to your new boss. The guy I locked up claims he thought I was introducin' myself. He's wetter'n a bathtowel in the boys' locker room. Swam across the Rio Grand-E and don't speak a word-a English. *¿Comprende?*"

"Doesn't speak English, or doesn't understand English? People can lie in more than one language."

"What's the stinkin' difference? Either way, they say I screwed up."

She studied his miserable face as he pulled out his wallet and dug through it with a sausage finger. Out came a twenty and a square of paper folded into quarters.

"Sure you want to be a prosecutor, Cézanne?"

"My whole life. I want it so much it hurts clear down to my red corpuscles. I want it more than sex. I need it as much as air."

"Got a client for you if you was to decide to go into private practice."

Her pulse throbbed in her throat.

He said, " 'Member that pimply-faced putz at the door when we first went in?"

B. Lewis.

"IA grilled him. He ain't as stand-up as you."

Even through the smoky veil, she didn't need to scrutinize the embossed seal on the unopened document to know Roby was dogpaddling in deep *kim chee*.

"The client's me, Zannie, if you want the job. Seems Mister Lewis ducked in out of the storm and overheard some things he shouldn't-a. They're fixing to ramrod me. Read it and weep." He unfolded the paper and shoved it under her nose.

"They're out for blood. Mine. Tomorrow morning? Nine o'clock sharp? They're gonna gimme a *Playboy* and a specimen cup and screw me with the results."

Chapter Four

If the previous evening's sight of a drunken handyman perched on the roof like a rickety weathervane was enough to give even the most good-natured homeowner an antacid moment, Chuck Crane's cement hawk profile froze Cézanne in place. The man should have been home with his wife making funeral arrangements, not hunkered over his desk scrutinizing reports at six forty-eight on a Saturday morning. He shifted his gaze, zeroing in as if someone slapped a painted-on bull's-eye between her brows. Her vision blurred, distorting his face in a house-of-mirrors reflection.

"Captain, I'm very sorry for your loss."

The torque in his jaw told her all she needed to know. Crane didn't want sympathy, he wanted blood. She slinked to her cubicle, unlocked their file cabinets and shoved her purse inside. When the DA's Office opened up Monday morning, she'd put in a call, try to wrangle an interview. With any luck, she'd get out of Dodge within the month.

Hooking her jacket over the Saddam Hussein coat hook, she made every effort to avoid placing herself within the trajectory of Crane's bullet-like glare. She dried her clammy hands against the tropical wool skirt and looked longingly at the phone before dropping into her chair.

She needed to see the Medical Examiner's report. Look at the photographs. Roby always said forensics played an integral part of an investigation, but pictures told the story.

And high-profile cases got speedy treatment. She reached for the phone.

A tap at the entry to her cubicle stopped her breath in her throat.

The presence of a woman shrink-wrapped in black spandex leggings and a chartreuse polyester blouse filled the opening, causing Cézanne's hair to stand on end. They'd never met, not formally, but she recognized her nemesis immediately—the spitting image of a photograph that once drifted down from the visor in Doug Driskoll's patrol car. She wanted the carrot-haired woman with freckles as big as chocolate chips to think she didn't have a clue as to her identity, but with the flicker of recognition, Darlene Driskoll's humorless jaw turned strong. Lips thinned to a crimson thread while coppery eyes narrowed into a predatory glint. A wicked knitting needle, poised for carnage, shined in her grip.

Cézanne's mouth went dry. Her Smith & Wesson lay just beyond reach.

"Captain wants to see you," Darlene Driskoll said in a strangled-chicken squawk. She relaxed her free hand and a ball of yarn swelled between her fingers. "And close your mouth. It's unbecoming."

The queen of spandex turned to leave. Cézanne watched the cauliflower-indentations of her backside ripple off down the hallway and privately wondered how someone as un-balanced as Darlene Driskoll passed the background check and landed a job with the PD. Especially if rumors of that unfortunate arson at her former workplace some years back were true. Somebody in Administration ought to take a pulse upstairs in Criminal Investigations.

Or, flat-out call an embalmer.

She opened her desk drawer, pulled out a mirror and

checked her reflection. Sure enough, her face matched the transparent alabaster of her blouse.

Captain wants to see you.

The creaky hinge eeriness of Darlene's words hung between her ears. She dreaded the walk to Crane's office. Leper colony stares of brother detectives tracked her every move, but Greta, her ample bosom heaving beneath an oversized checkered shirt and her eyes shielded by the glare from a pair of rhinestone glasses, looked away.

"Greta—"

"Not now, Shug."

"Do you have any electricians' tape?"

She needed to fasten a strip of black tape across her badge in the cops' symbol of mourning—to pay respect to a fallen comrade—and Greta was the official custodian of supplies.

Squaring her shoulders, Cézanne bellied up to the counter.

"What the hell's Driskoll's wife doing here?"

"Working."

"Oh, good." Her voice climbed in pitch. "That's reassuring because for a minute I thought she only showed up to kill me." Cézanne's eyes ricocheted in their sockets. "Since when does she work here?"

"A week or so." Greta ducked her head and rifled through a box of Post-It notes until she located the tape.

"Don't tell me she's assigned to Homicide."

"Pawn Shop Detail. Cézanne. . . ." The whiny voice trailed off, evasive and pleading.

Cézanne persisted. "What's going on up here?"

"Please, I'll get in trouble."

"Where's Roby?"

"Transferred." Greta shoved aside her props. With

shoulders slumped in resignation, she rested her hands in her lap. "They moved him to dogwatch. The lieutenant caught him at the door and sent him back home so he can rest up and report for duty tonight. There. Are you happy now? I'll probably get fired."

Before Cézanne could comment on the galling lack of due process, Greta excused herself in a cloud of cheap cologne.

A margarita would be nice. Or a lobotomy.

At the captain's door, she could see his lips moving and knew he must be praying. Watching Crane perform his private ritual, unaware of her presence, called up the image of Chicago's only surviving student nurse hiding under the bed in terror while Richard Speck led her roommates off, one by one. The picture stuck, clear, in Cézanne's head: while the girl may have wanted to save her friends, trying virtually ensured the same grisly end.

She took a shallow breath.

"Captain, you asked to see me?"

"Come in."

Anyone with half a brain could see the unshaven scarecrow was deep in the throes of grief; he didn't even need to glance up to give her the creeps. He slapped a case file closed and moved it off to one side of the blotter. With a shift of the eyes, he held her captive in his glare.

"Pack up."

"Sir?"

"Starting now, you report to Pawn Shop Detail," he said in a voice loud enough to chip the texstone off the walls.

With the realization that Crane had just stripped her access to the ME's report, pressure mounted behind both eyes.

She needed that autopsy report. "But—"

"Dismissed."

"For how long?"

She made no effort to move. She couldn't if she'd wanted to. It took several seconds to absorb the full meaning of such a transfer: siding with Roby exacted a high price. Her tongue felt as thick and inflexible as old shoe leather. With the electric current from the sting of his voice still tingling in her ears, a rush of air left her mouth in a desperate attempt to reclaim her position.

"Captain, there's been a misunderstanding."

"No misunderstanding."

"I'm a good detective. I'll get to the bottom of this."

"I want you out of my sight." Biting voltage in his tone raised the hair on her arms.

She no longer needed a drink, she needed a phone.

To call Dr. Kervorkian.

Hi there, Doc. How's your schedule? I get off at three. The oven's fired up and ready to go.

Crane may not have buried her in some maggoty, horseshit job the way he did Roby, but ending up in Pawn Shop Detail with Darlene Driskoll definitely put her on the blow-fly level.

Two weeks' notice looked better than ever.

The click of high heels against the basement floor echoed in Cézanne's numb skull, and she felt the weight of Captain Crane's foot on her career in every step.

Any second, the clock radio would go off. Fumble for the volume, turn down the oldies, drag her carcass out of bed. Practice her public relations skills for the DA interview. No more Doug "All-Good-Things-Must-End" Driskoll. No more pink slips ordering her to see the Department shrink because the

Mayor's idiot first-cousin-once-removed accused her of lipping off at a call. No more bolting upright at three in the morning in a cold sweat, reliving gasps of dying victims or the agonizing cries from their kin: "Find the bastards who did this and put 'em away—or we will."

Pawn Shop Detail was the place used-up, old flatfoots went to mark time until their pensions came in. In the undertow of whirlpooling thoughts, she heard the sucking sound of her career circling the drain.

And that wife of Driskoll's.

Darlene might be a civilian employee, but it would hardly matter if The Brass wandered in some morning and found a certain lady detective-turned-lawyer springing a leak on account of nobody bothered to inquire into whether the Texas Department of Public Safety issued Driskoll's spouse a concealed handgun permit.

At the dismal entrance to Pawn Shop Detail, she scanned the perimeter for incoming SCUDS launched by vindictive wives. Across the room, Darlene sat at a desk, pawing through a sack lunch and wearing a gimlet-eyed stare. With one hand, she reached into a drawer and pulled out a steak knife; with the other, she removed an apple from the paper bag. Michael Jackson's "Thriller" blared over a radio providing a nifty beat for Cézanne's stomach to moon-walk up her throat.

"Help you?"

The voice came from behind.

Dazed by ill fortune, she turned to meet the twinkling gaze of Aden Whitelark, police psychiatrist. The demon indirectly responsible for that ugly little five-day suspension she talked The Brass into running in conjunction with a three-day weekend. Giving her a grand total of eight shame-filled days to clear memories of Doug Driskoll from her hydrocephalic head.

"Why if it isn't Detective Martin." A tenuous smile played at the corners of his lips. "Apparently I've been misinformed. I heard you resigned."

"Don't act so glum. I plan to. What are you doing here on a Saturday?"

"Dropped in to pick up a couple of files. Shall we chat?"

"What about?"

"Roby Tyson." His gaze flitted over her. With a grandiose flourish, he sliced a hand through the tension and toward his office across the hall.

"I'm out of the Roby Tyson business," she lied.

"Good. Then you won't mind dropping in after lunch, shall we say one-thirty?" He lowered his gaze to the box in her arms. "Anything I can do to help?"

"Got any extra cyanide caps on you?"

"I beg your pardon?" His face mirrored her dismay.

She mumbled a pathetic 'scuse me and slinked through the doorway, into the first unoccupied eight-by-eight she came to. Still in the spandex queen's line of fire, she placed the cardboard box on the desk, picked up the phone and dialed an outside line. Only one person could identify with this kind of bad luck.

Roby's friend. A local constable named Jinx Porter.

Chapter Five

Most of Roby's law enforcement contemporaries considered Jinx Porter a butt kicker, the kind of man to puzzle over one minute, have all figured out the next, and by the end of the meeting, wander off completely baffled. But to hear Roby tell it, Jinx Porter was the smartest cop he'd ever met.

Which still made him pretty dumb in her book, considering police legend. Porter may have screwed over his girlfriend, a reserve deputy constable, but the girl—Raven—in a ruthless public gambit, turned the tables. She ingratiated herself with the most powerful woman in town and made Ol' Jinx wish he'd been stillborn.

While on duty and having breakfast at the Paris Coffee Shop, Roby had even toasted the feisty lady with a virgin screwdriver the morning he read the headlines. Raven announced her candidacy in the upcoming election for Jinx Porter's political seat. With high-schoolish vindictiveness, Roby wished the breath of a thousand buffalos on her. All on account of she set out to topple a local legend.

The way Cézanne had it figured, Raven loved the guy enough to force his respect. No one recognized her political prowess until it was too late.

And while people generally agreed Porter might have a peculiar side since he practically lived in his office, Cézanne found herself experiencing peculiar tastes.

Jinx Porter had something she wanted.

He kept his own database of thugs.

Which seemed strange since amassing criminal records was the job of the Texas Department of Public Safety. But even weirder was the fact that through years of painstaking research and recording, Porter's hobby became an obsession. He had compiled the largest database of unsolved homicides dating clear back to the fifties, and anyone in law enforcement worth their salt knew it. Including the DPS.

Porter might just have something to say about all this.

When she sneaked out of the PD to the Constable's Office in the old Criminal Courts Building next door, Jinx Porter was doing what made him a legend—dressing down another Tarrant County employee by telephone.

With his boots propped on the desk and a folded-open newspaper shielding his face, he yelled, "We don't have nine cars, we have five. If your records show nine, you idiots can by God trot your fat fannies over and scare 'em up on your own."

A short pause, then, "Do you think I told her to wreck the patrol car? It's your job to make sure she has a spare. Yes, I'm aware she's the Joe DiMaggio of collisions. I'm also aware that you drive a silver Lexus. What does that have to do with anything, you ask? We have a court order to serve a Child Writ and we're by God serving it today if I have to come out and commandeer *your* vehicle."

He seemed to be on *hold* because he broke into a tune.

"Took my old flame to the fireman's ball, but the firemen put her out—"

Cézanne cleared her throat.

Porter dropped the Metropolitan page low enough for a thick pair of wire-rims to show over the top.

"Top o' the mornin'." He sat up in his chair and gave her the visual once-over, then held up a finger, a sure sign someone had come back on the line. "A brand new

Chevy? Sure, we'll take it."

He hung up the phone. "Help you?"

Having caught him in a good mood, her confidence buoyed.

"Roby Tyson," she said, in a rush of self-consciousness, walking toward him with an outstretched hand. "I'm his partner."

"Not a chance."

Jinx Porter wasn't the first person who thought their shotgun, cop-marriage to be a mismatch but he recovered nicely. In a flash, his boots hit the floor and he made it to his feet. Light from the overhead fluorescents reflected off his bald head and she liked the way his shy grin and the warmth of his grip put her at ease.

"That old sonofagun, how's he doing?"

"Are we where we can speak uninterrupted?"

"I'm pretty sure this paranoid Sheriff the 'religious right' voted in has the building bugged, and my deputy's due in from overtime. Other than that, come on back."

He motioned her to follow him down a short hall to an office walled with "Dogs Playing Poker" pictures. As her gaze drifted over cheap paneling common to county decor, she felt the burn of his judgment.

"A close, personal friend gave those to me," he said.

The gleam in his eyes betrayed his words. Raven. He was still pining, lost without his playmate.

Dragging up chairs until they were facing each other, Porter continued. "Long time ago, your buddy Tyson saved my bacon. Covered me in a shootout at Butler projects. I owe him."

She knew the feeling. "When's the last time the two of you spoke?"

"It's been a month or so. We shared a table out at—" He

pulled up short, enough to cover his tracks and drawled, "Say, what's all this about?"

"Do you know Captain Crane, Constable?"

"That coward?" Porter let out a disgusted huff. "Only way somebody like that makes rank is to cut throats. And call me Jinx."

She checked her watch. Not much time.

"Crane's daughter's dead. She just graduated the police academy maybe six months ago and hadn't been on patrol all that long. Roby used to see her socially, back when she was still a cadet. Which stirred up a hornet's nest, let me tell you. We have a fair-to-middlin' suspect, but the captain's obsessed with pinning the tail on my partner."

"I didn't see anything on the news."

Unceremoniously, she cut him off.

"Of course you didn't. Right now, Chinese water torture couldn't get The Brass to comment." Her voice crescendoed with the reality of her words. "First thing they did was transfer Roby out."

"You shouldn't take it personally. I'm sure he doesn't. That's just a hallmark of good police procedure."

"The second thing they did was move me. Roby's on night shift, assigned to patrol Rose Hill cemetery, guarding the grave of Lee Harvey Oswald. And I'm buried so goddam deep in the basement it'd take a crew of geologists a month just to get a seismic readout on me."

Jinx exhaled slowly. "What do you want?"

"Roby once bragged how you have files of unsolved homicides on computer. Your own statewide databank. He said it was better than the Department of Public Safety's."

His eyes narrowed as if she'd presented him with something vile and asked him to swallow it.

"I want you to search for case similarities. See if you come up with any other suspects or victims. Can you do that?"

"And who gets to provide me with the details of this investigation, seeing as how you and Tyson are out of the loop?"

He had a point.

Her eyes roamed the walls, searching for an answer. She found it in the "Dogs". A picture entitled "A Friend in Need" showed a card-playing canine slipping an ace to the Heinz-57 seated in the next chair.

"Don't ask questions you really don't want to know the answers to," she said dryly.

They understood each other with a look.

Aden Whitelark still officed in the same intimidating hellhole as the time she'd been ordered to have her head shrunk—after Darlene Driskoll customized her Martha Stewart kitchen with lead, and after the two-timed Mrs. Driskoll's high-dollar divorce attorney told her Texas did away with alienation of affection as a cause of action. The woman knew just what to do to get even and did it. Went caterwauling to the Chief.

"Have a seat." Whitelark tugged at one of the more uncomfortable guest chairs, then eased into his own plump leather wingback and steepled his fingers under his chin. "How've you been?"

"Great." She perched on the edge of her seat, scoping out the exit, ready to take off like a scalded cat. "Really."

"Make yourself comfortable."

The look on his face had a way of prompting her lips to unzip, to make her words pour out in a pathetic effort to mask her uneasiness around someone she knew had the capacity to unravel even the brashest cops' tightly-wound emotions.

"Everything's fine. Perfect, actually. I'm getting along great. Except that I'm snowed-under. New job, you know." She decided she could reach the door in under four seconds. Three, if he came after her. "Mind if I go now?"

"Soon. You don't look all that thrilled."

"I'm dizzy with happiness." Sinking into the chair. "Life couldn't be better."

"How are things at home?"

She gave the room a visual scan and decided to spare Dr. Freud the sad-sorry-saga of Leviticus Devilrow. Of how the recent hailstorm left her gingerbread house with a Belgian waffle for a roof. And how it took less time to bear offspring than it did for Devilrow to slap on a few shingles and hang a gate. But in his usual annoying fashion, Whitelark pressed.

"A penny for your thoughts."

Make it a dollar—for the cuss-kitty.

She'd need it once Whitelark was out of earshot.

The guy wanted her to drop Roby in the grease and she wouldn't do it. Shifting her gaze, a photo of two cotton-topped children caught her attention. His, probably. She glanced up in time to find herself the beneficiary of Whitelark's unsettling stare. Her gaze flickered past the Campbell's Soup Kids to the medical texts displayed on the shelf.

He said, "You doing all right?"

She wanted to tell him not to bother with small talk, that she was onto him. That the only head problems she had came from Devilrow's incessant hammering. But this wasn't her first rodeo with the police shrink, and she knew, firsthand, that Whitelark relished his role as a psychic vampire sucking out his victim's most intimate thoughts. He was worse than the worst voyeur, peeking into the mental closets of unsuspecting cops, rummaging through their secret cubby-holes with the stealth of a cat burglar.

And once he'd fileted the patient's inhibitions with his mental scalpel and feasted on the host animal until there was nothing left but a skeletal mess, he'd lick his fingers and set about diagnosing problems that didn't exist. She might have to play along in the interest of public relations, but she sure as shootin' didn't have to provide Whitelark with additional material to sabotage her personnel file.

She cut her gaze from the psychiatrist's bible, the DSM IV, careful not to let him read anything in her face.

"If I recall," he said, pulling out an inch-thick file and thumbing through it, "you don't have any little ones, do you?"

He knew she didn't. She glanced at an accordion folder shoved off to one side. The one with the double rubber band. That would be Roby's.

"Do you have kids, Cézanne?"

"I try to make it a practice never to assume responsibility for anything that eats."

"Don't you want any?"

"Not if they don't show a profit." Inwardly, she cringed. *A simple 'No thanks' would do.*

"I don't recall why you divorced."

He didn't recall because she never told him. And she couldn't fathom doing so now. God forbid people should see her as an idiot savant at relationships. The bastard might still be living with her if Roby Tyson hadn't wisecracked about why some husbands had lower sex drives than others. She'd learned several lessons from Roby smarting-off: one, her ex's libido wasn't all that low, after all; two, it took a special kind of man to screw another man and duck pottery at the same time.

When she didn't answer Whitelark after a fashionable silence, he offered up a morsel of trite wisdom.

"It's the minor irritations that turn into major obstacles when trying to make a relationship work, don't you think?"

"I suppose if you call popping the zipper on my best dress a minor irritation."

"Come again?"

Time for Whitelark to buy a vowel, solve the puzzle.

"I'd say the eye-opener to my sad-sorry-marriage would have to be six formal gowns hidden in his closet, none in size ten."

The lousiest farmer could have cultivated crops in Whitelark's furrowed brow. He shifted uncomfortably as realization registered in his grimace. But it wasn't the same, a woman being jilted for another guy. Learning the man she'd chosen to spend the rest of her life with had a transvestite lover made the Doug Driskoll fiasco look like an invitation to the Jewel Charity Ball.

She felt the magnetic pull of Whitelark's naked ring finger, left hand, and knew that sometime between their last visit and this one, he'd been dumped, too. Which reinforced another unhealthy belief.

Any man footloose and fancy free was that way on account of somebody, somewhere, didn't want him.

"Does that mean you're burned out on dating?"

Her ears pricked up. "Depends."

"On what?" He picked up a pen and let it hover over a blank page.

"On whether you're asking for personal reasons or trying to gather enough information for a Borderline Personality diagnosis."

"I might be making polite conversation."

She wanted to tell him she'd sooner take a pair of pruning shears to a power cable than date. That the sparks would be just as exciting and a lot less messy. Instead, she shrugged him off. It took less energy.

His eyes shined with mild amusement. "So how does it feel getting transferred to Pawn Shop Detail?"

"If bad luck were music I'd be a brass band."

"And my office? How does it feel to revisit a place you swore you'd—now let me see if I remember correctly—" He permitted himself a chuckle. "—you'd rather be videotaped getting a barium enema on the Courthouse steps than cross my threshold?"

She refused to get suckered-in, and he seemed to find the ensuing void in conversation disconcerting.

He tried again. "It bothers you being here, doesn't it?"

"I feel a bit like the bride of the jerk who holds the World's Record for most marriages. I know what I'm supposed to do in the honeymoon suite. I'm just not sure it'll be that exciting."

"You're very funny. People often disguise pain with humor," he said.

Whitelark's cheeks plumped, and his eyes crinkled at the corners. She felt a personal sense of accomplishment wearing him down, eroding the stone mask of fake concern.

The guy wasn't bad looking, all things considered. His Ivy League clothes worked and he received a high mark for the Italian loafers. Her imagination started to free associate. Without warning, his clothes ended up in a pile on the floor, and she found herself fidgeting in her chair, fighting off a visual of herself blindfolded, wrists bound to the brass bedposts, Whitelark astraddle, probing more than just her thoughts.

Share your most decadent fantasies.

She said, "I don't understand why I'm here. I haven't done anything, and I don't know anything that will help you."

"I wouldn't go so far as to say that."

The lusty visual returned, this time more graphic. She studied the intensity of Whitelark's mouth, the tightening of his jaw. Behind the smoldering eyes lurked untethered passion. And although she tried to fight off these images, she imagined him taking his lips to her until she surrendered to his demands.

I want your darkest secret.

Pyramids of gooseflesh surfaced. She could almost feel his tongue snaking across her jugular and needed to place herself beyond his gravitational pull.

A prick of pain and it's over.

But it never would be. Because Whitelark's job was to go on a mental archaeological dig, emotionally stalking her until she 'fessed up. Why she only wanted emotionally unavailable men. And why, when she pushed them into leaving, she felt no pangs of grief, only relief. Why she put the squeeze on The Brass until they partnered her up with Roby Tyson—a man she thought she hated—then realized one day over a cup of foglifter, she not only admired, but adored. Roby Tyson taught her she didn't have to take shit off anyone even though she'd been taking shit off people since the day they buried her sister. And the last thing she envisioned on this, of all days, was to have a discussion with Aden Whitelark about poor, dead Monet.

The police shrink smiled. "You know whatever we talk about in here is confidential."

"Sure."

Like the last time, she wanted to say—when she fell for the same line, only to find out the Chief had access to all the records because Whitelark worked directly for him. Not that it would do any good to point that out. Whitelark would get off the Borderline Personality jag and head straight for Paranoid.

She shifted in her seat and tried to pretend the pain goring her chest wasn't serious. Worse, she knew he hadn't forgotton the purpose of her visit, a visit that was supposed to be about her partner.

"Tell me about your relationship with Roby Tyson."

"There's nothing to tell."

"The Crime Scene detectives found a hair next to Carri Crane's body. I believe it was from carpet they vacuumed. They're comparing it to Tyson's."

The news siphoned the oxygen out of her lungs. Blood seemed to coagulate inside her veins. She thought fast.

"Roby and I took the call. While he bent down checking for a pulse, I accidentally brushed against his hat. It fell off. The hair probably dropped out then. Doesn't make him a criminal."

"I hear they're trying *amino black*."

She wanted to retch. If it worked, they'd be able to find Roby's fingerprints on Carri Crane's body. He admitted he made love to her. She saw him smooth the long, blonde hair from Carri's bloody head. If he inadvertently touched his clothes, the guys in Forensics could ferret out the slightest trace. She glanced about the room for a trash can, her gaze settling on nothing.

"You'd take a bullet for him, wouldn't you?"

"I'd take a bullet for a lot of people. I might even take one for somebody I didn't know. Or didn't much care for."

"He wouldn't take one for you."

Yes, he would.

"Are you in love with Roby Tyson?"

No.

She said, "All my friends are important to me."

Whitelark digested this silently. Any minute he'd be asking her to describe her relationships. Her stomach squished.

"Tell me about your childhood. How did you get along with your mother?"

She uttered an unenthusiastic, "Swell," and wished he'd stop. It didn't make her feel good to tell whoppers, but she didn't see any reason to discuss Bernice, either. She'd trusted Whitelark with personal information the first time. Told him of her German heritage. Disclosed how her mother, a maladjusted, humorless bully, could keep her in line with a hiss.

Stop da racket. You want you should ask yourself, 'How will my television look wid a hammer through it?'

The click of Whitelark's pen cap snapped her attention back to the present.

"Do you like your mother?"

"Do you like yours?"

"Do you think Tyson's capable of committing premeditated murder?"

"No more than I am at this moment."

Two minutes later, he dismissed her with a clammy handshake and a formal appointment.

Shortly after eight-thirty that evening, Cézanne arrived at the Forestview Psychiatric Unit to check on Bernice. At first, she pecked on the glass until a hospital staff member appeared and mouthed, 'Closed' then tried to fan her away using a pantomime of hand gestures. But when she pulled out her badge and explained how events precluded visitation during regular business hours, a nurse showed up with a door key and permitted her inside.

When they reached the room, Cézanne saw the dim outline of her mother beneath the bedcovers, curled up asleep. With the rustle of linens, she could smell fabric softener in Bernice's clothes and the fragile scent of herbal shampoo in her hair.

"Your mother's had a bad day," said the nurse, shaking her head. "She had to be put in seclusion."

"When's the probable cause hearing?"

"They held it yesterday. Don't beat yourself up, Honey, you didn't need to come. The judge talked to her. It wasn't anything formal. Nobody ever gets out after a PC hearing, you ought to know that."

Cézanne was marginally relieved to hear her thoughts spoken.

"And the commitment hearing?"

"In a week or so."

"What does the doctor say?"

"The truth, Hon?"

She nodded at the lump on the bed.

"In layman's terms, she's batshit crazy."

Chapter Six

Monday morning, Cézanne arrived at HQ in a downpour. By the time she reached the portico at the top of the front steps, the hard rain whipping at her ankles saturated the hems of her slacks.

Inside wasn't much better. The foyer had a wet dog smell, and even though she wanted to remove the new navy blazer and give it a good shake before heading down to the basement, she knew the .38 snubnose clipped to her waistband would attract the attention of the ACLU protesters congregating at the entrance to protest their latest misperception of police brutality. She was making a point to flick off raindrops when she noticed a couple of has-been traffic sergeants—guys from the old school with accordion-pleated faces—waiting near the elevator. With their uniforms rumpled and posture sagging, she took note of her own damp khakis and hoped they would dry without spotting.

The sergeants were talking faster than a couple of Puerto Rican housewives. When she heard Roby's name spoken, she decided to ride along.

"G'dam that Tyson," said the tall one, a broomstick of a man with straw-colored hair permanently creased at the forehead from years of wearing a motorcycle helmet. "I'm gonna recommend them boys in IA to fire his ass."

"That's for sure."

"Mangy sonofabuck." The lanky one talking again.

75

"That's a firing offense, sleepin' on the job."

"Yep, sleepin' on the job. A firin' offense, for sure."

"G'dam Tyson. Didja get a look at his face? Sonofagun was prob'ly likkered up, to boot. That nose of his looks more like a Kojack light every time I lay eyes on him. Which, you ask me, is too g'dam much."

"Yep, too damn much."

A chime sounded, and the elevator doors slid open. The three climbed aboard, and she waited for one of them to select a button. The scent of wet hairspray hung heavy in the shared space.

The lanky one checked her out. "How do?"

"Real good." She forced a smile. "You?"

"Mighty fine."

He favored her with an admiring glance. She didn't look that hot in navy blue but she had taken great care matching the blazer with one of her grandmother's scarves. And an unexpected wink from the tall sergeant shored up her morale and made her glad she made the effort, even if she did feel like she was running on "E".

He refocused his attention on his partner. "Don'tcha think we ought to write it up, formal?"

"Yep. Formal's good."

"G'dam. Getting rid of him's gonna make us heroes."

"You can say that again."

The elevator hummed above its gentle sway, but the air grew fetid with the scent of their hard night's work. Finally, they lurched to a halt. The doors peeled back to expose Captain Crane blocking the way, his face beet red and a coil of smoke filtering up from his shiny scalp. Cézanne shrank to one side and watched the sergeants' grins melt into hangdog expressions. Crane seemed to look right through her.

"Hey, Cap'n." In stereo.

"I ought to give you two jackals days off." He flapped a memorandum in their faces. "I hope you don't need any vitamin-D in your diets because as long as I'm seven-to-three shift commander, you won't see daylight until I retire." He punctuated the bulletin with a hearty, "Gotdammit."

He pivoted on his heels, leaving them scratching their heads. They faced each other like matching bookends, shrugged, then trailed in his wake. Just before the doors slammed shut, Cézanne leaped off and ducked behind the nearest wall where she hoped Crane wouldn't see her.

"Whatcha talkin' about, Cap'n?"

"Roby Tyson, you dimwits."

"That's what we come to tell you, Cap'n." The beanpole spoke in an excited rush. "We're on the way upstairs to write him up. Me'n Billy Ray caught him snoozing in the patrol car." As if he needed to add, "Dereliction of duty."

Crane snarled, "And exactly what time did this infraction occur?"

Reflexively, they checked their watches.

" 'Bout two-thirty this morning." The beanpole looked to his partner for support. "Wouldn't you say about two-thirty?"

"Yep, two-thirty."

"Well it's nine-thirty now."

"Yessir?"

"While you were out doing Lord-knows-what, Tyson dropped by the station and scribbled out a couple of commendations."

"Come again?"

"He put your names in for the Medal of Valor. For saving his life."

"Do what?" In stereo again. Loud stereo.

"Claims he was overcome by carbon monoxide fumes and if you hadn't found him slumped over the wheel, he'd have died of asphyxiation."

The sound of Crane's foot stomps left the sergeants scratching their heads and Cézanne dashing for the stairwell. She felt the presence of his retribution long after the door clicked shut behind her.

Back in the basement, she checked in at the secretary's desk before dialing Roby's house from her office. He answered without her ever hearing it ring.

"You're not the only one in the penalty box," she hissed into the mouthpiece. "You'll never guess where they buried me."

If he didn't have an inkling of her whereabouts, the faint trickle at Roby's end of the line pinpointed his own location with the accuracy of loran.

"What is 'Pawn Shop Detail'?" she answered before his allotted number of *Jeopardy!* seconds expired. "And why do you answer the phone when you're in the bathroom? People'll think you're poorly bred."

"Turn me in to the latrine police."

A clunk of metal against tile sounded through the earpiece. Roby groaned and dropped the phone. When he came back on, he dismissed the clatter with an unapologetic, "Sorry."

"What was that?"

"Kidney stone. That was it you heard falling out. Pinged right into the bowl."

She wondered how he maintained his sense of humor when the ghouls at the lab might be looking at photos of his bloody fingerprints, raised by the use of amino black.

"Listen," she whispered, pausing to scout for eavesdroppers, "did you know they hired Doug's wife?"

"I heard there was a big push on for minorities. They must've been light on their screwball quota."

She flopped into the chair and threaded her fingers through the fringe of bangs drooping over her forehead.

"She's Pawn Shop's secretary. And she's got me in the crosshairs of her scope, right this minute."

Roby let out a low whistle. "Imagine. And me here wishin' I could trade places."

"People on Death Row wouldn't trade places with me. People in iron lungs would pull their own plugs to keep from trading places." She hazarded another glance. Sure enough, Darlene sat at the far end of the room sharpening pencils with a straight razor, and arced sparks from her eyes.

"At least you've got electricity," Roby said, his voice turning bitter. "I came in this morning, started flipping on switches and blew out my TV, my VCR, and a ceiling fan I got for a souvenir when they tore down the Chicken Ranch. When I complained to the electric company, the gal said, 'We only guarantee to furnish you electricity, Mr. Tyson, we don't guarantee how much.' "

"Electricity's the least of your worries. There's a couple of pissed-off sergeants wanting your hide, and I don't even want to think about what Captain's plotting."

Roby let out a sigh. The long pause that followed told her she'd struck a nerve.

"It's time you stop thinking like a cop and start thinking like a lawyer, Zan. When it's sports, it's 'Show me the money'; when it's a bar it's 'Show me your tits'; and when it's a criminal case, it's 'Show me the evidence.' "

"I wouldn't be so cavalier if I were you," she said miserably.

"They've got no evidence."

"No? Dr. Whitelark told me they found a head hair near Carri's body, and they're trying to match it with one of yours."

"Simple enough to explain."

"What about amino black? You touched her face. If they find your bloody fingerprints on Carri Crane's body—"

"Don't call me from the PD again. You want to talk, use a pay phone."

Chapter Seven

Jinx Porter had said he'd be in touch, but the sun was setting fast and he still hadn't phoned.

She used the drive time home to replace the memory of the dreaded visit to Aden Whitelark with fretting over Roby. He paged four times during the day. But with the sudden influx of The Brass roaming in and out of Pawn Shop, engendering a climate of paranoia, returning calls didn't seem such a hot idea.

Worse, news that she aligned herself with Roby spread through the District Attorney's Office with the speed of a California mudslide. Which made the chances of getting hired on virtually nil. The last thing the DA needed was more bad publicity. It wasn't as if the highest law enforcement agent in the county ran a tight ship. Hell, more than a handful of prosecutors had publicly disgraced the office the previous year. Judges sentenced their fair share of drunk-driving attorneys to *pro forma* probation. One Assistant DA even danced topless after downing too many scotches; according to office gossip, another, high on coke and short of car fare, played a tune on the cabbie's organ to settle the tab.

But homicide?

Never had she heard of anyone at the DA's Office being asshole buddies with a murder suspect.

Half a block from her driveway, Levi Devilrow played kickball in the street with an empty pizza box. A shard of sunlight through the windshield made it impossible to tell whether Levi waved or flung sweat at her. But since she felt pretty comfortable with the notion that the father-son team hated her, she settled on the latter. She blinked away the sting of the sun's brilliance and zipped into the drive with a spirited scatter of pea gravel. Then, she screeched to a halt with such suddenness, a faded, seven-month-old warning citation for no headlight—left on the dash as a reminder she still needed to change the burned-out lens—shot to the floor.

She hadn't counted on the wrought-iron gate she'd contracted the senior Devilrow to craft, blocking the entrance —the impenetrable gate she originally expected she'd need once she started purchasing art treasures with that nice salary as an Assistant District Attorney.

She cut her glare to the shiftless Devilrow, sacked out on the porch. Surprise turned to fury.

Devilrow came up off the porch like Dracula rising from the coffin. Wiping sleep from his eyes, he lumbered over in a halo of dust, smelling of pepperoni and extended a catcher's mitt hand, palm up, in demand.

"I come for the other half o' my money."

She climbed out of the BMW and shifted her attention to hideous twists of iron. Mercury percolated to the top of her head. An invisible boa constrictor wrapped around her lungs. The air grew thin.

"No." Denial came out like the low of a wounded calf.

"I did what I's s'posed to. Now you do your part."

She waited for her heart to defibrillate, and when the gate didn't vaporize after a couple of dedicated eye-blinks, she allowed its magnetic pull to draw her near.

"No eff-ing way."

"What-choo mean?" Devilrow's irritation turned sinister.

She clutched at a wrought-iron spear to steady herself. A trickle of sweat slid down the small of her back.

"This isn't what I ordered." A thousand dollars down the rathole, and the nightmare of a gate blocked her path like a permanent bad dream. "This is hideous."

Grotesque, corpulent figurines perched atop each end post seemed to track her moves through slitted eyes.

Devilrow relaxed.

"Don't worry," he said in his usual laid back way that made her wonder if he wasn't fixing to slip into a coma. "I ain't gonna charge extra for those."

"Not charge me?" she yelled. "You ought to be glad I don't find a way to charge you with intentional infliction of emotional distress. What in the hell are these things supposed to be?"

"Gargles."

"What?"

"Gargles."

"Oh, good. I'm so relieved, you know, because for a minute I thought I was looking at angels with hard-ons."

She checked her hands to gauge whether they would fit around Devilrow's thick neck. Her fingers clutched at her chest, where she became only moderately aware of a heartbeat.

"I think it looks good, myself," Devilrow said.

"It would look better with a shovel taken to it. Beat it into the ground until there's nothing left but a dark stain."

Come to think of it, the idea might work on Devilrow.

With the last bit of self discipline, she huffed out her disgust. "This is not what I ordered. I asked for grapes with vines. I did *not* ask for gargoyles."

"I couldn't put a arch on it or them foo-foo swirls." Behind narrowed slits, anger fanned the embers burning in his maroon eyes. "If I did, would-a made it over five feet. So I threw in gargles."

"Are you trying to get me arrested for obscenity? Look at the size of the goddam things. What did you do, mix Viagra in the metal? Pinocchio's nose didn't even get this big."

He lurked nearby, biceps twitching. For a fleeting second, she thought he'd slap her silly. She searched her vast vocabulary for just the right words to express her displeasure—something a man of Devilrow's caliber could understand, possibly even relate to.

"It fucking sucks."

"I figured you would accept this." He enunciated each syllable. "Make do."

So he considered her a pushover.

Accepting Devilrow's shoddy workmanship would make her a prime candidate for an EEG. Get this synapse problem she seemed to be having defined. Locate which wires crossed. Determine how many neurons were being siphoned off to the "Oh, that's okay," part of the brain instead of the part that should have had her snapping to attention, screaming "WHAT?" at the top of her lungs.

Devilrow moved in, crowding her. The sour taste of bile rose to her throat.

"This looks like a prison gate."

"That's how we was taught to make them."

"Somebody actually taught you to do this?" Her hands fluttered in frustration, like a dying pigeon twitching against a pile of fire ants. "Who, in God's name, teaches shit like this?"

"Prison."

"You've been in prison?"

She gave him a slow blink of ultimate distrust, enough to let herself absorb the surrealness of the catastrophe, then silently vowed to kill Doug Driskoll for recommending an ex-con as a handyman.

Without fanfare, she made a visual examination of the rest of the gate and experienced the lightheaded rush of dread.

Devilrow had sunk the iron gatepost a good eight inches onto the neighbor's side of a neon orange surveyor's flag.

Normally she would have viewed eight inches as good news. But this eight inches encroached over the property line. And the homeowner was selling, with the closing due any day. Her arms snaked around her midsection in a pitiful attempt to keep lunch down.

"It's got to go."

Devilrow reared back, snot-slinging mad.

"Nobody ever complained on my work." He stood over her with menacing calm, but his nostrils flared wide enough to park a Volkswagen beetle in each one.

She wanted to tell him his luck just ran out. And she would have, too. But a Jeep Cherokee with a magnetic real estate company sign barreled through the intersection. It bounced over the curb, flattening the CONTRACT PENDING sign in the neighbor's yard. A beet-faced realtor sprang out of the four wheel drive, leaving her speechless and her diaphanous blouse ringed in sweat. Not so stunned she didn't notice pushbars on the bumper of what appeared to be a patrol car sneaking into position, though. Extra antennae and recessed emergency lights in the grillwork cinched her suspicions.

Boy was that realtor going to be pissed.

Then again, maybe not.

The spider-legged lawman wrenched himself from the cruiser and strutted past the realtor with his sights set on her.

"Cézanne Martin?"

He pushed aside the western-cut jacket enough for her to see the glint of a badge. With one hand hidden behind his back, he extended the other for a shake. She knew the drill. She'd done it to others a thousand times in the span of her police career.

Hi ya, Pod'na, howzit going?

Pump, pump.

Pull them towards you, slap a court order in their paw.

Have a nice day.

She refused to take the bait.

Frothing at the mouth, the realtor glanced up from a blown front tire and made positive ID.

"That's her. That's the lady who lives in that house."

The afternoon sun sapped her remaining strength, draining the fight right out of her. With shoulders drooping, she owned up to her pedigree. The deputy thrust a bulging document so close she could smell the ink.

Her guilty mind went through a series of warm-up exercises. Doug Driskoll's wife must've decided to leave him and pointed the finger in what was certain to be the bloodbath of divorces.

Or Bernice. She'd escaped. Maybe torched another mattress at the nursing home.

"What's this?" she managed to say through her teeth.

"Fort Worth Marshal, Ma'am. Injunction." The marshal sucked at the insides of his cheeks, turned his head and arced a mouthful of amber spit into the street. "Gateposts have to go."

She unfurled the voluminous sheets. Her eyes focused on legal mumbo-jumbo with the capacity to put the fear of God in an avowed atheist.

It began with: COMES NOW.

Not to fret.

She cut her gaze to the realtor. "It's a simple misunderstanding."

He speared the ground with the mangled sign stake, righted it and nudged a clump of dirt into the gaping hole with the toe of his docksider.

Just because Devilrow was standing there with his arms folded like Hell's butler didn't mean she couldn't volunteer him to dig up the posts. She'd yank them out by the roots herself, if she had to.

"I'm confident we can work this out," she said.

"If our closing falls through because of this half-wit, my company will sue."

That ripped it.

Devilrow might be a half-wit, but he was her half-wit.

Cézanne could hardly believe her ears, the way her mouth opened up and sided with Leviticus Devilrow in a way that sent the realtor running for the Jeep. With a sense of triumph, she turned to the marshal. He studied her wrists as if to calculate how many clicks it would take to secure handcuffs around them.

"Anything else?" she wanted to know.

"Just this." He arced another spit stream onto the neighbor's grass and forked over a document.

"Now what?"

"Summons. You didn't get a building permit."

She swiveled her neck to peer at the brass buttons on Devilrow's overalls while the marshal angled back to the cruiser.

"You didn't get a permit?" Her words climbed in a three-octave, third act, everyone's-dead-and-I'm-next voice. "I gave you plenty of money to cover the permit."

"Homeowner's ultimately responsible," the marshal called over one shoulder.

"Speakin' o' money, Miz Zan, I'll be wantin' what's due me."

Left choking in the officer's smoking tailpipe, she started to unleash three days' worth of unvarnished fury. But Devilrow's son stopped his pizza box soccer game with such abruptness she took notice.

Rounding the corner, a Channel Eighteen News van skidded up even with the curb. In the time it took to blink, a cameraman trotted up with a petite blonde reporter in tow.

"Cézanne Martin?"

"Yessum, she sho' is." Devilrow grinned big and pointed a finger the size of a burned frankfurter, the traitor.

Her mouth turned to sand, and the cardinal rule of police work flashed into mind.

Anyone with a camcorder trained on them had problems.

Blinded by the spotlight, she raised a hand to shield her eyes about the time the reporter shoved a microphone under her chin.

"What's your opinion of the District Attorney convening a special Grand Jury to indict Roby Tyson for Capital Murder?"

Cézanne came out of her disoriented state slumped against the arm of a Chippendale wingback with Leviticus Devilrow smacking her cheek with his calloused hand. His son curled up with his dirt-caked feet digging into a crocheted throw on her couch, glued to the six o'clock news. Worse, an overstuffed sandwich cupped in both hands oozed mustard.

"Here 'tis, Daddy," he hollered. Lettuce dangled from one corner of his mouth. "Miz Zan on the groun.' "

Television filled in the blanks of her out-of-body experience.

Entranced, she watched how Devilrow dislodged her belt off a gate spike. He wiped away a thread of blood running down her temple and shouted for Channel Eighteen to get the "F" out of the way before the guy holding the zoom lens got an internal probe with it. While the story ended with the entire Metroplex pondering the whereabouts of Roby Tyson, she focused her energy on Devilrow.

"I'm gonna kill you," she said with conviction.

The boy shifted his gaze and paused in mid-bite. Luminous brown spheres widened in their sockets.

"Don't fret, Son, she just devilin' me," the big man said. To Cézanne, he mumbled, "Ought to be thankin' yo' lucky stars, you axe me." Devilrow smashed his own sandwich against a set of meaty lips. "Wasn't for that gate breakin' yo' fall, you'd a-split yo' head wide open."

"Is that my roast beef?"

"Did you know you got green stuff growin' in yo' fridge?"

"I'm gonna kill you."

"Ought to treat people kinder, you axe me. You lackin' in compassion. Yo' mama didn't teach you proper. Take me: you left me favorin' my back out in them hedges the other evening. I could-a took one look at you tangled up in my prize gate and said, 'No-sirree, I ain't studying Miz Zan', but Leviticus Devilrow' mother taught him to turn his face on hate."

She raised up on her elbows. "Don't do me any favors."

"No'm, I ain't."

After convincing Devilrow she didn't need anybody fussing over her, Cézanne shooed them off and doctored the scratch plumped up near her eyebrow.

Around eight-thirty that night, the telephone rang.

Jinx Porter.

He didn't say how he managed to get her unlisted home number. "What's going on?"

"I was hoping to hear from you before I left work," she answered coolly.

It wasn't as if she'd already started a law practice and was billing by the hour, but Roby might be cooling his hocks in the county jail, for all she knew. He damned sure wasn't answering his telephone.

"Well, it was kinda hard to fulfill your assignment, stuck at my desk all afternoon."

"I thought you had this stuff on computer."

"You don't think I keep this kind of information at work, do you?" Agitated. "The county's so screwed up the only thing I keep in my office that's worth a tinker's damn are the Dogs Playing Poker. Not a day goes by somebody doesn't raise my blood pressure. And the last thing I need to piss me off is to have to make two trips to the car, moving out."

"If you say so."

"I was about to grab a bite." His tone grew considerably warmer. "You know Cosmo's?"

Fort Worth's number one pick for hardening the arteries with mouth-watering barbeque? She did.

"I show up once a week, come hell or high water. Meet me and we'll talk."

She didn't need convincing. If he had a lead that could help Roby, an evening with Jinx Porter would be an investment in her partner's future.

"Be there in fifteen."

She found him seated in a corner booth away from the crowd, singing some half-baked ditty between sips of Coors Light.

"I call my baby 'Honey' 'cause she likes to feel my

stinger. I call my wiener 'Frank' 'cause it plumps up when I—" He stopped in mid-tune. "Top o' the mornin'."

She slid onto the opposite bench.

He held up a piece of meat, smoky and red, seasoned to perfection and falling off the bone. "Rib?"

"May as well." She shared his plate while he flagged down a waitress. "Cola," Cézanne said between bites.

Jinx wiped the grease off his fingers, tossed the napkin aside, pulled out a paper and passed it across the table. Looking over six names, she caught him studying her.

"I did a search." His voice oozed pride. "Check 'em out."

"This is it? This is all there is in the whole state?"

His eyes narrowed, and she knew she'd frayed a nerve.

"I'm sorry, Constable, I don't mean to appear ungrateful. It's just that I'm half out of my mind with worry. Did you see tonight's news?"

"Looked like somebody hung you on a meathook."

"Then you know about the Grand Jury investigation?"

"Reckon you'd better get crackin'. I wouldn't mind helping out." He settled against the seat back. "Matter of fact, it'd be my pleasure. Maybe we could get together at your place, have a couple of—"

"JINX."

The crow-in-heat screech of his name sheared the attention of everyone in the room. Cézanne jerked her head around and stared straight into the cleavage of a woman twice her size. Not to mention a masculine face covered in troweled-on makeup.

With the most enormous, unfeminine hands she'd ever seen.

And an Adam's apple.

One look at Jinx Porter's shocked expression told her he couldn't fall through the floor fast enough.

Haloed in a musky fragrance, the drag queen positioned himself at the edge of their table.

"Love your scarf, Dearie. Is that real silk? I'm Glen Lee Spence, but you can call me Leather Devotion. I see you're enjoying the company of my friend, the constable."

She gradually became aware of her mouth gaping open.

"And may I ask where you bought that positively glorious angora sweater you're wearing? From a distance, I thought you had on Buckwheat's head."

Glen Lee leveled his gaze at Jinx.

"I do not wish to disturb you, Jinx, but I promise I will have all of my stuff removed from the apartment by tomorrow afternoon. And I would appreciate it if you would look after Pookie so that he does *not* run out into the street. I think it's the least you can do, considering you picked the fight."

With that, Glen Lee Spence twirled around and prissed off in his tight knit skirt and garish pashmina. Cézanne sat, unblinking, until the bizarre apparition disappeared from sight.

Roby's friend had some explaining to do.

"You know this person?"

"It's not what you think."

"I really don't know you well enough to think anything." Nor was she at all certain she wanted to.

"I can explain. I evict—"

She silenced him with an upraised hand.

With a hang-dog expression, he dropped a couple of bills on the table and wrenched himself out of the booth.

Roby was right. Jinx Porter was a first degree masher. When she was certain he had left, she did something she hadn't done in days.

Laughed herself into a cramp.

Chapter Eight

For an early morning service, the funeral home was crammed.

But not so packed Cézanne's keen eye didn't spot a couple of headhunters collaborating with a few self-ordained sneaks from Narcotics for a bit of amateurish surveillance.

In the vestibule, she signed the registry with her bold, slanted script and took a ceremonial program embossed with angels from a pasty-faced funeral employee. Mourners filed past, and each time the solid walnut doors opened, she felt the influence of Captain Crane like hot breath on her neck. Her eyes drifted over the page before she allowed herself a peek inside the room.

At the front, surrounded by a garden of floral arrangements, with her marble statue complexion barely visible over the frills, lay Carri Crane. An honor guard shared the first two rows with pallbearers on one side of the chapel; on the other, a blend of uniforms settled in among middle-aged folks and clean-cut college kids dressed in their Sunday best.

The scent of carnations mingled with a blue-haired lady's magnolia fragrance, tightening Cézanne's throat. In her thirty-two years, she'd only attended one funeral, but snippets of that horrible day pelted her memory with the vengeance of a Biblical stoning.

Halfway through the doorway, her feet turned to lead.

It wasn't the idea of a lengthy service that triggered her decision to bolt from the room. Nor was it the critical expressions forming on the faces of brother officers, and the elbow jabs that dominoed along the pews and brought similar disapproving looks. It was the bloodless hand of a funeral employee reaching into his pocket for a photograph, studying it momentarily, then signaling to several suits flanking the chapel's entrance.

She tracked the men's gazes to the unexpected sight of Roby filling the entrance. Gold-plated smiles of compassion melted into disdain. They moved in a fluid motion, gliding over to form a well-choreographed shield. Lemminglike, Cézanne followed.

Whatever happened, she and Roby were in it together.

One of the men emerged as the leader. He spoke in a voice straight from the tomb.

"Excuse me, Sir, would you mind coming with us?"

"I wouldn't stick anything within a three-foot radius of me I wasn't prepared to lose, if I was you. Including that puny little flipper of a hand you're trying to pass off as a clamp."

"Sir, your presence is unwelcome."

Not to mention potentially disruptive. The few cops loitering in the foyer obviously weren't TV watchers, or Roby would have already had hands latched onto him. She linked arms with her partner. His muscles grew taut beneath his sleeve.

"I've come to pay my respects."

The director said, "The family requests your immediate departure."

"Come on, Roby, I'll go with you."

"Only way I'm leaving is carry-out." The set to his jaw told her he meant business.

"Please, just give us a moment." Her gloved hand lingered on the pale man's sleeve. "I swear it won't be a problem."

The employees exchanged glances. Nothing in their movements suggested they planned to leave Roby unescorted, but upon the abrupt nod from the guy calling the shots, one of his cronies ducked inside the chapel.

She hissed, "He sent for reinforcements," and gave her partner's arm a violent yank.

"She was my life. She made me young."

"Come on." The tug turned ferocious. She backtracked him to the outer steps. "The Cranes don't want you. Right now, as far as I can tell, you're only trespassing. Keep putzing around, you'll end up in lockdown."

"It's a public place."

"You're persona non grata." Her eyes rimmed with tears. "And you may be a wanted man. For all we know, the Grand Jury handed down an indictment, so for God's sake, quit fighting me."

His massive shoulders slumped under the weight of her stare.

"Aw-right. Let's git."

They ended up in a corner booth at a café down the street. It wasn't until she pulled off her gloves and warmed her hands against a mug of coffee that the subject of Roby's impending arrest came up.

"I had a dream last night," he said, his dismal mood mirroring the overcast sky. "You got to be a prosecutor—"

"Fat chance."

"—and sent me d'rectly to the electric chair."

She allowed herself a wry chuckle. "What happened to lethal injection?"

"All I know is, I had electrodes sprouting out of my head

and an executioner with an itchy trigger finger."

The silence between them grew. When he finally downed the rest of his coffee, he dropped a bombshell.

"The Boys borrowed Mother Goose yesterday."

She knew immediately he was talking about the Crime Scene detectives and wondered if a go-getter nicknamed "Slash" had processed the pick up truck.

"Don't think our brother officers missed a spot. One fellow knew me by reputation and said he was gonna extend a little professional courtesy." Roby let out a facetious *harumph*. "Reckon I ought to be glad I got Mother Goose back without any holes cut out of the seats instead of being bitter over spending yesterday afternoon chiseling off *Super-Glue* and wiping down fingerprint powder."

"They SuperGlued your vehicle?"

"Misted it with Ardrox, too. Guess they didn't want to miss a single opportunity to see me fry."

With her mind on autopilot, she visualized Slash diluting the neon chartreuse liquid with ethyl alcohol, pouring it into a mister and spritzing the stubbornest latents brought up by the SuperGlue fumes. Then, whipping out the fluoro-scope and the digital camera and snapping close-ups of the prints fluorescing under the UV light so he could preserve them for later comparison. Make a dandy impression on a jury. He'd probably bring the light to trial and squirt his hand. Hold the UV next to it, let 'em see it turn blue. Juries loved gimmicks, just ate that forensic stuff up. Roby's voice buzzed in her ear and she became aware of him speaking.

"When I got my truck back, the whole inside looked like dirty snowflakes. Do you have any idea how much time it takes to scrape SuperGlue off with a razor blade?" He gri-maced. "They luminoled it, too. While I was doing the windshield, I had the misfortune to nick myself. I bled on the seat. If they come back for seconds it'll light up like a torch."

Inwardly, she shuddered. If they fumed his vehicle they were gunning for him.

About that time, their waitress breezed by with a fresh pot of coffee and barely stopped long enough to splash a re-fill into their cups. Roby signaled for the check before she flitted off.

Cézanne asked, "Acid phosphotase?"

"Might as well test for the presence of *spunk,* they checked for everything else." He touched the mug to his lips. At the last moment, he set it down without taking a sip.

"I could-a told 'em they'd find her hair. Could-a prob-ably even pointed out stains. That pick up got quite a workout the last few weeks. Sugar—I mean, Carri," he cor-rected himself, "liked parking lots. Don't ask me."

"Don't worry, I won't."

She'd never seen him lower his chin with the shame of a five-year-old. It was always Roby embarrassing somebody else, not the other way around. She never knew him to be anything but brazen about his sexual escapades.

"Did they get a search warrant for your house?"

He nodded. " 'Course they didn't plan on me having a housekeeper who's scared of germs. They only ended up taking the bedsheets when everything else came up clean as a whistle, but now the maid wants time-and-a-half for having to scrub the place all over again."

"They're just doing their jobs."

Roby snorted in disgust. "You sound like a prosecutor. Why don't you just go ahead and ask me if I did it?"

"The Crime Scene guys're supposed to be professionals. Whatever they find or don't find could winnow you out as a suspect."

"Do you think I'm bothered by the fact they're doing a bang-up job investigating me? I'm not. Do you think it pisses me off having those dickweeds hanging back until I drop one of my Marlboros on the pavement and grind it out? Hell, if they want my spit to work up a DNA profile that bad, let 'em have it. I can only hope when they finally get it outta their gnat-brains that I did it, they'll put half as much work in on the miserable fuck who really did."

She wanted to believe him. She *did* believe him.

"I met Jinx Porter."

Amusement mixed with surprise. "Did he try to get in your drawers?"

"I think it was headed that way."

"Should-a let him." Roby winked.

"Me sleeping with Jinx Porter carries the same odds as a politician keeping his zipper fastened."

"He's a card. Used to be my closest friend 'til you came along. He wouldn't begrudge me, though. I always did find women easier to get along with. Reckon he does, too."

Cézanne studied the steam coiling from her cup. She took a deep breath, and when she sighed, the hope she felt when they first arrived seemed to go with it.

She said, "I'd give anything to go back four days."

"You ain't a-kiddin'." Roby dug into his pocket and pulled out an envelope. "Didja get that job at the DA's?"

She sniffed. "Not hardly."

Instantly, his load seemed lighter. "How come? You've been breathing it ever since we first met that night at the laundromat."

She didn't want to point the finger. On account of she believed in him. Trusted him. And yeah, doggone it, loved him. It took the duress of the moment to recognize what

Carri Crane saw behind the gunmetal gray eyes. Roby had a genuine soul, and for a man nearly forty thousand miles out of warranty, perfect bone structure under the weather-beaten skin. She could imagine how Carri Crane must have rested her head against his chest after a wicked tryst, listening to the beat of his gold heart.

Her eyes cut to the window, and for a brief moment, she marked time scanning traffic.

"How come, Duchess? How come you don't want to be a *persecutor?*"

She mumbled something about having plenty of time to pursue her dream, first things first, and watched the mourners snaking down the funeral home steps like a never-ending anaconda.

Roby downed the last of his coffee and broke her concentration with a slap to the Formica tabletop.

"I'm gonna make you a star," he said. "I'm gonna give you a chance to put yourself on the map."

"What are you talking about?"

He removed a paper from the envelope and read from it. "Fifty thousand dollars cash, Zan. That's all I could scrape together on short notice."

"I don't understand."

"Let's just run the ambulance right up to the front door." With the passion of Romeo, he dropped the bank statement on the table and sandwiched her hand between his. "I'm asking you to be my lawyer."

Her lungs collapsed. The euphoric rush that followed after they reinflated gave way to despair.

"You need an attorney who's made a name for himself. Somebody who—"

"Believes in my innocence."

"For God's sake, Roby, I don't know anything about defending people. I've spent the last few years of my life locking them up."

"Bullshit. You defend people every day. You protect them from bad shit happening."

"I don't protect and defend criminals," she said, her thoughts hotwired to her tongue. "I protect and defend people *from* criminals."

"You think I did it."

"That's not what I meant."

"Don't you see? You don't even have to be on my side, Zannie. Why can't you just be for the truth?"

With a sharp intake of air, she sat up straight. "I'm not a defense attorney. I don't have the mindset."

"I'm not asking you to create facts," he said, his corded arms folded across his chest. "The facts'll take care of themselves. You say your job's to protect and defend? Fine." He yanked his necktie loose and opened his shirt down to the third button. "Look at it from another angle: protect my rights. Protect Carri's. Defend me from a bum rap. Defend Carri's memory by pointing them in the direction of the maggot who did it."

This is how Moonies work.

"I'm a born prosecutor," she said, editing out the rest of the thought pinballing around inside her head: that she would have been a shoo-in if he hadn't gotten in the way.

"That's why you're perfect. You know how they think. Stop looking at me like I just insulted you."

Everything in the room came into sharp focus.

"It's more money than you'll see in a year. Hell, more than you'd make being a State's attorney."

Her jaw went slack. She couldn't believe Roby's crust— the smooth-talking way he propped her up and that gold-plated smile full of sin.

"Some of this may have to go for bail. I ain't staying locked up with a bunch of queers. But what's left is yours. I'll get you some more, soon as I can. Say you'll do it, Duchess. Say you'll take me on as your client."

"Insanity," she mumbled, plotting impossible strategy while staring into a tunnel that didn't exist. "It might work, because, see, I could tell the Court you were crazy enough to hire me—"

A cashier's check thrust under her nose stopped her in mid-sentence. Pay to the order of: Cézanne Martin. He already knew she wouldn't let him down, probably knew the second the idea occurred to him.

"My life's in your hands now, Girl."

That's what she was afraid of.

Chapter Nine

With its windowless walls and mausoleum ambience, the dismal atmosphere of the PD's basement transcended that of the funeral and seemed just as permanent. For the hundredth time in four days, Cézanne found herself longing for an upstairs office where she could throw open a window and suck in a deep breath of fresh carbon monoxide from passing cars.

The only person in Pawn Shop Detail when she arrived around one o'clock that afternoon was Darlene Driskoll, seated at her desk, applying nail polish. Darlene paused in mid-stroke, screwed the cap on the bottle, held up a metal nail file and raked it across her thumbnail in slow, deliberate whacks.

Jesus H. First the knitting needle, then a steak knife and straight razor, now a nail file as big as a survival knife. Each time they crossed paths, Driskoll's wife had something sharp in her hand.

Cézanne slipped into her cubicle for some down time before meeting Whitelark. Before the Grand Jury returned an indictment, she needed to figure out how to deliver Roby to the booking desk and bond him out at the same time. If she became his attorney of record, the conflict of interest would force her to quit the PD. But if she left the PD, accessing Carri Crane's homicide file would be next to impossible, even with the Rules of Discovery.

Okay, maybe not impossible. But harder.

Darlene waddled in with a stack of papers and dropped them on one corner of the desk. Instead of returning to her station, she stayed put. The pink in her plump cheeks turned as crimson as her newly lacquered nails. Gold-flecked eyes dulled. For several seconds she did nothing but stare.

The pulse in Cézanne's throat throbbed, but she forced a smile and kept her voice level. "Was there something else?"

"Dr. Whitelark set your appointment back an hour."

Darlene presented a message slip and placed it on the edge of the desk with cold deliberation. In the time it took Cézanne to blink, the woman produced an antler-handled letter opener and stood tapping it against her palm.

"Want I should slit your throat—mail? Your mail. I meant mail. I can open your mail for you, or you can do it yourself. Whatever you want."

Cézanne's mind gathered speed. Purse in the drawer, five seconds away. Gun in purse, useless. Darlene within the lunge. Herself, disabled in a flash.

Talk it out. See what she wants.

"Pull up a chair." The idea didn't seem so outlandish, given the alternative.

Darlene took a seat across the desk and sat contentedly on her brisket. "Your name's spelled funny. I always thought it was Suzanne." Her voice strident at the end.

"My mother worked in a museum. The kids were named after her favorite painters."

"So how do you say it? Your name, I mean."

Bernice pronounced it *Say-zonne.* But this was Texas, where most everyone else said *Suh-Zan,* accent on the last syllable.

"You're not the first to mispronounce it. I'm used to it.

Most people just call me Zan but I pretty much answer to anything that's not profane."

"Cézanne." The pronunciation of the majority rolled off Darlene's tongue. "From now on, I'll remember."

The thought brought no comfort whatsoever.

"Who does your hair?" Darlene's hollow stare held its focus. "I used to fix mine that way, but I could never get the color right."

"Your hair's nice." Cézanne scrutinized the dried-out tumbleweed. It was the polite thing to say, and in no way reflected her true opinion. "You should keep it the way it is."

Darlene grimaced. "It's brittle." She pulled at a curl until it straightened. "I won't ever go blonde again. It's just not the same. Anyway, I'm growing it. My hair grows fast. In a couple of months it'll be where yours is."

Her eyes glazed over, and her mind seemed to retreat to a faraway place. "I used to wonder what you were like in bed."

Every fiber in Cézanne's body cried out. She spread her palms in surrender. "It's you he loves."

"Do you play music when you seduce your victims?" Darlene asked in a voice cool and wistful. "Doug never wanted music before you."

There was no right answer. And judging by Darlene's distant gaze, she didn't expect one. Beyond the cubicle, a phone rang. Neither made a move to dial into the extension and answer it.

"Tell me what you said to him. What you did to make him your slave." She returned to the present. Her eyes sparked fury. "It's the least you can do."

"Let it go, Darlene."

Knuckles whitened against the letter opener. "He never

would've looked at you if it wasn't for we were having money troubles."

In a valiant attempt to keep her voice ingratiatingly pleasant, Cézanne awarded Driskoll's wife a minor victory. "I'm sure that's true."

More phone lines lit up, their tones shrill and unnerving.

"I'm going to answer this," Cézanne warned. She reached for the receiver.

"Don't. We're the only ones here. Nobody'll know."

The air grew stale. Spicy cologne, mingled with Darlene's sweat, turned rancid. The stench of fear invaded their shared space.

"Now he's in Narcotics, he never thinks of you at all."

"I'm glad." Cézanne swallowed hard. "I had no idea he transferred. I don't keep up with him."

With her voice steeled in conviction, Darlene said, "I'd do anything to keep my family together. Anything."

Cézanne thought of the cashier's check in her wallet. Of the list of names Jinx Porter gave her to run down. How she wanted to tell Whitelark and the others to shove it, walk out and never look back. But she couldn't. On account of a little thing called *work product*.

Even a rookie knew an investigator's work product was off limits to defense attorneys. And that was the hangup. She couldn't leave.

Not until she no longer needed access to their files.

So for Roby Tyson, the best friend and partner she ever had, she'd sit right here and eat Darlene's shit with a sterling shrimp fork if that's what it took to save him.

The unexpected creak of a door brought instant relief to Cézanne's knotted muscles. She said, "Somebody's here."

The desk sergeant, normally an unwelcome sight, waited at the entrance, jerking his head toward the inner office in what seemed to be an animated conversation. When Darlene lingered unfazed, Cézanne stood bracing her hands against the desk and ladled up some crow.

"I apologize for any grief I may have caused you."

Darlene's blanched face registered shock. "Grief?" She indulged herself a mirthless chuckle. "Grief is what the Captain's feeling."

"We should check on our guests."

With reluctance, Darlene rose. She loosened the grip on her letter opener, letting the color flood back into her hand. With all the *chutzpah* Cézanne could muster, she summed up the disastrous liaison with Darlene's husband.

"I wish you both the best."

In retrospect, she couldn't remember a Tuesday in her life that started out as bad as this one.

Chapter Ten

The only person with a clue how it felt to be surrounded by crazy people also happened to be the very person Cézanne didn't want to have anything to do with.

A forty-five minute visit with Aden Whitelark, still dressed in funereal splendor and steepling his fingers the whole time as if he were superior to nine-tenths of the population, left her gnawing a hole inside of her mouth. It didn't seem unusual for him to have so much documentation on Roby's quirky behavior—supplied by others, of course—but he wasn't able to wring anything out of her to add to it. A person couldn't very well cough up stories if they developed amnesia early in the interview.

She barely made it back to her desk when Darlene, carving into a large package with a box cutter, stopped long enough to put a hair raising call through.

Bernice.

Grappling for her purse, Cézanne high-tailed it to Forestview.

After the doctor's urgent message, they must've shot Bernice up with enough juice to send her frolicking through the loblolly pines. One could only hope the shrieks would subside in the time it took to make the ten mile drive.

She'd know soon enough.

An attendant unlocked the door and keyed off the elevator. The click of Cézanne's heels echoed through the corridor leading to the hospital's psychiatric wing. She reached the entrance to Bernice's room, only to have the pungent smell of disinfectant invade her nostrils. A doctor, clipboard in hand, hovered over all ninety-five pounds of her mother, furiously jotting down God-knew-what.

Bernice seemed to be resting quietly.

Hey, bartender. A round of Prozac for my friends.

Cézanne tiptoed near enough to tug his sleeve. When he turned to peer at her over his smudged horn rims, she noted his name tag.

JEREMY HILL, followed by a string of initials unique to the medical and psychiatric professions.

"I had no idea she'd be asleep," she whispered.

"She's faking."

Dr. Hill punctuated his written entry, then cocked his head in her direction. The glasses slid out of the permanent dents on either side of his prominent nose, and he pushed them back into place with his thumb.

"The nurse went for restraints."

Cézanne recoiled. "You're not putting Momma in a straitjacket."

"We're not going to fight her again."

Cézanne got a closer look at the blood splatters staining his smock. She shifted her eyes to her mother's peaceful face before performing a visual scan on the exposed parts of her body for bruises.

"I'm here now. I'll watch her."

"No, Ma'am." He appeared unflappable. "Your mother's a force to be reckoned with."

Tell me.

A chubby nurse with salt-and-pepper hair waddled in with a fistful of straps.

Cézanne tried again. "That won't be necessary. I can handle her fine."

"Can you?"

"She knows me. She'll feel safe." Her throat heated up with an acid burn. She hated the sound of her own childlike pleading.

The nurse locked gazes with the doctor. He shook his head.

"NO." Cézanne knocked aside a chair in her lunge for the restraints.

Dr. Hill stepped between them and gave the attendant the go-ahead. "Ms. Martin, you don't seem to realize the gravity of your mother's psychosis."

The nurse bypassed her, heading to the far side of Bernice's bed. Cézanne made a wild grab for the doctor's sleeve and hung on.

"It's you who doesn't understand." Tears spilled over onto freshly powdered cheeks.

"We have a court order."

Up came the first strap. At the sight of the tattoo on Bernice's arm, the nurse's face contorted into a mask of disgust.

The cloth touched Bernice's wrist, and she came to life. She balled up a fist and took a swing. The pie-faced nurse went sprawling to the floor, her hat zipping across the linoleum and coming to rest within an arm's length of the wall like the Stars' winning hockey shot.

"Where are da scissors?" Bernice shouted. "I shall cut out your heart."

Off flew the sheet. Over the side of the bed lopped a scrawny leg.

Dr. Hill stepped aside. Depressed a wall switch.

Cézanne knew the drill. Bernice never laid a hand on her all the time she was growing up. Never laid a hand on any of them except for that one time. Brute force wasn't needed. The woman dominated her offspring with mind control. They obeyed out of fear and threats. So she wouldn't hurt her now, of that, Cézanne was certain.

She rushed to her mother's bed side. "Don't worry, Momma. I'm here."

Bernice oscillated her head into a grotesque angle and stared through glazed eyes. Slowly, her dilated pupils contracted into pinpoints. Embers ignited. Steel-blue irises blazed in a backdraft of fury. She hoisted her leg back up onto the mattress. Maneuvered into a new position.

"YOU." At the top of her lungs. "I shall see you dead dis minute. You are da one, gave da orders to kill *mein Mutti*."

"Momma, what're you talking about?"

"Kush meer in tochus."

"She's speaking in tongues again," muttered the doctor.

"You're wrong." Cézanne maintained eye contact. "This is Texas. I'm your daughter. Don't you know me?"

Sobs hung in her throat waiting to break free.

"Kush meer in tochus," Bernice screeched through bared fangs. "I watched you kill my brother. You are evil, and I shall rip out your heart wid my bare hands, Nazi schwein."

"Look at me. Don't you know me?"

Cézanne watched the hatred mellow into mere contempt, and for a split second, she knew they connected. Bernice recognized her. With arms outstretched, Cézanne reached out to embrace her mother. Bernice lifted her arms—

—and locked her small hands around Cézanne's neck.

A thin gold chain resting just below her collarbone broke, snaking into her bra. Frantic, she pulled at the taloned fingers enough to vacuum in a deep breath. With her free hand, she dug out the ornate, cylindrical drop and held it inches from her mother's face.

See the mazuzzah, Momma. See the Torah rolled up inside.

The woman's strength crushed the voice right out of her. Tightened around her pulse points. Cut off blood flow to the brain. Lightheaded and nose to nose, what little oxygen she took in mixed with the stench of Bernice's fetid breath. The mazuzzah slipped from Cézanne's grip and disappeared into folds of percale sheets. Both hands prying couldn't lessen the stranglehold.

"I shall watch you die, *Shikse*."

Dr. Hill's once commanding voice rang out, tinny and distant.

They'll need an atom splitter to separate us.

Cézanne's knees turned to mush. Each gasp for air became more precious than the one before. At the sensation of capillaries popping in her eyes, she threaded her fingers together. Shaped her arms into a tee-pee, the way she'd learned street survival in rookie school. In a last ditch effort, she drove the powerful wedge up between Bernice's outstretched arms and broke the choke hold.

Attendants appeared out of nowhere, converging on them. The nurse leaped forward to clamp a bony arm.

"No," Cézanne gasped.

Bernice reared back. Took another swing. Connected with Cézanne's cheek. Stung like a belt sander and set off Westminster chimes in her head. Off to one side, her eye caught a splotch of white moving in.

"Get away. I'm the one getting the shit beat out of me, not you."

Bernice popped her a good one. Grabbed a hunk of hair and pulled her onto the bed with unbelievable strength.

"Momma, don't. I'm Cézanne."

"She can't hear you." Dr. Hill talking.

Bernice put up a valiant resistance.

"Mamzer. Groyser putz."

"She hears." Cézanne not only felt the hair rip from her scalp, but heard it.

"Increase the dosage." Dr. Hill, barking orders.

"Don't. I can make her understand."

The nurse disappeared in a blur.

"Momma . . . see my . . . face."

"Ugliness."

Bernice cleared her throat and spat out a wad of phlegm, putrid and thick. It slimed down Cézanne's temple, into her hair.

"I shall stomp it da way you did Herman's. He only was five, you evil bastard. You shall shake hands wid Hitler in hell."

In an instant, the war ended.

Bernice relaxed her grip. Her arms fell limply at her sides. A flicker of recognition reappeared, and her cold eyes warmed.

"Monet? It is you?" The madwoman's eyelids fluttered. Focusing her vision seemed a challenge. "I knew you would come. You are my most wonderful child. I always loved you best."

The news had the impact of severing an aorta.

"I'm Cézanne, Momma. Monet's not here."

Monet's dead. Monet's been dead for years.

Bernice slumped into a dune of pillows. "You do not wear your grandmother's mazuzzah?" Tears glistened against parchment skin.

Cézanne scoured the covers for the holy mazuzzah, the only tangible heirloom Bernice's family didn't lose to the Germans. The day Bernice presented it to Monet, she explained how their grandmother managed to keep it secret.

While the Nazis thundered up the stairs to their flat, she'd ripped it off its chain and turned it into a sacred suppository.

Gold glinted against a flap of sheet, newly unfurled.

Found it.

Cézanne held it up for the pathetic creature to see.

"You must keep it close to your heart, Monet. Protection." Bernice's lids fell to half mast. "You are so beautiful. I never had trouble to tell you apart from Cézanne like da others. Even babies in da bassinets, you were prettiest, always."

She spoke the truth. Teachers didn't have a clue Monet took Cézanne's math tests. Or that Cézanne sat for Monet's history exams. The "F" in algebra should have been obvious after her twin died, but the school counselor wrote it off to depression. It was, but with an added slant. The Martin family harbored a secret more shocking than the legendary mazuzzah.

"You must have Cézanne to show how to fix your face. It is a mess."

"Okay, Momma." She choked on the words.

Bernice's eyes closed completely. With the cadence of her breath, shallow, and her words, sluggish, she whispered, "Promise me, Monet."

"Anything, Mommy." Her spirit dying inside.

"Watch Cézanne. She is not—

—so strong—

—as you."

The lines in Bernice's face relaxed. With a fist to her mouth, Cézanne held back a sob. Tension drained from her mother's body as Cézanne stroked the garden-hose veins in her feeble hand.

"Cézanne . . ."

"I'm here, Momma."

"Cézanne is . . ."

The last words from Bernice's mouth, before she faded out for the afternoon, came out strong. Determined. Disgusted.

". . . such . . . a weakling."

Chapter Eleven

Collapsed in a chair in Jeremy Hill's office, Cézanne refused his offer of a tissue and claimed the entire box. Emotionally spent and physically exhausted, she let the container rest in her lap and slumped against the chair back. Her eyes traveled over several framed Renoir posters on a blue-hued wall, to a fake ficus in one corner and finally, to a wall devoted to Hill's medical credentials.

Dr. Hill broke the silence. "So?"

He was waiting for her to say something. He must have asked a question.

"What does *Kush meer in tochus* mean? She says it whenever I come into her room. 'Kush meer in tochus.' "

Cézanne gnawed the inside of her lip and mentally weighed the consequences before offering up a translation. She decided not tell him it meant, "Kiss my ass."

"It's Yiddish. It means your glasses are slipping."

"Mrs. Martin's a Jew?"

The words hopped out like warty little toads. She recognized the grimace that followed. She'd seen it before, all through grade school. And now he was scrutinizing her face. Another *groyser putz*, expecting her to have a schnoz like a toucan.

Without comment, she watched him open a drawer and pull out a small cloth. He removed his horn rims, polishing them for what seemed like forever. After seating them back in their place, he consulted a small mirror, licked his fingertips and plastered down a patch of wiry growth jutting out from his scalp.

She decided then and there, she hated him.

For good measure, she planted a wickedly suggestive seed in the hope it might germinate.

"You have a Dr. Mandelbaum on staff?"

"He's Forestview's director."

"Well, I noticed when we passed Dr. Mandelbaum's office his eyeglasses were slipping." She could almost see a light go on in Hill's attic as he finished preening.

The mirror went back into the drawer.

"So you're Jewish," he said with fake cheer.

"My mother's Jewish. I'm nothing. Didn't you hear her call me a shikse?"

The doctor stretched against his chair back. "I beg to differ with you, Dear Girl. If the mother's Jewish then the offspring's automatically—"

"You don't have to school me on my birthright, Doc. I know my heritage. My father raised me Lutheran."

"Who's Monet?"

The question iced her over. Her mouth went dry, and it took several swallows before she regained her composure.

"Monet was my twin. She was Momma's girl. Monet was raised in the Jewish faith."

"Ah." His eyes lit up with excitement. "Then your sister did the *bat mitzvah* shtick."

Clearly, he wished to show off his cultural awareness by blathering *drek*.

"Monet never made it. We were twelve when she died."

"And Matisse?" He reached for a pen. His eyes searched the desk until he excavated far enough through the clutter to unearth a pad.

"Henri Matisse." After a ragged sigh, she set the record

straight. "Henri is my brother."

She anticipated the next question. It happened all the time.

"My mother was a museum curator and was mostly fond of impressionist and post-impressionist painters. As for Henri, his birth certificate says Matisse but he changed it himself through the court system. Henri was the only one who could ever stand up to her."

"What happened to Monet?"

Cézanne dug for a tissue and came out with a stack. She lifted her chin in defiance and tried not to give in to the pain pulsing behind her left eye.

"How is this information necessary in order for my mother to receive proper treatment?"

"Your mother's a very sick woman."

"Then make her well."

"I need a complete family history."

"Have you spoken with Henri?"

Her eyes darted around the room. Took inventory. Anything to avoid Dr. Hill's unnerving gaze. She checked out the fake ficus. Then the Venus di Milo miniature featured on a pedestal behind her. When she could no longer ignore the dreadful pull of his stare, she yielded to it.

He extended his arm far enough across the desk to dangle a message slip with a telephone number scrawled on it.

"That's Henri's," she said without enthusiasm. "What'd he say?"

"I believe his exact words were, 'You can butt a stump for all I care.' "

A sick smile spread across her face. Still playing like James Dean. In seconds, an unintended chuckle swelled into a hearty laugh. In even less time, her emotions escalated to tears.

"Henri's an asshole." She gouged at her eyes with wads of Kleenex. Crunching the damp mess in a fist, she reminded the doctor, "You're not putting my mother in a straightjacket."

"Restraints."

"No."

"Then we'll get the net."

Cézanne bucked so hard the tissue box tumbled to the floor. She gathered her purse and readied herself to bolt.

"You've got a lot of chutzpah mocking my tragedy, you schmuck."

Jeremy Hill jumped to his feet.

Over a slew of Yiddish epithets, he shouted, "Ms. Martin, the net is a tentlike mesh that will confine her to the bed, yet allow freedom of movement. We can just erect it, zip her in—"

"Don't be a *shmendrik*. I'm not an idiot; don't you be. She's already been confined. Don't you get it? She's paid up to last five lifetimes."

"Calm yourself." He spread his arms helplessly. "This institution isn't equipped with enough personnel to watch her around the clock."

She froze in place. "Then I'll move her."

"I'd gladly invite you to do so. Unfortunately for you, none of the other local facilities will take her. We tried. The next stop is commitment to the North Texas State Hospital in Wichita Falls. I don't think you want that."

Cézanne banked the crumpled tissue off one wall and watched it circle the lip of the waste can and disappear from sight.

"Why don't you sit back down and tell me what happened to Monet?"

She beat him to the door. "My mother's not crazy. You

can medicate her. Just don't overdo it. I'll satisfy the bill, long as she's here." She lifted a finger and pointed it in his face. "But do not tie her down, or I swear I'll file suit."

"What happened to Monet?"

His arm came up to clothesline the doorway.

She ducked beneath it.

"Do you have a therapist?" he called out after her.

Images of Aden Whitelark came racing back.

"Get *shtupped*."

She picked up her pace to elude the memories. Heels clicked hard against the floor tiles. Desperate to leave the hospital. To flee the building. Retreat into the elements. Anywhere that would take her out of Bernice's life and away from this depressing place with its permanent smell of decay.

She reached the rubber mat at the exit. At the touch of a foot, the automatic glass door to freedom swung open. In the distance she could still hear Dr. Hill's torturous call, and it hung between her ears the entire drive home.

What happened to Monet?

Chapter Twelve

After stopping by the house to swap her blouse for one that still had all its buttons, Cézanne came up with a dozen reasons for not returning to Three-fifty. But the reason she should plagued her. And by the time she came within a mile of the PD, the rhythmic thump of windshield wipers and the scent of rain wafting through the vents coaxed some of the tension out of her shoulders. The shower let up as she zipped the BMW into the community parking lot, but standing on deck waiting for the trolley, her neck muscles corrugated all over again.

A cable car rolled up and braked in a spirited squeal.

The lunatic with the "National Rodeo Finals" jacket sat at the controls. Three sets of doors banged open. He swiveled his head in her direction, and their eyes locked in a murderous bent.

Several people brushed past to claim a seat. Soon, all attention hinged on her. Cézanne refused to budge.

The driver slapped at a switch. The third set of doors banged shut. He hit another toggle. The middle set closed. He shifted his eyes to the DO NOT TALK TO DRIVER WHILE CAR IN MOTION sign and pressed the caution bell.

Seconds passed.

She should get on.

Crazy speed demon wouldn't dare pull any kamikaze shit like last time, not with witnesses aboard.

She took a step. His hand covered the switch.

She hesitated, then took another. The brakes spewed out a warning. One more step, and he slammed the last set of doors in her face before she could climb aboard. Wheels ground against the rails in an eerie screech.

As she watched the shuttle sway gently down the tracks, she caught his reflection in the side mirror and thought she saw his lip angle up in a sneer.

Furious, she trudged through the mist, up the killer hill to HQ. With each burning step, she plotted the driver's undoing in her head. She'd report him, make a formal complaint. Maybe even demand his job. That'd get their attention, the sons-of-bitches who put him behind the wheel.

She crested the hill, breathless, her sleeves damp with sweat and her hair falling limp around her chin. By the time she reached the basement, blood seemed to course through her veins as if it were fuel-injected. Before she made it into Pawn Shop Detail, Darlene's electric laugh pierced the level of background conversation in the hall. When Cézanne opened the door, the sight of a lush arrangement of lilies placed prominently on Darlene's desk sickened her.

But not as much as the glinting scissors Darlene used to trim a red heart fashioned out of construction paper. Nor the kisses she smacked into the mouthpiece of the telephone. A sobering reminder that Doug Driskoll had only loaned himself out. He was never hers to begin with.

She bucked up and entered her cubicle where a new infusion of paperwork exploding from her desktop brought her to a standstill.

Beyond her line of vision, a chair scraped against the floor. In seconds, Darlene Driskoll appeared with an armful of printouts containing serial numbers of pawned items needing to be checked.

"Sarge said bring you these." Her lips thinned into a smirk.

"Set them over there if you don't mind." Cézanne pointed to a chair. When her nemesis didn't leave, she added, "Nice flowers."

"Aren't they? My Dougie sent them."

Cézanne wanted to tell her they looked like the kind of arrangement that belonged upstairs on Captain Crane's desk, but she opted to streamline conversations with Driskoll's wife and repaid the unstable woman with an unenthusiastic smile.

Characteristically blunt, Darlene asked, "Are you rich?"

"Where'd you get that idea?"

"Your house."

Chills raced over Cézanne's flesh like icy fingers. Her breath grew shallow.

Darlene Driskoll knew where she lived.

She dried her clammy hands against her knees. Tomorrow she'd wear a thigh holster.

"You came to my house?"

"I saw it once, driving by." Darlene's eyes grew wide. "I wasn't stalking you. I have a friend who lives in your neighborhood."

"And who might that be?"

"The Smiths." After an uncomfortable silence, Darlene blurted, "You wouldn't have met. They just moved in."

"I understand." She tried to act as if she meant it and let Driskoll's wife off the hook. It was enough to know the woman had it in for her. She made a mental note to tell Devilrow to be on the lookout.

"Dougie says you'll quit the force. He says you can't withstand the pressure."

"Like most Americans who've overextended themselves, I have bills." Cézanne lifted her chin convincingly to dispel any false impressions. "School loans, mainly."

"Don't lawyers make lots of money?"

"I predict they do," she said, influenced by wishful thinking. If only Darlene would go work somebody else's frazzled nerves.

"What size do you wear? I tried to diet, you know, but eating's not like smoking. You can't just quit cold turkey."

Interaction with Driskoll's wife was starting to feel like a B-grade film rethreading itself, and she'd seen enough.

"I hate to run you off, but I have cases to clear."

"Did he ever give you flowers?"

Violets, orchids and purple statice, mostly. And, once, a lavender rose. To complement her eyes, he'd said.

"Darlene, don't."

"Did he? I never got any until now."

Yoked with the guilt of upending this corn-fed girl's world, Cézanne viewed Driskoll's wife with what she hoped would be interpreted as a shameless expression of pity. She embarked on a set-to, long overdue.

"I didn't even know you existed," she admitted truthfully. The heat of shame crept into her cheeks. For God's sake, Driskoll was a cop, the lousy bastard. Telling the truth should've been a way of life. "I took him at his word. Once I began to suspect he was married, he conned me into believing he had filed for divorce."

"You could've asked around."

"I did. The ones who knew him best gave him the benefit of the doubt. Finally, to ease my conscience, I checked with the District Clerk's Office for a docket number." Cézanne shrugged. "There wasn't one."

Darlene, with her robust frame wrapped in a loud print

that would be considered bizarre by even the most lenient of standards, stretched the fabric to capacity and glumly absorbed the particulars. During the short time-out, she seemed to take the news under advisement. Seemingly nervous and unfocused, she finally asked the hurtful question.

"Did you love him?"

Cézanne shuddered inwardly. She needed an ambiguous answer that wouldn't encourage a tirade.

"I'm not the Jezebel homewrecker you take me for. If I had the power to design a man from scratch, he wouldn't be anything like your husband."

"Then why me? Why him?"

She didn't know, herself. "Relationships are insidious. Things happen. Even so, it's no excuse."

With a glassy stare and a sad smile disappearing into her face, Darlene's tone turned confidential.

"I was down in the dumps for a long time, you know. I never picked on you. I didn't even know about you until. . . ." The thought faded out, and her speech slowed to a sleepwalker's pace. "I didn't deserve what happened."

"No, you didn't." Cézanne's heart tightened in her chest. "He betrayed us both in the worst possible way, that much is true. And I'm not saying you should forget. God knows, no man ought to get off the meathook that easy, but let me make a suggestion. By taking him back, you've given him a clean slate and a chance to do better."

"There won't be a next time." Pinheads of perspiration beaded up on Darlene's nose. "Did you love him?"

She would rather have taken two thousand volts of electricity than answer. Darlene would smell a lie. She formulated a question designed to change the subject and delivered it with a lack of endorsement.

"What can I do to make this up to you?"

"I used to want you dead," Darlene said airily. "Now I just want you to be my friend."

"You want *us* to be friends?" The unexpected logic left Cézanne cold. "But why?"

"Because if we could be friends, I know you wouldn't have the guts to hurt me again. Not if you could help it." And then, "Did he ever give you flowers?"

By close of business, Cézanne made a decision that placed her on a bench outside Deputy Chief Daniel J. Rosen's office. When Rosen's secretary hadn't cleared the way for a visit after a ten minute wait, Cézanne helped herself to a cup of coffee from the credenza before barging in and plopping down in one of the guest chairs inside his private chamber.

Rosen, seated near the window and peering out through binoculars, turned to look.

Beyond Cézanne's view, the secretary's chair rolled against the floor and banged against something solid. Rosen's right hand woman appeared in the doorway, sputtering.

"Detective, you can't just—"

"It's okay, Ellen." Rosen fanned her away with his hand, then opened a drawer and returned the field glasses. "I've been expecting Detective Martin. Close the door on your way out."

Her superior rose from his seat and moved from behind a great mahogany desk, slicking a hand across lush black hair turning silver at the temples. For a man almost Roby's age, he still made a magnificent specimen, undeniably dashing in dress blues.

When they were alone, Rosen gripped her hand with the

confidence of a Heisman Trophy winner and pumped out a greeting.

"You're holding up nicely," he said, returning to his leather wingback and settling in. A gold-fringed American flag and its Lone Star counterpart flanked the windows behind him, promoting an impressive aura of integrity. "How's Bernice?"

She decided she didn't like her chair, and pulling one from the conference table and moving it closer to his desk gave her something to do while she decided how much information to trust him with.

Melting against butter-soft leather she answered, "Momma's back in the psyche ward at Forestview."

"Sorry to hear. Anything I can do to help?"

"Do you have a sawed-off shotgun, maybe something with pistol grips?"

"Stop putzing around." He lounged against his chair. "You've handled it before. How's this any worse than last time?"

"Go easy on the questions," she pleaded unenergetically. "I didn't come here about Momma. I need intervention."

"If you're referring to your transfer—"

"I want my old job back."

"—you just need to lay low until you can rehabilitate yourself with the Commander."

She found herself bolt upright and bristling at having to defend her position. The whole idea scalded her, and she held forth in a throaty voice, pronouncing each word with fierce determination.

"I want my old job."

"Crane's a valuable employee."

"So am I."

Behind Rosen's stony façade, intense blue eyes hinted at cosmic mysteries.

"Look, Zan, we agreed before you ever started working here that—"

"No, Sir, you agreed. *You* agreed." She stabbed a finger in his direction before turning it on herself. "I never agreed. And I never asked you to bail me out of any trouble I got myself into, never."

Seemingly nonplussed by the outburst, he let her vent her spleen uninterrupted.

"I never asked for favors. Not even on that bum rap out of IA, did I?"

Rosen's jaw slacked enough to ease into a half-smile on his noticeably reddening face, where he remained unruffled throughout the angry display. And except for a mild tic near the outer corner of his left eye, she wouldn't have thought her visit made an impact at all.

"And that deal when I first got on the force? Don't play dumb, Danny, you know the one I mean. I never asked you to run interference for me then, either, did I?"

At first, Rosen had seemed unimpressed. But when he craned his neck ever so slightly in his bored attempt to glance out the window, she detected the pulse throbbing in his throat.

She pounced. "I want back in Homicide."

"What do you expect me to do?"

"Transfer me. Darlene Driskoll's in Pawn Shop. She's a whack-o."

"You can handle it. Besides, she's a bad shot. The way I heard it, she couldn't hit a buffalo in the balls with a boat oar. You got off light."

"Cheap shot. You think I deserved that?"

"You were doing the hokey-pokey with her husband. She

had a right to be pissed. Why don't you find yourself a nice Jewish boy?"

"I'm thirty-two years old. If I *do* find a nice Jewish boy I'll get arrested."

"Driskoll's wife isn't going to do anything to jeopardize her job here."

"She wants the name of my hairdresser. While I don't expect you to understand the significance of that, the bottom line is *I didn't do anything to merit getting plucked out of a place I worked my ass off to get into.*"

"The bar results should be out soon, shouldn't they?" he asked.

"I passed. I just haven't had a chance to get sworn in. And don't think I don't know what you're trying to pull here. I learned the same tactic at the knee of the master, so let's get back to my transfer."

He gave a slow nod, but when she geared up with another deep breath, he shushed her with an upraised hand. "The best advice I can give you is: go be a lawyer."

"There's a lot at stake here."

"This is about Roby Tyson, isn't it?"

"Only a tiny part," she lied, measuring a smidgen with her thumb and index finger. "Momma's hospital bills have gone into the ionosphere, and I haven't even made a dent in my student loans."

When she knew he didn't buy it, her hands came up in surrender, and she delivered her words with the conviction of a street preacher.

"Swear to God, just get me back in Homicide, I'll be gone by summer and out of your hair for good."

His gaze traveled up to the ceiling, where he seemed to be mentally ciphering.

"That's still nearly seven months off."

"Please, Danny. Restore me to my position. I'll find Carri Crane's killer."

"We have Carri Crane's killer."

"If it turns out you don't, I'll find him. If it turns out you do—" The thought made her sick to her stomach. "—I'll help you convict him."

Rosen uncapped a pen and let it hover over a sheet of paper, where he seemed to consider its point. She took it as a good sign.

"I can move you to Auto Theft without a mutiny."

"So I can wear crappy clothes and get grease all over me from checking out VINs?" Nobody liked wiping down vehicle identification numbers on car engines. "Homicide."

"You'd be good at Sex Crimes."

"Is that supposed to be funny?"

"Or Vice. You'd like Vice. You'd make a good decoy."

"What? Prostitution? Are you taking another swipe at me?" Silence between them grew. "Homicide. Put it in writing."

He looked up expectantly, and she thought it wise to replay her hole card.

"I'll be gone by the first of summer."

"*You* put *that* in writing." He reached for the phone and pressed the intercom. "Ellen, draw up a transfer for Detective Cézanne Martin. On letterhead. To Homicide. Effective immediately."

"You're the most wonderful guy in the whole world."

He shushed her with a finger. "And draw up her resignation. Date it June Sixteenth and make it effective June Thirtieth." To Cézanne he said, "That takes care of your two-week notice."

"What reason do I give for her resignation?" Ellen again, her voice wickedly delighted.

"Just put that she's going to work as an attorney." He disconnected the intercom.

Cézanne said, "About Captain Crane—"

"Stay out of his way."

She regarded Rosen with the somber nod of someone who'd been there. "What if he raises Cain about me coming back?"

"You weren't worried about that when you came in here."

"But what if he goes to the Chief?"

"Then I may be forced to rethink my decision."

A soft tap at the door preceded the secretary's entrance. The prim, impeccably suited woman held one corner of the transfer by two fingers as if it were a soiled diaper. As for the resignation, she offered it gladly. Without awaiting further instructions, she pivoted on the ball of one pump and prissed out of the room. Rosen scrawled his signature on the transfer sheet and exchanged paperwork. He dropped her resignation in a bottom drawer.

"Make a copy of your transfer, and then post it. And don't get in any more trouble." He eyed her dubiously. "And remember our deal, the one we made when you first got on the force."

Her eyes drifted over the page. "I haven't forgotten. Thank you so much. You'll never regret this."

"I already do." Capped off by, "Just make sure *you* don't."

Chapter Thirteen

It took a cop to stay one step ahead of one.

By mid-week, a rumor that the Grand Jury had enough evidence to indict Roby when they reconvened on Monday had circulated the Department—given credence by the District Attorney—and the PD buzzed with speculation as to Roby's whereabouts.

He was on the lam.

At large.

Bon voyage.

Truth was, they had only to stake out his house if they wanted to catch him. He divided his time between home, the cemetery and casing doors along Hemphill, conducting his own investigation. If anyone had bothered to ask Cézanne if she knew where he was—and they didn't—she had only to tell the truth.

She had no idea.

Two hours before Pawn Shop Detail officially opened for business Wednesday morning, but only minutes from the starting pistol in Homicide, she let herself into the musty smelling office to box up her belongings. The last person she expected to encounter when she flipped on the lights was Darlene Driskoll parked at her desk, dozing with her cheek on the blotter.

The sleepy-eyed woman lifted her head. Drool crusted at the corners of her mouth. For a second, Cézanne though she'd entered the House of Mirrors. Darlene's copycat hairdo, slicked back with a turquoise cloth headband twisted so tight that the pattern was lost, did nothing for her bland complexion; but the new shade of auburn looked even worse.

And the freaky clothes.

Oy vey.

She'd dressed in the closet with the light off again.

Good taste seemed beyond the woman's frame of reference. Chartreuse and orange spandex might be considered interesting to her followers but to her detractors, she cannibalized thrift shops for a hobby. When the woman stood up, Cézanne saw red.

Actually, she saw fuchsia and hot pink and splashes of merlot. The oversized silk coverup that Darlene tried to fit her bulk into happened to be an original *Flora Kung* Cézanne recognized as her own. It had been missing since . . .

. . . she fled Doug Driskoll's house wrapped in a *Laura Ashley* bedsheet.

Darlene was the first to recover from the surprise encounter. The electronic crackle in her voice sent goosebumps across Cézanne's shoulders.

"What're you doing here?"

"I had the same question for you."

"I rode in with my Dougie. They had another shake-up in Narcotics, and he rotated out. Roll call's at six-thirty, so I'll be hitching a ride with him to work from now on."

"Won't that be fun," Cézanne said dully.

"It'll give me more time to spend with my Dougie, which I love, but we have four kids and they all need rides to school."

"Four? Y'all don't have cable?"

Her humor fell on unappreciative ears. She wanted to

tell Darlene that an evening of CNN would be just as much fun and twice as informative, but Darlene's dedicated glower quashed any further attempt at levity.

No longer fascinated by Darlene's unenigmatic presence, she turned away in silent rebuke and hurried to her cubicle to load the cardboard box. By the time she raked the last of her belongings off the desk, Darlene reappeared with anxiety lining her face and what looked like a tortoise shell icepick.

For a handful of seconds, Cézanne forgot to breathe.

Darlene bunched up her hair and drove the pick into the twisted wad until it stuck. "What're you doing?"

"Packing it in."

"You're leaving?" Her voice seizing up.

"Transferring out. Effective immediately."

"You can't leave." Darlene's tone carried a shrillness that would jar the nerves of a catatonic patient. "Where're you going?"

"Back to Homicide." She eyed Darlene's nails with a scornful stare.

Well, well, well. Look who helped herself to the BARELY NUDE polish in the top drawer.

Without comment, Cézanne picked up the box and angled past.

Darlene's face scrunched into a grimace of desperation. "When're you coming back?"

"Never, I hope."

"But what about me?"

Cézanne kept walking. The woman's reaction seemed almost comical. It was as if any second, Darlene would lock arms around an ankle to keep her from leaving.

"Get the door, will you?"

"Let's do lunch. You can show me where you shop."

"You name it." It was her ambiguous response to all such announcements.

"I like your skirt and sweater. I wish I could wear knits. Where did you find it?"

"Banana Republic."

"What color do you call that?"

"Persimmon."

"You think that shade would look good on me?"

She wanted to tell her if persimmon didn't make the air traffic controllers at DFW Airport steal her away from the PD to direct 747s, nothing would.

Instead she answered, "Dandy."

She continued her slow tread but before she could clear the door, strong fingers sank talons into her arm. They were close enough to smell each other's breath, and Cézanne couldn't believe her own eyes when she looked in Darlene's. Periwinkle contacts floated over Darlene's jasper-colored irises, rendering Cézanne speechless. The woman made a bad copy.

"I didn't know you wore glasses," Cézanne remarked.

"I wanted a change. They don't have a prescription." Her brows knitted. "I'm thinking of getting my tongue pierced. What do you think?"

"I think it's disgusting."

"I hear it makes oral sex better."

Touché.

"Stay in touch?" Darlene said. "That's what friends do."

Enemies, too, if they were smart.

With an innocuous, "You got it," she disengaged herself from Darlene's clutches.

Driskoll's wife must be sleepwalking. Either that, or the sausage casing she stuffed herself into had deprived her brain of oxygen. By the time Cézanne reached the elevator, she remembered a line from her favorite comedienne, and the thought put a smile on her face.

Friends are just enemies who don't have the guts to kill you.

Only the act of head-butting a telephone repairman marred Cézanne's return to Homicide. She didn't even mind that the cardboard box collapsed on impact a few feet from the door, emptying office supplies at her feet. While re-forming the container, she made small talk with the brown-eyed stranger who stooped to recover her belongings.

"Trouble with the phones?"

"Something like that."

"What kind of trouble?"

He shook his head and dumped the last handful into the box.

"I don't think I'd much care to work here." Without waiting for comment, he headed off down the hall toward the elevator with the content of his tool belt slapping against his thighs.

Greta was the first and only one to welcome her.

"You're over here by me now, Shug," she said, pointing to the cubicle directly across from her desk. "Some of the guys swapped offices after you left. Get the frown off your face. They didn't know you'd be back."

Cézanne stowed the box under her desk. She knew better than to unpack before taking a pulse. The Chief could still veto Rosen's order.

"How'd the captain take the news?"

"Capt'n didn't say too much. By the way, what's civil disobedience?"

Cézanne ignored the slap and made a mental note to buy Greta a better brand of perfume. Preferably something expensive. Something that didn't smell like phosgene gas and only half as fatal.

"Do I have any cases?"

"Lieutenant's in the process of assigning some."

"Who's working the captain's daughter's?"

Greta's cheeks lost their color. She leaned in close with her hand cupped to her mouth.

"We don't talk about it, Shug," she said in a conspiratorial whisper, "and you ought not, either. I can tell you this much, though, Capt'n knows everything that's going on with it. It just breaks my heart to see him this way."

Cézanne took a smug breath.

The captain didn't know *everything*.

And he wouldn't. Not for awhile, yet. And as much as she enjoyed Greta, her sixth sense kicked in the moment she got a peek at her new digs. Captain Crane didn't get to the top by being stupid. He got there by stepping over the bodies of men with only half the killer instinct. Greta was supposed to get her spyglass out. Privately, Cézanne wondered how far her friend would go and what The Brass promised to make it worth her while.

She threw her jacket over one chair and slid into the spare. Picking the phone up with a flourish, she dialed.

"Municipal court?" she asked loud enough to keep Greta from straining to hear. "Put me through to Code Enforcement. I want to talk to somebody about a screw-up with a building permit."

Chapter Fourteen

Shortly before noon, Captain Crane appeared at Greta's station practically incoherent. His suit looked slept in and the purple half-moons beneath his eyes brought back memories from patrol days of a one-two punch in a barroom brawl. In less than a week he'd aged a lifetime. Anyone with a thimble of sensitivity could tell by the void lurking behind the accusing glare that losing his only daughter had broken his back.

But two years of sidestepping his tirades gave Cézanne a leg up on Crane's personality. His back may have been broken by his daughter's death, but it hadn't paralyzed him.

"Greta, tell Sue-zanne Deputy Chief Rosen wants to see her in his office. Now." Greta glanced over sympathetically. Crane vaporized.

"You heard the man, Shug. You don't think they'll move you again, do you?"

Before taking the elevator to The Penthouse, Cézanne stopped at the ladies' room to check her appearance, halfway expecting to see a "Contents Under Pressure" label stamped across her forehead. When she arrived at Rosen's office, Ellen refused to meet her gaze and merely pointed to his door.

Cézanne entered completely unprepared.

Rosen sat behind the desk with his fingers flexing like a spider doing push-ups on a mirror. To her right, coiled the Chief himself. To her left, Captain Crane swizzled cream into a guest cup. Lieutenant Binswanger, a figurehead of a man people occasionally glimpsed during administrative functions, closed the door behind her.

Inwardly, she groaned.

A flash of midnight blue caught her eye. Binswanger propped himself against the conference table and folded his arms across his chest. Under the circumstances, she may as well have been naked with her legs trussed up like the family Thanksgiving turkey.

"Sit down, Detective," Rosen said. "Would you care for some coffee?"

Not trusting herself to speak, she shook her head and shrank in her chair.

Crane growled, "Take it," and pushed the cup, sloshing, within her reach.

For one dizzy moment, she caught herself trying to pass out. Bright spots danced before her eyes as she lifted the coffee and took a searing swallow. It jolted like a wet hand on a live connection; she made a mental vow to resign before they could fire her.

"Are you all moved in?" Rosen's attempt at polite chit-chat.

"I travel light."

"I'm sure you're wondering why you're here."

She said, "Contraceptives weren't what they are today. But why worry about a mistake that happened so long ago?" She wanted to tell her audience they shouldn't hold her responsible, just because the rubber broke.

Rosen tightened his jaw, but the corners of his mouth turned up in ever so slight betrayal. The lieutenant kept his gorilla posture but Captain Crane appeared dazed. She rehearsed her resignation in her head.

I need Emergency Family Leave. My mother's sick. Kiss my

ass and mail my check.

"You're out of Homicide. Starting tomorrow, you report to Narcotics."

Rosen may as well have whipped out his alter-ego and peed on her. The rest of his monologue faded out to a tinny buzz. When his mouth stopped moving and the silence became deafening, she stood up, completely recovered.

"Would you gentlemen be kind enough to permit me a moment alone with Deputy Chief Rosen?"

The Chief attempted to wither her with a look, but he rose to his full height and snapped, "I'll be in my office, Daniel."

With the room cleared, the silence stretched a couple of beats. She dropped into her chair and they stared at each other making quiet assessments. Her stomach went hollow. Her heart bounced around in her chest, and the little hairs on her arms bristled.

Her voice dissolved to a whisper. "I didn't want to have to do it this way."

"Do what?"

Uncowed, she sat up straight. "It may not be a felony to bag a seventeen year old babysitter, but I'll bet the Chief would have plenty to say if he found out your latest trophy was his great-niece."

Anger pinched the corners of his mouth. "What the hell are you getting at?"

"Your four year old walked in. You were so caught up in the moment you didn't even see her peering through the door. You ought to be glad she asked me what you were doing to that girl, instead of running to your wife for an explanation."

"Oh, God." He did a panicky review of the room. "What'd you tell her?"

"What I said isn't important. What I want, is."

It didn't take him long to put it together. He gave an almost imperceptible nod. Pressed his lips together until they turned blue.

Blood pounded in her ears. She knew from his expression he wanted to curl his fingers into her cashmere sweater and heave her through the glass. "Homicide."

He tapped the intercom button. In a voice tight with controlled fury, he said, "Ellen, please ask the gentlemen to come back inside."

It took less than seven minutes to clear the room and speak her peace before the players reassembled—less time by Cézanne's calculations than it took men their age to have decent sex. Behind the desk, with the tan siphoned out of his gaunt cheeks, Rosen about-faced The Brass's position.

"Detective Martin will remain in your unit," Rosen said.

Crane's face sagged and his frame seemed to melt under the wrinkled suit.

"If you have a problem with that, Commander, say the word, and we'll see that you get a lateral transfer. Maybe something a bit less stressful while you're trying to put your life back together."

Crane squared his shoulders and accepted the first condition of defeat. The second followed with the swiftness of an executioner's axe.

"I assigned Detective Martin the Carri Crane file."

The news was more than the commander could handle. He buried his face in his palms and let out a low, tortured moan. When his startling reaction ended almost as soon as it had begun, Crane shot her a lethal glare.

"Pension or not," he growled at the lot, "the only reason I don't tender my resignation is because I have a vested interest in this matter. I expect this—this woman—to report directly to me during the pendency of this case."

His tone left no room for doubt. On this, he would not compromise.

"Fair enough." In one of the more familiar gestures of dismissal that had made him famous, Rosen rose to his feet and clapped his hands together. "Let's get back to work, shall we?"

She knew by the way he smiled, and the way Captain Crane left snot-slinging mad, that she ranked maybe one needle-jump above a pervert in their estimation.

"All except you." Rosen stopped her from trailing them through the door.

When the last one filed out, Rosen motioned her back into the chair. Neither seemed eager to open a dialogue. After an uncomfortable silence, Cézanne cleared her throat.

Rosen said nastily, "I imagine you're proud of yourself right about now."

"Not really."

The tiny lines around his eyes tightened, and the pinched corners of his mouth suggested what he really needed was a suppository, a newspaper and a half hour to himself.

"How dare you strongarm me? You have skeletons in your closet, too."

Her stomach knotted. "What happened, nobody would blame me. You stand to hurt yourself as much as me, stirring up shit that's better left buried."

"I'd like to blister your butt," he snapped. "If you screw this up, I'll nail you."

"If I screw it up, I'll nail myself."

"Get back to work. I don't want to see you until that case is closed."

"I'm already gone."

At the door, she let her hand linger on the knob long enough to vector the secretary's location. "Before I go, Uncle Danny, let me just say—"

Up went the hand to shush her.

"Sorry—Deputy Chief Rosen. I want you to know that I, for one, never believed your meteoric rise in rank had any connection with those vicious rumors about you and the Chief's daughter."

His eyes lost their luster. "Perhaps I should remind you, there's no statute of limitations on murder."

At once, she knew he didn't mean Roby.

A shrill tone rang between her ears as if to warn of an emergency drop in cabin pressure. The ringing grew louder, and when she heard the sound of her voice over the white-water raging between her ears, it came out small and far-away as if she were speaking from within a vacuum.

"Not a day goes by I wouldn't trade places."

His lips moved, but if he said anything she didn't hear it.

"You actually blame *me* for what happened, don't you? For God's sake, what's wrong with you? I was a little kid. I didn't want to die."

"You didn't feel that way three years ago when Tyson kicked in your front door and peeled you off the bathroom floor, though, did you? How does it feel to cheat death twice?"

It wasn't until quitting time that she remembered the comment that ended their conversation.

In retrospect, it dallied in her head, ominous.

There are worse things than an office in the basement.

Chapter Fifteen

Twenty-four hours passed before Cézanne reconciled Rosen's prophetic words.

Alone in her cubicle, hunched over the crime scene photos and examining a faint bruise pattern on Carri Crane's neck with a magnifying glass, a shadow fell across the desk. The scent of *Angel for Men* brought her up rigid. She looked over at the man filling her doorframe, and her heart flopped.

Doug Driskoll.

The air thinned. Every hair on her body stood at attention. Seconds passed before she realized her mouth gaped. In disbelief, she sealed her eyes. When she opened them, he hadn't disintegrated.

"Hey, Babydoll."

The mere presence of his five-feet, eleven-inch frame lounging against the entrance freeze-dried her mouth and made the blood in her veins ice over. Writhing inwardly, she could almost hear the anguished screams of Darlene Driskoll piercing four floors.

When her heart finally jump-started itself, she chose her words carefully and delivered them in a whisper.

"You have to leave. We can't even be seen in the same zip code."

"You haven't heard?" The bemused twinkle in his eyes turned to delight. "Quarantine's been lifted."

"What?" Her voice had all the shrillness of a piccolo.

"It's true. The Chief assigned me to Homicide." He shed his coat and loosened the tie she'd given him on his last birthday.

There are worse things than an office in the basement.

Over a low moan, she pushed her chair away from the desk and melted against the seat. Rosen played a mean game of "Gotcha Back".

"I get it," she muttered, trance-like. "How stupid could I be? It's *quid pro quo* in reverse."

"What?"

"He said there were worse things and there are, and I'm here and you're there, and I could just kick myself because I'm the most snake-bit person on the planet."

"Simmer down, Babe."

"Don't call me that. Don't call me anything. Don't talk to me." Her eyes darted around the cubicle. "Where's my gun? One of us should die. I think it should be you."

"Now, lookie here, if you think—"

"I take it back. I don't want to kill you. I just thought I wanted to kill you, but it's not you, it's me I want to kill for being so," she paused to swallow the curse word teetering on her tongue, "naive."

She took a shallow breath and shook her head. Not staring evil directly in the face helped her think straight.

"It was just too damned easy. Shit just fell into place, and I should've known better because I don't get anywhere in this department without practically having to draw blood." She hammered a fist on the desk, then took a chance and met his alarmed gaze. "I have two words to say to you. Go away."

His lips parted, and his teeth flashed. She found it depressing that he still possessed the same magic smile that made the elastic fall out of women's panties.

"Go away? Babe, I just got here."

"Then I'll go away." There wasn't enough oxygen in the room for both of them. She slapped the Crane file shut and groped for her jacket. "You just don't get it, do you? Swear to God, you may be the only person stupider than me. Matter of fact I know you are. Know why?"

She must look foolish babbling like a seventy-eight record when her body wouldn't move faster than thirty-three-and-a-third. But the truth was, he still did it to her—turned her left brain to pablum. She only had to look into his tempestuous eyes to call up images of tangled sheets, hungry kisses and hot tongues exploring each other's erogenous zones. She rose.

"Don't leave me, Babydoll."

She pulled up short. She heard right. He didn't say, "Don't leave." He said, "Don't leave *me*."

The Brass might be the intellectual author of this script, but she didn't have to star in it. Just because Doug had the biggest—

—ego on the force, didn't mean she had to fall all over again.

"Captain said to pick a desk, but since you already staked out that one, I'll sit here."

"You know what? Take both. Take anything you want, but don't take me for an idiot. You're a loaded gun—no, worse than that—you are a friggin' bazooka, and I'm not about to commit professional suicide."

She forced a smile and rubber-banded Carri Crane's file. At the last minute, she snatched up a scrap of paper and wrote an IOU for the cuss-kitty.

"You know what? You'll enjoy it here. Greta'll get you started. I'm sure Lieutenant Binswanger can find something for you to do."

"Whatcha got there? That's it, isn't it? That's the rookie's case." He moved close enough for her to see the light go out of his eyes.

"Don't you dare take another step. I don't even want you close enough to spit watermelon seeds at. Let me by."

She detested the alarm in her tone, but there was no way two people could fit through the opening without exchanging lint. If Rosen's idea was to stick her under a microscope, the last thing in the world she needed was a single fiber from Doug Driskoll's pants. She crooked a finger to snag her coat from the wall peg and shooed him back out into the corridor with a flick of her hand.

"Since you didn't know they were moving me, I guess it's safe to assume you don't know why, either."

"I have an idea."

Detective Driskoll, as she decided to think of him, cocked his head.

"I've been assigned to help you with Carri Crane."

The news floored her. She thought The Brass just filled Roby's vacancy at her expense. She must have taken leave of her senses to have picked such a fight.

"This is too goddam much for any person to have to go through at one time. Don't hound me today, come back tomorrow. Tomorrow I'll be able to deal with being number one on their hit parade, but today? Today, you just keep your distance. Tomorrow I'll be the architect of some rules, and we'll stick to them."

"The only thing I want to stick to is you. Want to get a bite?"

Her eyes widened, incredulous. He was looking at her neck.

"You're the most fucked-up person I know. What kind of dement would get his wife a job at the same outfit his former girlfriend works at? You people slay me."

146

"I want to help you close the case."

"The only way you can help me close this file is if you knew her."

He shrugged. "No more'n anybody else."

"Then fat lotta good you are. You're just like the others. You're out to skewer Roby Tyson."

"Maybe I'm here to lend a fresh perspective."

"My ass."

She fought the urge to take a hundred dollar bill and spew out every curse word she knew—in English and Yiddish. If there was a God, she'd forget Driskoll's second-skin Wranglers by the time she made it to the parking lot, located the key to the cruiser and drove to Trinity Park to meet Roby; she wouldn't even remember the plaid shirt that brought out the green flecks in his irises, nor the birthday tie she'd like to noose his neck with.

He hadn't changed a bit. If his psychotic wife mixed fabrics like throw-up after a roller-coaster ride, Doug Driskoll dressed better than a seven course meal at the Petroleum Club.

Worst of all was the realization that the guy could still put her into a tailspin. She spotted him in the rearview mirror, taking long strides in her direction. Without hesitation, she cranked up the engine and bounced down the parking garage incline, leaving him coughing in a swirl of exhaust.

Roby would've been a sight for sore eyes had he been where he said he'd be, but the moment she rolled up near the men's restroom and spotted the Vice cars, she knew he'd skedaddled.

She flipped through a MAPSCO of Fort Worth and studied the directions to the captain's house before striking out.

Fresh perspective, my ass.

Chapter Sixteen

Everybody on Northside knew Agnetha Svedborg, the daughter of a wealthy grocer. By the time she celebrated her fifteenth birthday she had worked afternoons in the family stores—every one of them—extending the same line of credit to those who couldn't pay as her lionhearted father.

What most people didn't know was the story that led the old man to red-pen her from his will. A neighborhood regular called Chucky, who stopped by the market for a Moon Pie and Big Orange soda each day after rookie school, stole her heart. That he had a thirteen year jump on her in age didn't help matters, but he was willing to wait. At least until she was legal.

Only a father could affix blame.

Agnetha inherited her mother's honey-blonde waves, berry-stained lips and Dresden doe eyes and, according to neighborhood gossip, she could soften the bitterest of men. Chucky fell under her spell and his hope of marriage never faltered. He promised Agnetha if she'd only come with him, he'd moonlight three jobs to move Heaven and Earth for her.

To anyone who appeared at the ornate wrought-iron perimeter of the sprawling old Victorian on Grand Avenue, it would seem Captain Charles Crane more than kept his end of the bargain.

Cézanne stood at the stained glass door and rang the bell. She clutched her coat tighter, but the winter chill from a fast-moving norther whipped underneath like icy fingers.

The door opened a sliver.

"Mrs. Crane?"

She wished the tiny woman with the chiseled features and ringed, swollen eyes would speed it up, invite her inside and seat her near the logs blazing in the marble-faced fireplace she could see from her place on the doormat.

"I'm Cézanne Martin." A flashed badge. "I work with—"

"I know who you are." The answer came out soft, unhurried and expected. "Roby Tyson murdered my daughter."

Cézanne stammered from the cold. "C-could I come inside a m-minute?"

Agnetha Crane let her in.

Cézanne brushed past a Chinese fishbowl with an enormous fiddle-leaf fig tree that branched within a wisp of pressed tin ceiling tiles. While she made a quick, visual inventory of Hepplewhite furnishings, the lock snapped shut behind her. Potted plants from the funeral were clustered near the entry and on the dining room table, dozens of flowers, still fragrant, wilted in their vases. On the coffee table lay pink parchment embossed with interlocking "C"s, a pen, and the funeral guest book. And she knew by the stamped envelopes that Agnetha Crane had already begun writing thank-you notes.

She turned to offer condolences, only to find Mrs. Crane staring up at her, arms folded across her bosom.

"What is it you want?"

"It's not my wish to intrude upon your sorrow. I just have to ask a few questions. Your husband wants this case wrapped up, and so do I."

Lines of mistrust deepened, then melted into coifed hair the color of expensive champagne. Momentarily, the disapproving glint vanished. Agnetha Crane emerged a smaller, more refined version of her daughter. And without the hard edge of misery pulling at her face, the same physical beauty people saw in Carri radiated from her.

"I'll take your coat."

Cézanne gave it over. Without invitation, she took a seat on a brocade settee near the fire, away from the prism of colors playing off the stained glass, and tried out some charm school tricks.

"Your taste in antiques is exquisite. I love Hepplewhite."

"It's Sheraton, although the untrained eye might confuse the two."

"Maybe you could do something with Captain's office."

They shared a much needed smile.

"I'm afraid it was my mother who had a flair for quality. As the only daughter, I inherited her furniture and jewelry. I always planned for Carri—" She rubbed her palms against her wool slacks. "Can I offer you something? Coffee? A sandwich?"

"They don't let us accept food. It's policy. Not that anyone would try to poison us. It's just the rule."

"Rubbish. I'll brew some coffee. I never knew a policeman who didn't take an IV of the stuff."

Agnetha Crane breezed out of sight. Beyond the parlor, a drawer slammed and flatware clinked. Cézanne took the opportunity to study the room, get a feel for the Cranes as a family. What she saw came as no surprise.

Pictures of Carri sprouted up everywhere. On the mantle, photographed astride a dappled gray. Prom night on the arm of some pimply faced jock. A huge canvas of a cotton-headed toddler clutching a fistful of bluebonnets hung above a burled walnut writing desk. Her police academy photo, uniformed and stern-looking, with her mother's eyes and her father's stubborn jaw. And another. A teenaged Carri in a turquoise wraparound with birds-of-paradise, silhouetted against a Hawaiian sunset, her face aglow with the promise of unfulfilled dreams.

"She loved the print of that island skirt so much she wore it year round." Mrs. Crane reappeared with a teakwood tray and placed it on the coffee table, a marble-topped beauty with ornately carved rosewood legs. She pulled a dainty sewing chair so close that their knees almost touched. "We took her to Oahu for her birthday that year. She even talked her father into buying her a sundress in the same fabric. Poor Chuck. Men just don't understand about women and their clothes. I didn't know what you take so I brought cream and sugar."

"Just cream."

"Carri's the only one around here who drinks—" Realizing her mistake, Agnetha Crane began to tremble. She put down the creamer until she got herself steadied. Their eyes met, and she said gravely, "It hurts something terrible. I pray you never know this feeling."

"Yes, Ma'am." Meek.

"My daughter took *crema mexicana* in her coffee," she said, starting over. "It's like half-and-half, only thicker. Chuck always teased her that it would make her fat. But she ate right and worked out with a personal trainer, so I kept it for her."

"Thank you."

Cézanne accepted the cup, a delicately fluted piece of bone china decorated with pastel pink roses and rimmed in gold. Made it hard to imagine Captain Crane with his pinkie up. She took a sip and the bitter brew warmed her raw throat.

"Delicious." A white lie. The cream clotted in the cup,

and Cézanne knew in an instant it had been more than just awhile since Carri dropped by. She would eventually steer the conversation back to that very point, but for now, she changed the subject.

"I love your home. It must have been wonderful for Carri, growing up in the biggest house on the block."

Agnetha Crane's eyes lit up. "Dear, I'm the one who grew up in the biggest house in Bellevue Terrace. My father, Pere Svedborg—"

She pronounced it 'Swenburk'.

"—everyone called him Swede, he had the biggest house." She squared her shoulders with pride. "Until Chuck bought this one and added an extra two thousand square feet onto the back and upstairs."

"Did your father visit often?"

"Never."

"So he didn't get to know your daughter?"

"On the contrary. Carri had a half million in trust as soon as she let out her first yelp."

Instead of smiling at the happy ending to the Crane's love story, Cézanne found good reason to frown.

"Did your daughter have a will?"

"Nothing we consider valid."

"I don't wish to appear pushy, Mrs. Crane, but this could be important."

"We get everything. The only difference between Carri's written will and the law of intestate succession is that she named that scoundrel Executor of the estate and gave him a token bequest," she said with a sniff.

"You mean Roby?"

"We want nothing to do with him. If he doesn't voluntarily withdraw as Executor, our attorney will petition the Court to have him removed. Same for disclaiming the gift.

He'll not see a crying dime as long as I draw breath."

Cézanne tightened her jaw. Roby should have told her. Unless he didn't know.

"You were that man's partner." It came out a guarded accusation. She couldn't even say Roby's name.

"For awhile."

Cézanne tried out an innocuous comment. One that couldn't backfire if things went sour.

"You think you know someone. . . ." She let her voice trail. Took in her surroundings and waited for the Captain's wife to respond.

It didn't take but a second.

"Bad news is what he is. That man made her do things she'd never have done on her own. Carri couldn't wait to slip out after we went to bed."

"Sounds like a typical kid to me."

"Chuck put a stop to it, I assure you." Hostility festered in her voice. "He had a security alarm installed and refused to give her the code."

Cézanne hoped her smile didn't betray her thoughts: Crane was an asshole.

"So," she went on, "my daughter rebelled. She got an apartment with another girl, somebody she met at the gym. Chuck and I couldn't keep her from seeing that man once she left home."

Nobody ever said anything about a roommate.

Cézanne pulled out a pen and spiral pad for field notes.

"Carri lived with someone?"

"Michelle Parks."

She scribbled furiously. "Where do I find her?"

"I have no idea. I understand she already moved out."

"Where did they live?"

"You mean you don't know?"

"The reports show Carri lived at this address."

"In some fleabag near the hospital district. She wouldn't say where. Probably too embarrassed, but it upset my husband something terrible, his only child keeping him on a need-to-know basis." Agnetha Crane pulled a pack of skinny cigarettes from her sweater pocket and shook one out.

"You mind?" she asked, then reconsidered. "What am I asking you for? This is my house." She produced a lighter, snapped the flint and puffed until the flame caught. "They should've fired that drunken bum years ago. Chuck says—"

"I'm sorry, Mrs. Crane, but I have to ask something while it's fresh in my mind. This roommate, what else can you tell me about her?"

"If I bothered to invite you into my home you may call me Agnetha."

"Agnetha," Cézanne repeated, obedient. She suspected it wouldn't be long before they were addressing each other formally again. "About Michelle—"

"A dancer."

"A ballerina dancer? A dancer with the Fort Worth Dallas Ballet?"

Agnetha permitted herself a cruel laugh.

"No, Dear. An exotic dancer. I believe the police refer to her kind as a titty-dancer." She took a long draw on the cigarette and blew smoke in the direction of an ornate brass ceiling fan swirling lazily overhead. "Chuck and I didn't approve, but he ran her name through TCIC and NCIC and she didn't have a criminal record, and the girls seemed compatible. Carri worked day shift at the PD, and Michelle worked nights at the club."

"Which club?"

"I haven't any idea; Carri wouldn't say. Apparently,

their lifestyles didn't conflict. Except for. . . ." Her voice trailed off, and her gaze flickered to the wall and beyond. Whatever the thought, she brushed it away with a flip of the hand and a soft sigh.

Cézanne poised to write. "Except for what?"

"The night before." Agnetha Crane's eyes glazed over with the thousand-yard stare of a combat veteran. "Carri phoned our house. She said Michelle was waving a gun, planning to commit suicide. Carri asked me to talk some sense into her."

Cézanne barely breathed. Gooseflesh popped up on her arms until the hair pierced her sleeves like a thousand tiny needles.

"It's ironic," Agnetha said, her voice tapering off to a whisper, "how Carri tried to keep her friend from killing herself and the next day, and then it's Carri who ends up—"

Her eyes misted. The whites turned iridescent pink and tears rolled along the rims in precarious balance. It didn't take long before the reservoir spilled over her cheeks in rivulets. She stared into oblivion.

"I feel so guilty now, bickering with my child. If we hadn't been so against it, maybe she'd have stayed put. I shouldn't have said that about Michelle not being our kind. Just because we disapproved of her occupation, she's still a human being. Carri said we were *ragging* on her unnecessarily."

"I'm listening."

"Michelle was very distraught really. She even asked permission to come to the funeral. I never heard such a thing."

Chills turned into frostbite. Something didn't set quite right. Stank like a cesspool, in fact.

"Why would anyone need to ask permission?"

Agnetha closed her eyes and tilted her head back until

the tears disappeared into her hair. "The other mothers banned Michelle."

"What other mothers?"

"Her other roommates'."

"Banned her from what?"

"Their funerals."

The news took a second to soak in.

"Michelle's previous roommates committed suicide? Does Captain Crane know this?"

Agnetha's eyelids snapped open. The room temperature dropped.

"Only two of them. I know what you're thinking. You want to close this case as a suicide. Carri did *not* commit suicide. That man killed her."

"Mrs. Crane, don't you think it's a little bizarre—"

"Sick people attract sick-os. Chuck always says if you put two of them in a room with a hundred normal people, they'll find each other in the crowd."

"Did you discuss this with the captain?"

"My husband's a walking dead man. I'm not about to saddle him with a bunch of tripe when he can barely hang onto his sanity."

"Did anybody even bother to interview her?"

"I'm telling you, that man killed her. You know it—"

She rose to her feet.

"—I know it—"

Went for the overcoat.

"—the police know it—"

Rammed the wrap so close Cézanne almost got a snoutful of angora. So close she whiffed her own perfume.

"—the District Attorney knows it. You just need to do your job. Put that animal behind bars, and get him the needle." Her voice rose to a shriek. "I hope to God I live long enough to see them strap him to the gurney. I want to watch him take his last breath. He murdered our Carri."

The massive stained glass door opened with a yank, and the wind blasted through Cézanne's hair. In the time it took to make a final plea, the definitive slam sounded behind her, and the deadbolt shot home. But the worst was yet to come—the unearthly scream on the other side, a scream to be heard from Hell to Heaven.

A cry that carried a message.

Do your job, or we'll kill him ourselves.

Chapter Seventeen

Unfortunately, the only man smart enough to catch Carri Crane's murderer also happened to be the one everybody thought killed her.

When Captain Crane ran Michelle Parks's name through the Texas Crime Information Center and National Crime Information Center—what the cops referred to as TCIC-NCIC—he didn't find a criminal history for her. At least not under that particular surname. But she had one now, thanks to traffic citations for *No Drivers License* and *No Seatbelt* issued by one of the PD's motor jocks. When she let the unpaid tickets turn into warrants, they booked her. And she listed her place of business as Ali Baba's, a seedy strip club on the outskirts of Fort Worth.

Around nine o'clock that evening, Cézanne sat in the parking lot of Ali Baba's and studied Michelle Parks's mug shot. Long, dark hair drawn back in a ponytail. Knowing eyes, hardened by the experience of running with a rough crowd. Thick makeup and an "up yours" grin. The kind that came from having memorized the phone number of a good bondsman and an even better lawyer.

And the girl in the picture was a dead ringer for one Michelle *Parker*.

No wonder Carri didn't give the captain Michelle's true name. Because Michelle Parker, AKA Michelle Parks, had a rap sheet as long as her legs, and a fairly recent booking photo.

Three charges for prostitution, zero convictions. Lots of traffic citations, especially for driving with a suspended drivers license, a charge that originated from not carrying car insurance. A felony possession charge, pled down to a misdemeanor with credit for time served. Three days in jail. A Cowtown sweetheart deal suggesting, once again, that it wasn't who to know, but who to blow.

The drumming beat of dance music coming from inside the building vibrated Cézanne's windows. With the BMW sandwiched between a rusty pickup and a Cadillac, and parked beneath the only burned out streetlamp in the back row, she wondered what kind of scam she'd have to pull to get inside without blowing her cover. She tucked the photos above the visor, opened the car door, and swung out a leg.

Once across the threshold of the dimly lit cave, she never even saw the beefy goon appear out of the shadows with a toothpick clamped between his molars until he was towering over her like a partially shaved albino gorilla. And she knew without asking that whoever did the shaving didn't survive the process.

"You the new chick?" He spoke in a raspy monotone as if someone tried unsuccessfully to rip out his vocal cords. "Boss's office is 'round the corner. Third door to the right."

He pointed.

She hesitated a fraction of a second too long. Why would he mistake her for a dancer? She wasn't stacked.

He must have read her thoughts. She didn't like the way he studied her breasts before making eye contact.

"Where can I find Michelle?" Cézanne's eyes adjusted to the darkness.

"Hollywood's in back."

"Hollywood?"

"Michelle."

A strobe light above center stage pulsed on a scrawny dancer. The fuzzy-haired blonde pranced about in spike heels wicked enough to gouge out an eye. Men approaching geezerdom bellied up with dollars threaded between blue-collar fingers, enticing the girl to gyrate her shaved pubic area in their faces. Or worse.

The gal managed to pull off a parlor trick—actually squatted down and snatched up a folded bill with her—

Lord Almighty.

She couldn't have done it any quicker with a remote control clothespin. Overhead, a digital message encased in plexiglass scrolled by in flashes of bright red.

DON'T TOUCH THE DANCERS. IT'S THE LAW.

Not that there was much danger these old coots had the energy to cop a feel. Jesus H. Anybody desperate enough to patronize a sleazy joint like Ali Baba's probably couldn't get it up with a crane and guy-wires.

Cézanne made a move toward the curtained hallway where a sign designating EMPLOYEES ONLY hung overhead.

Brutus blocked her path. "Can't you read?"

Music drummed so loud that empty chairs vibrated against the floor.

"I need to talk to her."

"Then getcha a man, pay the cover charge, grab a seat and catch her after her stint. We don't allow women, stag."

"I'm not paying cover to talk to my sister."

"Bullshit." His eyes traveled over her in a head to toe inspection. "Michelle don't have family."

When she didn't move, he took a step closer. Tried to intimidate her into retreating. He gave the smoke-filled air an exaggerated sniff.

"I smell ham."

The only odor she could make out through the thick haze was foul aftershave. That and the fact that Brutus's time-release deodorant clocked out around noon.

"I smell cigarettes," she said. "And marijuana."

He shook his head. "Not me, I smell pork. Bacon. Swine." He eyed her with the cool dispassion of a killer. "I think we got a pig here."

"Do I look like a cop?" she asked. "If you must know, I set her up for a private party this weekend. She was s'posed to work for two hours dancing at a femme ceremonial uniting, but the couple wants her four hours or not at all."

"Huh?"

"Lezzies, numbskull. A dyke wedding. The butch gets a bachelorette party. Now I've got to re-negotiate the fee."

He gave her a blank stare.

"I've got about three minutes," she said, tapping a fingernail against her watch crystal. "You don't let me back there to discuss this, you just tell her the deal's off and not to call. I'll find somebody else who'll work for five hundred smackers."

"Bullshit."

A naked redhead with a dollar bill threaded through a ring protruding from her navel sashayed up smelling of sweat and baby powder.

"Somebody need a dancer for a party?"

Brutus snapped his fingers and thumbed at a table of construction workers. With a backward scowl, the redhead jiggled off, dragged up a chair and leveled her thirty-eights inches from a gawker's moustache.

Cézanne played her ace. "I can have a fire marshal here in under three minutes."

She fished for her badge case and held it up like a silver cross on a garlic pod necklace. Even in the dark, she thought she noticed a flicker of fear. Ten to one, the Brylcreamed behemoth had warrants, but since he probably had the IQ of a school zone speed limit, she spelled it out.

"When the fire department comes, the cops aren't far behind. You know—cluttering the parking lot with marked cars, jotting down license plates, running warrants. And if that doesn't work, we always have TABC. I swear those guys over there are drinking, only I didn't see a liquor permit posted by the door when I came in."

That got his attention. The boys from the Texas Alcoholic Beverage Commission didn't much care if they crippled business.

Whaddayaknow.

The SOB pointed out one of several corridors spoking out from the main floor and stepped aside. She navigated her way through a trail of zoo print lingerie strewn across the floor, stepped over a pyramid of tacky platform shoes and entered a dressing room with a construction paper star tacked on the door.

HOLLYWOOD.

She found Michelle Parker lounging on a day bed like a mermaid draped over a rock, enormous floatation devices jutting out from beneath a sheer kimono, veins blue from transparent skin stretched taut. For Cézanne, a two-word description summed up the paragon of virtue in the provocative pose: speed whore. A meth user with boobs the envy of South Texas melon farmers, and hair bleached lighter than a cow skull in the desert. The girl from the mug shot dropped a copy of the *National Enquirer* low enough to reveal a face troweled in theatrical makeup.

"You the new chick?"

Cézanne commandeered a wrought-iron bistro stool and

parked herself beneath the glaring bulbs of the vanity, nearest the *Frederick's of Hollywood* catalogue. She anchored her heels into a patch of threadbare carpet. Prepared for a long chat or a difficult removal, whichever. Fleetingly, she wondered if Detective Driskoll might've stuck around longer if she'd tried out some of the get-up featured on the *Frederick's* cover.

Hollywood dropped the *Enquirer* on the floor and boosted herself up on one elbow until she could reach the edge of the Formica countertop.

"Here, Sweetie," she said, handing over a business card. "You wanna work here, you need to see this guy."

A local plastic surgeon specializing in breast augmentations. No job too small.

A painful flash from childhood exploded in Cézanne's head. She was fourteen again, riding home from school with Bernice.

Why it is, your face is so long as a quarter horse?

I didn't make the track team.

You should not eat donuts, I told you dis very morning. You are da most stubborn mule.

I'm fast, Momma. I beat two girls and the trainer ran me against Mindy Silverstein. He had to go back and watch the film, it was so close. I would've won, but Mindy chested-out.

Chested-out? Talk English, Cézanne.

It means I'm flat, so I lose.

In an instant, the memory vanished along with the doctor's card, crunched in her fist and jammed deep into her coat pocket.

"I'm here about Carri Crane."

Michelle Parker's face went translucent. Her eyes misted, and a florid giveaway raged up her neck to blotch her cheeks. She reached into the robe pocket for a smoke, crushed the empty *Virginia Slims* wrapper, gave it an angry toss in the direction of the nearest waste can and snorted in disgust.

"You're a cop."

Cézanne shrugged.

"How the hell'd you find me?"

"Next time, pay your traffic tickets."

The stage music came to an abrupt halt, and the frizzy blonde hurried in flicking beads of sweat from her bare breasts.

"I just made fifty bucks," she panted, grabbing an aerosol can from the vanity and dousing herself. The locker room smell from a corner clothes hamper disappeared in a cloud of raspberry spray. "Gonna do a table dance, but the guy likes black. You got anything black?"

Hollywood shook her head.

"Goddam these losers, always demanding freebies." The blonde rummaged through a locker, snatched up a chiffon wrap and raced for the door. At the last minute, she turned to Cézanne.

"You the new chick?"

"No."

"Oh." The dancer shrugged, then brightened. "You here to party? 'Cause Hollywood don't do women. But me and Reno do."

"Thanks anyway."

"Your loss." With that, the girl pranced out.

So that's what life boiled down to. You didn't have a man velcroed to your side, made you queer.

Hollywood broke the spell. "See my lighter anywhere?"

Cézanne glanced across a pile of cosmetics, located it, and sent it airborne. In the time it took to glance away, Hollywood produced a cigarette out of the blue.

She lit up and pitched the lighter aside. "I'd offer, but it's my last."

"Smoking was never one of my vices. Too slow a death. I prefer more agony. Dating married men seems to work."

The words came out spontaneous and without guile, but Michelle fell victim to an uncontrollable cough. She'd hit a raw nerve.

"You married?" Cézanne asked.

"Separated. But me and my old man're getting back together. This thing with Carri made me realize how much he means to me."

"Happens that way sometimes."

Cézanne's antennae went up. Something not quite right here. Better proceed with caution. Not too many questions, too fast. This girl would summon Brutus, and out she'd go.

"Were you and Carri close?"

Michelle shrugged. Took a long drag and blew the smoke out in a slow, deliberate thread. "Hardly saw her. You know how it goes."

"I suppose." Cézanne forced a smile. She didn't like this girl. In a risky move, she bet against the house. "But you were there the night she died."

"Killed herself." Michelle inhaled deeply and held it. Finally, she said, "Yeah, I was there, but I was passed out."

"You heard the shot?"

"What I heard sounded like a door slamming." Michelle's eyes narrowed into cruel slits. "I just figured the bitch had another go-round with *Five-O*."

"Pardon?"

"That cop."

Cézanne fished out a black and white copy of Roby's ID photo. "Ever seen this man?"

Hollywood leaned forward. "Sure. That's old Needle-Dick."

Cézanne stuffed the picture into the same pocket with the surgeon's card. "He's been in here?"

"Sure. He used to come gawk at one of my roommates. Sat there and drooled like *Paloff's* dog when she'd trot out."

Damn Roby anyway. Cézanne pulled out a small, spiral notebook and a pen. "What's her name? Where can I find her?"

"Who, Glennis?" Michelle gave a wry laugh, took the last drag off the cigarette and stubbed it out in the white sand of a floor ashtray. "Poor kid bought the farm."

"She's dead?"

" 'Fraid so. Corked herself."

Cézanne frowned.

But Michelle, avoiding eye contact by picking at her perfectly manicured nails, cleared things up. "Glennis was one fucked-up bitch. And screwing that cop dude didn't score any points."

So Roby had a thing for skanky dancers.

Cézanne let the interview come full circle. "How come you never gave a statement to the police about Carri Crane?"

"Nobody asked. I go on after this number," she said, straining to listen. Drumming bass rattled the walls.

"Who were those Mexican dudes?"

"How should I know? In that part of town, people come and go all the time."

The redhead with the navel ring scampered in with big news.

"Tiny just tossed some sweathogs." She caught Cézanne staring at the metal loop in her belly button.

"Like it? You should get one. It only hurts a little, and

166

guys love 'em." She hiked up a leg, settled a platform heel on the edge of Cézanne's chair and tilted her crotch up way too close. "I got this'un three weeks ago." She parted the tender flesh wide enough to show off a tiny gold ring piercing her

God bless America.

"Takes six weeks to heal," the redhead went on, "then I'm gonna replace it with a bigger one. That's why Tiny threw the hammer-slammers out. One tried to fit a buck in *that*." And then, "I'm Reno. You the new chick?"

Hollywood stopped picking at her bloody cuticles and intervened. "She's The Heat."

Down came the leg. The girl recoiled. "Shit, Hollywood. I told you they'd come."

Three strides, and Hollywood slapped the dancer's face. She grabbed Reno's shoulders, and gave her a rough shake. "Get the fuck out, and don't come back."

Reno grabbed the nearest smock and dashed off. Hollywood rifled through the clutter of cosmetics until she hocus-pocused another cigarette. Out came the lighter and up went the flame.

"You spoke to Mrs. Crane the night it happened," Cézanne said.

"I dunno. I forget."

"You did," she said, firmer this time. "You were upset."

Hollywood stood. Shed the robe and adjusted the T-back disappearing between her cheeks. Pulled a scrunchy off her ponytail, shook her hair and admired her reflection. She smoothed a slow hand over one bare buttock and held Cézanne's mirrored gaze with her own.

"Whatcha thinkin', Sister?" Sensuously, she swayed to the music, letting her fingers serpentine across her breasts and down her torso. "If there was enough money I'd get Reno . . ."

She threaded her thumbs through the skimpy gold lamé triangle, stretching it enough to show off a patch of close-cropped hairs bleached platinum.

". . . the three of us could spend some time together."

"I thought the blonde said you don't do women."

"I like to watch."

The rest went unsaid. Hollywood mocked her with a grin.

"Your roommate before Glennis, tell me about her."

"Bethany? A head case." Hollywood caressed her mammoth breasts. "Whatcha thinking, Lady Dick? You giving it some thought?" She pulled at her nipples until they hardened. "The doc did a great job, don'tcha think? You can't even see any scars."

Cézanne stayed on keel. "Mrs. Crane said the girl killed herself."

"He cut through here," Hollywood explained, drawing a taloned finger across one rouged nipple, "so it wouldn't show. Then he shoved the implants through that little slit." The dancer reached out to take her hand. "Touch them. So you'll know in case you want to use the same doctor. Some turn hard as rocks but these are . . . Jell-O."

Cézanne slipped from her grasp. Hollywood grinned, circling the flat of each palm against an erect nipple.

"What happened to Bethany?"

"Went haywire. Ended up in the ol' ice box." Michelle stopped the show long enough to take a puff, then snuffed out the cigarette in a styrofoam take-out of half-eaten Chinese. "Love to visit, but I gotta split."

"Just a couple more questions." Cézanne tried out a feeble smile. "You and Glennis were living in Fort Worth?"

Michelle's shoulders dipped in a frustrated slump. She shifted her stance. "Burleson. Hey look, Whoever-You-Are, I don't perform, I don't get paid."

Cézanne rose. Especially when she saw Michelle move to the door and press a button recessed in the door jamb. Brutus would be on the way about now.

"Your roommate, Bethany. What happened to her?"

"Blew her brains out. I have a knack for picking them."

Cézanne cemented her initial impression. Michelle was crazier than a rat in a drainpipe. Brutus burst through the door, filling the framework. Michelle stepped aside. Gave him a look.

Now or never. Another hunch.

"You and Bethany were living in Burleson?"

"Nope." With an artful twist, Michelle slid past the goon.

"Where then?"

Brutus advanced.

"Don't even," she warned, reaching into her purse, snaking her fingers around the butt of the Smith.

Last chance.

"HOLLYWOOD."

The dancer didn't so much as return a glance.

"What was Carri's address?"

As Michelle headed down the dark hallway, her backside swinging in sync with a Britney Spears hit, her words melded into the metallic beat.

"You want anything else from me, talk to my lawyer."

Chapter Eighteen

Roby finally came up for air around midnight, and not a moment too soon.

When he suggested meeting Cézanne someplace nobody would be looking for him, it didn't surprise her at all when he picked the laundromat of their first encounter. After the last person emptied out, she yanked open the door and stalked inside. Instead of reveling in the presence of a man who cut a snappy picture in his tweed jacket and tartan pinpoint oxford, she reared back with a closed fist and delivered a right hook to his middle.

A new black cowboy hat toppled off his head and came to rest upside down, on the floor. With Roby doubled over and gasping for breath, she lit into him.

"You duplicitous bastard! You could have saved me three hellish days by telling me you were screwing every 'ho' in the Metroplex. I thought we were friends. I thought you trusted me. I'm supposed to be your lawyer when they finally cart your sorry butt Downtown, and you can't even tell me the goddam truth."

She stuffed the cashier's check into his shirt pocket. With some effort, he righted himself enough for her to catch him wincing. The well placed lick brought tears to his eyes.

He vacuumed in a breath. "Zannie? You gone crazy?"

"Yes, I have. I was crazy to think you didn't do it, Roby. You killed her, you lying son of a bitch, and probably those other girls, too."

The heat of outrage lapped at her neck like white-hot flames.

Ashen faced and still clutching his abdomen, he straightened to his full height. "What girls?"

She studied his face with cold scrutiny. It was so like him to insult her. "You know what girls. Strippers. I bought your story. I believed in you. I trusted you. I hate your guts."

"Titty-dancers?" His eyes narrowed in a confused squint and one brow arched into a question mark. "Zannie, I don't know—"

"And don't ever call me Zannie again. My sister was the only one I let do that, and you're not family."

Snorting fury, she balled up her fists to take another swing. Roby stepped back, his eyes wide, but not far enough away to take any more of her shit and she knew it.

"I never got any tail off a topless dancer in my life. Least not that I know of."

"Hollywood said you did."

"Who's Hollywood?"

"Like you don't know." Infuriated, she tightened her jaw. "Michelle Parker."

He picked his hat up off the floor, propped his rump against a washing machine and rubbed the sting out of his belly. "You're not making sense."

"Where'd your girlfriend live? Huh? Tell me. Or maybe there's a reason you don't want me to know."

"With her parents."

"Lie."

"She was a mama's baby," he said, still short of breath. "She lived at home. Ask them if you don't believe me. Which explains why I could never pick her up there."

"I get it," Cézanne said nastily, "it's like pizza, right? 'We deliver.' "

Roby's eyes stormed over. "If you were a man, I'd—"

"Get off it. You pulled the wool over everybody's eyes."

Her eyes flickered to his hands, and she saw he'd clenched a fist. He wanted to knock her block off.

"She knew you, Asshole. From your picture. So don't act like you never heard of her."

Roby shook his head. "Is this gal a dancer?" He relaxed his hand.

"Yeah. Did you do her, too?"

Roby snorted in disgust. "Now lemme see here. Some skank says I banged her—"

"Not her. Her roommates."

"—and, how long've you known this—this—this Hollywood person?"

He made it sound ludicrous. She swallowed some of the rage, letting the bitterness ooze down her throat.

"Zannie—Zan. I don't know what you're talking about."

"Don't waste my time."

His shoulders bowed under the weight of her judgment. "Long as I've known you, who'd have thought you'd turn on me?"

His bold observation whittled her down a notch.

"How long have you been staking out Ali Baba's?" she demanded.

He favored her with an unlikely grin. "Not me. You couldn't zap me in there with a cattle prod."

"Hollywood said she knew you."

"So do half the people in this town. Don't make me a killer."

She wanted desperately to believe him. Almost more than she wanted to slug him.

172

"Hollywood recognized your photo. Said you took a shine to one of her roommates."

"So?"

"So you just had the cods to stand here and tell me you never went to Ali Baba's."

"No, Ma'am." He took a deep breath. "What I said was, I couldn't be zapped inside with a cattle prod. Make sure you listen to what people say when they answer your questions."

"I pay attention to what they say," she snapped, "but I pay even closer attention to what they don't say."

The beacon of a lone headlight swept the parking lot before landing in front of the laundromat. Roby settled his hat on his head and tugged at the brim. In no time at all, a new batch of illegal aliens would migrate in with a week's worth of dirty clothes.

"I stopped by Ali Baba's once, and that was enough for me."

"You ogled her roommate." When he maintained his silence, she pressed. "Why would she lie?"

"Don't know."

"I'm thinking you do. And by the way, I hate your new Stetson. Big hat, no cattle."

"The Crime Scene boys confiscated my Texas High-Roller. The one *you* knocked onto the carpet. That nasty shag saturated with blood? The same type blood they'll likely find on my hat."

"That's right, find a way to blame me."

"Tell you what, Duchess," he said with a sigh, "if you've got half as much faith in her story as I do in your ability to ferret out the truth, I'm still in good hands. So far, you've done real good. Now why don't you take a day off and get laid? You're starting to scare me."

Chapter Nineteen

This time when Cézanne arrived at the Crane's Grand Avenue estate, Agnetha Crane didn't even try to put on a good front. From the flower bed, she pushed herself up on all fours, got herself balanced at the knees and rose the rest of the way wielding a garden spade. Her eyes filmed over with the dull glaze of roadkill, and she raised an arm to wipe the sweat beading along the kerchief securing her hair.

"See these? Potted plants from our friends. Left over from the—"

The lady couldn't bring herself to say the F-word, much less talk about the service. Misery shrouded her face, still every bit as fresh as the newly tilled earth.

"So," the captain's wife continued, "if you haven't come to share news that your brother officers picked up that man, then get off the property."

"All I'm asking for is a couple of minutes."

Agnetha Crane flung the spade at the ground. It nicked a shrub and chopped off a pansy as it hit the dirt. Anger turned to shock. She dropped to her knees, sandwiched the petals between gloved hands and wept.

Cézanne gave the neighborhood a furtive once-over. Jesus H. Five-thirty on a Friday afternoon, and folks corralling their kids into station wagons for flag football practice. God only knew what they were thinking. Police brutality.

Without explanation, she joined Carri's mother on the grass and found herself getting misty-eyed.

Weird. She didn't even like Carri. Didn't know her, really. But she knew Roby. And people wanted him to fry.

"Mrs. Crane, there's nothing I can say that'll make it better. Believe me, I'd rather be incarcerated in a Turkish prison than come here. But I think you know something—information that might turn out to be vital to your daughter's case—and I have to find out what it is."

The woman snapped to attention, parting her palms. The crumpled flower stuck to one glove in a purple smear.

"I told . . . you everything." Between sobs. "Please . . . leave me . . . alone."

Cézanne reached out a hand. Touched Mrs. Crane's shirt sleeve, half expecting the lady to knock it away. She didn't.

"The girl, Michelle. I went to see her."

Agnetha's eyes ignited with a thousand "whys".

"She wouldn't know anything. She's a," the captain's wife sniffled away the last of the sobs and spat crudities, "titty-dancer."

"We need to go over the phone call. The night Carri asked you to talk to the girl."

"I told you already."

"Tell me again. Tell me slowly. Tell me verbatim."

Mrs. Crane looked skyward. Searching for words? Scouring the Heavens for signs of her daughter? Without warning, her shoulders slouched.

"It was about seven in the evening. Carri called, crying. She said she wanted to move back home. That she'd made a big mistake. That Michelle was upset."

"Did she say what upset Michelle?"

"Something about the girl's husband. And Michelle had a gun. That part scared me. I thought. . . ." Agnetha Crane glanced across the street, lifted a hand and exchanged

175

waves with an elderly man walking past.

"Thought what?"

"I don't know what I thought. I just told her to get out of the apartment. I even offered to pick her up on the nearest corner right then and there if she wouldn't give me the address. She said, 'No, I can make do for now. Besides, I have a date. Talk to her, Mom. She wants to die.' That's what she said."

"Then what?"

Agnetha sighed. Looked around. Searched the plants for answers. After a long pause, she said, "I talked to her."

"Did Michelle say why she wanted to die?"

"No, she just cried a lot. Said she didn't have any family. And how lucky Carri was that we loved her. She asked if she could call me 'Mom.' "

"And you said what?"

" 'Sure.' "

"Then?"

"That was it."

"What can you tell me about the gun?"

A flash of recall lit up Mrs. Crane's eyes. "A pistol. Carri said, 'She has a twenty-two caliber, Mom. She's waving it around.' I asked if the girl was on drugs. Carri said, 'No, just drinking.' "

The refreshing scent of a newly scalped lawn drifted over on a light breeze. Cézanne took a deep breath. A chill rippled up her sides. Mrs. Crane had no idea.

"Did Michelle own other guns?"

The woman nodded. Brushed away a gnat. "Oh, yes," she answered, matter-of-fact. "She was on the shooting team in the military. Carri said she kept a shotgun. For intruders. And others. I don't know what kind."

"She did military service?" Cézanne found the news astounding. "What branch?"

"Didn't I tell you?" Mrs. Crane looked as though Cézanne had sprouted horns and a tail. "I'm sure I did."

No, because that little nugget would have been important.

"Was she Army? Air Force?"

Mrs. Crane lifted a non-committal shoulder. "I don't know. Apparently it didn't last. She got booted out for something. Carri took up for her. Said it wasn't her fault. But Chuck says anything less than an honorable discharge is bad."

The sun disappeared behind the clouds. In seconds, the evening chill sent a shudder across her shoulders.

"Do you know where Michelle was from?"

A headshake.

"Did your daughter say anything else in that conversation? Anything at all?"

Seemingly defeated, Agnetha shrugged off the question.

"Please. If there's anything else, it's important."

"Just when she first called, crying."

A car roared by, white vapors coiling out from the tailpipe, disappearing into the air like Mrs. Crane's thoughts. Cézanne glanced down the street. An unmarked patrol car rounded the corner.

Captain.

Every second counted.

"What about when she first called? Why was she crying?"

"She just kept saying, 'I can't take it anymore. I can't do what they want me to do.' "

"*They* who?" Captain Crane's cue-ball head became visible through the tinted windshield. She rose to her feet. Snatched up her purse. "Who's *they?*"

"I don't know, I didn't ask." An agonizing whimper escaped Agnetha Crane's throat. "My daughter was crying. I just wanted to make it better."

"The roommates, where were they from?"

"I don't know."

"Do you know how they died? Anything?"

"Just that they shot themselves."

Lord have mercy.

"Anything else? Anything at all?"

Mrs. Crane spotted her husband even before he screeched up to the curb. Her eyes conveyed a message. That Cézanne better leave went without saying.

"Did Carri say who she had a date with?" Cézanne moved toward her car. The door to Crane's cruiser popped open. "Can I call on you again?"

"We'll see," came the reply.

She already had one leg inside and her bag slung across the seat when Agnetha Crane called out.

"Don't you want to know her name?"

"God, yes."

With Crane's long strides, it took only seconds to reach his wife's elbow. He pulled her to her feet and menaced Cézanne with the kind of glare to undermine even the most confident person's self-esteem.

"Her last name was Faust," Agnetha hollered.

Crane lifted her up on tiptoes.

Bethany Faust! A name on Jinx Porter's list.

Now all she had to do was call Johnson County for the low-down on Glennis Somebody-or-Other, or find Bethany Faust's friends and family and interview them. With only two-hundred-fifty-three other Texas counties to check and God knew how many in the other forty-nine states, no big thing. Not to mention she'd never been able to get Jack-Shit from Louisiana or the military.

Chapter Twenty

It wasn't that a handful of detectives stopped what they were doing when Cézanne walked into Homicide at six-forty-five Saturday morning that made her check her hole card, but the alarm in Greta's widening eyes as she intercepted her in the corridor between cubicles.

"What are you doing here on a weekend?" Cézanne said.

"Shhh. Captain's got me working time-and-a-half until this thing's over."

How transparent.

"And I thought I was the only one working straight through."

Clear as a diva on opening night, the voice of Darlene Driskoll sang out from Cézanne's cubicle.

"I guess if we get any more bills, you're out of here, huh?"

"No, you are," came the husky retort of her sometimes-husband. "I want to see the credit card balances. Now."

"They're in my desk."

"Then get them. Better yet, I'll get them."

"But why, Dougie? Why can't I just call the companies and tell you the balances?" Her usually determined voice degenerated into a falsetto whine.

"You're not calling from this phone because I said so. If you want to phone for the credit card balances, do it from your own office."

"But what's the big deal?"

"I don't need the whole Department knowing my business. You never know who's listening in."

Cézanne's eyes bulged in their sockets. The head-on collision with the telephone repairman that didn't seem important at the time suddenly made sense. Her breath came in shallow gulps.

Trouble with the phones?

She tightened her jaw and grew a titanium spine. Over Greta's dismay, she sauntered on in expecting to see Darlene Driskoll dressed like an explosion in a textile mill. What she got turned out to be more than a routine visual assault. Festering in a red polka-dotted sarong like a bad case of measles, Darlene's bulk draped over the chair's edges. She toyed with a wicked stickpin until the gold lamé flower securing the fabric at one shoulder stood up like a misplaced cyclops.

Cézanne swallowed hard.

"Good morning, Darlene," she said, forcing cheer, then turned to her new partner with a scowl and an irritably nasty, "Doug."

He was whittling pencils with a small, plastic pencil sharpener she recognized as her own, and she glowered at him for taking it without permission and felt her blood pressure rise over the mess of sawdust he made on the floor.

"You're in her seat," Driskoll prompted his wife.

"You didn't tell me you were working with her." Twelve-thousand volts of electricity arced out in Darlene's speech.

"Now you know."

"There's been a misunderstanding," said Cézanne. "He's apparently assigned to Homicide, but he's *not* working with me."

"You're in his office," Darlene whined.

"No, he's in mine. And don't bother to get up," she said, injecting a cheery lilt into her tone. "I'm just here long enough to check in, and I'll be out of your hair. And speaking of hair, may I say how exciting yours looks, Darlene. I never realized hair that length could be moussed into spikes."

Conscious of unfriendly eyes boring holes, she breezed between the pair to rifle through the file cabinet for a fresh spiral pad.

"Wanna have lunch at that new Greek place, Dougie?"

"No. *Zany* and I—"

Cézanne whipped around. "Don't call me that. Don't *ever* call me that."

"Lighten up, Babydoll, I didn't mean anything—"

She shot Darlene a furtive glance. Fake periwinkle eyes dulled, and her pudgy jaw unhinged. Cézanne's gaze flickered to Detective Driskoll reaching for his jacket as if he expected to tag along.

She extinguished his hopes with a glower. "Don't you have something to work on?"

"I'm supposed to be helping you."

"And you can. You can buy your wife a cup of coffee; I'll treat. Darlene," she said, turning to the pathetic woman as she slapped a handful of pocket change on Driskoll's desk, "it was great seeing you again. Let's do lunch."

"Really?"

"I wouldn't say it if I didn't mean it." She shifted her eyes to Driskoll and replaced her contrived smile with a glare. "If you borrow my stuff, at least have the decency to put it back where you found it."

Nobody had to tell her she had dodged a bullet. And judging by the way the rest of the noodle-spined Homicide gang flattened against the walls and practically drew down

181

in anticipation of a shootout, they knew it, too.

She headed out the door, leaving the brothers with a parting shot. "Am I the only one around here with any work to do?"

One thing for sure, Cézanne thought, she couldn't trust the telephones anymore. At least not the ones at the PD. And for the past four months, ever since Crane first slit open the bill to the cell phone assigned to her, combing for evidence to link her to Driskoll—and did so with the kind of fanaticism normally associated with gorillas picking off fleas—the best bet for running down "possibles" on Jinx Porter's list seemed to be via pay phone.

At a corner phone booth a block north of the Crane crime scene, Cézanne stood outside the unmarked cruiser in the chill, plunked some coins into the slot and tapped out a number on the keypad. A lowrider with license plates lit by purple neon tubing slumped heavily down the road, belching smoke. On the third ring, she covered her free ear to reduce the noise.

"Johnson County Sheriff's Office," drawled the unappealing baritone.

The Johnson County line might be fifteen miles from Downtown Fort Worth but, culturally, it was thirty years behind.

Which meant she got some hayseed on the line.

Cézanne gave her name. Let him know he was dealing with a sister officer, maybe get a little professional courtesy.

She said, "I need to speak with a homicide detective."

"Somebody get killed?"

"No—"

"Then you don't need to report a homicide."

"No, but I need information on one."

"So somebody did get killed."

Bonehead. She tried again. "Yes but—"

"Why didn't you say?"

"I guess we misunderstood each other."

"Not me. I understood you fine. You said you wanted a homicide detective, then you said nobody got killed, then you said somebody did. You're the one maybe doesn't understand."

She couldn't tell if he was ribbing her or not. He sounded as inert as a gas. Come to think of it, "moron" must be a job qualification for dispatcher positions in rural areas—if, in fact, that's who she had the misfortune to be dealing with.

"Perhaps I should start over." Something told her to keep it simple. Something a person with a room temperature IQ could understand.

"Do you have a Criminal Investigator?"

"Ware."

"Where do you think?"

"I dunno. You're the one asking questions. Hold on, I've got another call coming in."

"Don't put me on hold—"

Click.

George Strait crooned a familiar tune. Wanted the listener to pity him now that he'd done her wrong, standing on the porch, thumbs through his belt loops, watching her high-tail it out of there. She couldn't scatter gravel fast enough.

Hell, half of Fort Worth's male population saw relationships that way. Left-brain thinkers never considered the consequences, just followed wherever their divining rods pointed them, seeking out the nearest wet spot. So even if George did tune up in torment, the gal had a gutful. What'd he expect?

Now Loretta Lynn? There was a butt-kicker.

Click-click.

"Sorry 'bout that. I'm the only one 'round to catch the phones. Eunice—she's our secretary—Eunice ran down to the Tiger Tote so I'm filling in. They got those little Cokes in the glass bottles on special—"

"Spare me the sad, sorry saga. Just answer me this: do you people even have an investigation division?"

"Ware."

"In your office, where else?" She covered the mouthpiece long enough to mime "stupid fucker" and pictured him leaning back in his chair, a half-wit smile breaking across the face of this rusty cog in the slobbering-good-ol'-boy machinery.

"Lady, you're confusing the dickens outta me."

"I want to talk to a detective, an investigator, a deputy— whatever term that's not foreign to you—just put me in touch with him."

"Does it have to be a *him?*"

Her ears pricked up like a K-9 on alert. The concept sounded too progressive to be true.

"Thank goodness. Put her on."

"Only lady works here's Eunice. You don't wanna talk to her. She cain't he'p ya."

"But you just said—"

"No, Ma'am, I was just making sure you weren't one of those militant types. Can you believe there's still folks prejudiced against women deputies?" This time he sounded wickedly amused. "Hold please. Got another call comin' in."

"NO. Don't put me—"

Click.

—on hold, I'm at a goddam pay phone and the car fumes're worse than the showers at Treblinka. Stinking polecat.

Her ear hurt but she didn't want to let off the pressure. If she did, she couldn't pretend she didn't see the upraised middle fingers and the beginnings of road rage in the intersection long after the light turned red and the last car's tailpipe hung out in the middle of the street.

Click-click. The nightmare returned.

"Now, where were we?" he asked, cheerily.

"I want somebody who works homicides, on the phone."

"We don't work homicides on the phone. We have to send a man out to the scene. Matter of fact, I never heard of any department working homicides on the phone. 'Less maybe New York City does it. Cain't tell about Yanks."

"What the hell are you talking about?"

"A deputy has to go out to the scene to do the investigation."

"We're not on the same page."

"I wouldn't know. I'm looking over the sports section of the *Cleburne Times-Review.* Where're you?"

She started to tell him she was staring at the number listed in the phone book, wondering if Cleburne, Texas had a mental institution and she'd inadvertently misdialed.

"Where's your homicide investigator?"

"Yes."

"Yes what?"

"Ware's the investigator."

"Oh good grief." She pulled the receiver away, held it out as though it were a cobra and said, "I'm talking to *Rainman.*"

When she pressed it back to her ear, judging from the sound of the guy's breathing he was either doing something raunchy or he just took pneumonia.

"All I want is a homicide detective," she snapped.

"Same here, but there's not enough in the budget. We have a deputy that answers all kinds of calls, though. Even homicides."

"Now we're getting somewhere. Put him on the phone."

"Thought you said nobody got killed."

"That's it." She slapped her hand against the top of her car. "I'm not discussing this with you. Who's in charge?"

"The Sheriff."

"Fine. Put me through."

"He's jaw-jacking with some city slicker."

Cézanne grew testier. Oozing sarcasm, she injected enough syrup into her voice to start a cavity. "Look here, I don't care who I get as long as I'm talking to a commissioned peace officer."

"Then your answer's Noah."

"Am I to understand you're refusing to transfer my call?"

"I just told you Noah's here."

"I know no one's there. Just tell me when, goddammit."

"Nguyen? You want Nguyen? Why didn't you say that in the first place? Cain't he'p ya."

She slammed down the phone in frustration and kicked a nearby trash can hard enough to leave a dent. Stupid-ass motherfucker. She took a cleansing breath, dropped some more coins down the chute and redialed. A couple of drag racers in the distance were bearing down hard to beat the yellow light. She pressed her hand to her ear to cut the loud mufflers.

"Johnson County Sheriff's Office."

The hayseed again.

She kept her voice even and metered. "Who's there that I can speak to about a case?"

"Noah."

"No one?" She could no longer temper her fury. She patted her pocket for a pen. "I want your name and badge number."

With a swarthy, South-o'-the-Border inflection he said, "We don't need no stinking *batches*."

"I don't fucking believe this." This time, she didn't bother to cover the mouthpiece. "The inmates have taken over the asylum. Jesus H. Christ."

"Now we're gettin' somewhere. He's here."

"Who?"

"Jesus. Jesus is here. Matter of fact, you want to find Jesus, all you gotta do is spend the night in jail. More people find Jesus behind bars than in church. Hold on a sec."

"Don't you dare," she shouted. A group of pachucos across the street took notice. "I'm on a pay phone—"

Click.

The guy was pricking with her.

Click, click.

"I think we should start over," she regrouped, blood percolating behind both eyes hard enough to make her retinas pulse. "I want to talk to somebody. I don't care who, where, or when, so long as you give me a name and don't put me on hold."

"Why didn't you say that in the first place? Nguyen's our interpreter. He only comes in if we pick up an Asian. You want Nguyen, you have to call Arlington Police. Jot this down: it's pronounced 'when' but he spells it

N-G-U-Y-E-N. Be sure and tell 'em when you call, avoid the confusion."

This time, it was Cézanne who said, "Huh?"

"We don't have a 'Who', but when Nguyen's not available to translate, we use Michael Wu. He's with the PD over in Dallas. Task force, I think. Works Asian gangs. And Ware's retired. He does have a son, works for us. Gonna be our investigator soon as he graduates from the police academy, seeing how he's got a college degree from Texas A&M and all. But the kid's still technically classified as a cadet, and you did specify you wanted a *real* officer. Plus he's an Aggie and that don't set well with Tea-Sips, you know. Hope you didn't go to TU."

He just insulted her alma mater.

"I've had it," she hollered over the rush of cars. A disembodied chuckle at the other end of the line turned into a rollicking belly laugh. "Don't call me a Tea-Sipper and don't refer to The University of Texas as TU. I want to speak with the Sheriff himself. If he's too cotton-picking preoccupied with some yokel—"

"Some crackpot's bendin' his ear, all right."

"Never mind. Here's my office number. Have your fearless leader call me when he's finished yapping." She rattled off the extension and bashed the receiver into its cradle before he had a chance to induce a brain hemorrhage.

Collapsed against the plastic casing shielding the pay phone, Cézanne wondered if anything would fix the jackhammering behind her eyes besides a gunshot wound to the head. She climbed back into the driver's seat and ransacked the glove compartment looking for over-the-counter meds.

Unexpectedly, the dispatcher announced her call sign over the air. "Go to 'Talk-One.' "

With her attention neatly diverted from the contents

188

strewn over the floorboard, Cézanne punched the channel selector until the digits for the informal radio frequency flashed on the display.

She grabbed the hand mic mounted on a clip near the dash and cleared her throat. "Unit calling?"

Greta had gotten hold of a hand-held. "Cézanne, did you just call Johnson County?"

Finally. See about this. Redneck shit-for-brains needed a demotion, sonofabitch'd be cleaning horse stalls with a toothbrush.

"Bobby Noah from the SO is holding for you. Says it's important. Says he's the Sheriff. Oh," she added, "he said something else, too."

Cézanne closed her eyes tight and hoped she was wrong.

"Let's see," Greta said over the shuffle of paper, "I have it in my notes. Here it is. This is a quote."

Cézanne held her breath.

"He said he'd been waiting to pull this stunt for years and you should just accept it as a Noah-Nguyen situation."

Chapter Twenty-One

Most detectives didn't work at all on Sundays, much less come in early. But then most of them weren't up to their craw in a high profile murder case, either. Cézanne pulled out her key card, swiped the control pad near the door and quietly let herself into Homicide.

First she peeked around the corner to find Crane's chair empty. An unintended blessing. Since the funeral, he'd haunted the place like a ghoul. Halfway down the corridor, her ears pricked up at the rustle of paper.

She held her breath and listened to the skittering of rodent-like claws. Someone beat her in. And the rat sounds were coming from her cubicle.

She backtracked, traveling the hallway opposite Greta's desk until she had a bird's-eye view of her office. She blinked away the stupor of someone freshly awakened.

Darlene Driskoll, dressed in cheetah stretch pants and a matching shirt, sat in her husband's chair rummaging through drawers. By the looks of the mess, she'd been there long enough to settle in and work herself into a lather. Separated from a stack of papers were several wallet-sized photos.

Cézanne decided to watch from afar before making her presence known. For one thing, Driskoll's wife produced a wicked letter opener and was slicing through an envelope she unearthed from her husband's outgoing mailbin.

Jesus H.

Darlene's shoulders tightened with the instinct of a bird dog on point. But as her eyes drifted over the page, her whole body went limp. A low groan held captive in her throat escaped as an eerie wail. She cleared the desk with a sweep of the hand, smashed the letter opener into the drawer and slumped over the desk until her head came to rest atop crossed arms.

For several seconds she didn't move, seemingly not even to breathe. A uninformed bystander might have mistaken she'd fallen asleep, but it wasn't long before the anguish gave way to rippling shoulders and breaths expelled in sobs.

Paralyzed with guilt, Darlene's private drama became Cézanne's personal hell—intolerable to watch.

She probably had the same reaction to me.

Cézanne straightened her shoulders. Time to bring down the curtain.

She retraced her steps until she stood at the entrance to Homicide. Halfway down her corridor, she whistled "Hi-Ho". Even before she came upon Darlene on her knees gathering papers off the floor, she heard the vermin-like scramble.

"This is a pleasant surprise. What brings you here on a Sunday morning?" She decided to be a sport and furnish the pathetic woman's answer. "Doug forget something?"

Darlene sniffled through a nod.

"Let me help you. Your husband can be such a slob. I don't know how you stand it. You ought to be canonized for sainthood."

She set her purse—the one with the .38 buried at the bottom—on Doug's desk.

On top of the wallet photos.

Glamour Shots.

Dropping to one knee, she fleetingly wondered if

stooping to Darlene's level would put her at a disadvantage, relaxing only when no hat pins or ice picks appeared out of the blue. And after they finished straightening the mess, she planned to slide those pictures away with her bag and identify the people in them at her leisure. Even if Darlene suspected she took them, she probably wouldn't have the nerve to confront her.

When they were done, Cézanne stowed her purse in the file cabinet and appraised her adversary. The department cat burglar nearly pulled off a caper.

"Want to talk girl talk?"

Darlene shook her head. But she reclaimed her chair and settled in as if she craved nothing more.

"Something I can help you find? Is he working a case?"

Darlene sniveled. "Some bills I left."

Cézanne wasn't falling for it. "Your hair looks different. What'd you do, get it cut?"

"Shaped."

"It's—" The truth. "—different."

Darlene's gaze flickered to the blotter and down to the open drawer in the middle of her husband's desk. A look of panic crossed her face. She leaned over and scanned the floor, then returned to an upright position with confusion etched in her forehead.

The photos.

Cézanne's heart thudded with anticipation. "Lose an earring? Contact lens?"

Darlene shook her head. Amber eyes glittered, frantic.

Cézanne nestled her shoulders into the chair back. Darlene didn't have the guts. She felt a sadistic mixture of sympathy and triumph play out in the corners of her smile.

"You don't look happy, Darlene. I think I know just

what you need. Want to run up the street for a light break-fast?"

Darlene's eyes narrowed. "You mean it?"

"Sure." Fake cheer. "I'll buy."

"That's awful nice."

"It'll be fun." Like having tonsils lasered off without anesthesia.

They were getting into the patrol car when Cézanne pointed to a silver Explorer parked in a metered space on the street.

"That yours?"

Darlene clammed up as if she'd just been Mirandized.

Cézanne played a hunch. "You can park your POV in the lot on weekends. Didn't anybody tell you when you started working here?"

Darlene shook her head.

"Well you can. That's about the only time they don't tow our personal vehicles. Come on."

At the end of an uneventful meal, Darlene asked, "Where do you buy your scarves?"

"You like this?" Cézanne pulled the scarf ends bunched at the collar and gingerly retied it. "It belonged to my grandmother. I have all my grandmother's scarves."

An unhealthy memory returned.

She kept them in a Smith & Wesson box in a dresser drawer, the six shot snubnose with bird's-eye maple grips that once belonged to her father on the bottom, and the scarves loosely stacked on top.

She wouldn't tell Darlene that every great once-in-awhile when things got really bad, she took out the gun, ejected the hollow-points and stood in front of the mirror with the cold barrel pressed against her temple and practiced. Nor how she'd done so the night she learned Doug was married, after his infatuation with her played out in some sick testosterone conquest.

It wouldn't do to tell Darlene her grandmother's scarves had a kind of magical power to them. That on more than one occasion they kept her from reloading. . . .

She became aware of the quiet.

Of Darlene, sizing her up.

"Sometimes when I feel blue, I take a scarf out of the box and hold it to my nose, just so I can smell her." Her voice trailed and her mood plummeted.

"Your granny's dead?"

"Has been for a long time."

"Mine's alive," Darlene said. "I don't think she likes me though."

Injecting a false lilt, Cézanne said, "There's a little boutique called *Fantasia* on North Main. You should stop in. It always lifts my spirit. Sometimes I swear I smell my grandmother's lilac."

Cézanne could almost see the wheels turning behind Darlene's flat forehead.

Back at the lot, she pulled the cruiser up even with the Explorer. Without warning, Driskoll's wife lunged. With no time to react, Cézanne found herself crushed in the woman's embrace.

Darlene pulled away, cranberry-eyed.

"You won't tell him, will you?"

"About the snooping? I'd have done the same."

For the first time that morning Darlene smiled, smug in their secret. While she stood beside the Ford fumbling with the keys, Cézanne touched the electric window opener and slid the glass on the passenger side halfway down.

"Thanks for the company."

Darlene nodded. "Let's do it again, can we?" Followed

by, "What's the name of that perfume?"

As Cézanne pulled into traffic, feeling worse than ever like a man-eating vamp, she wondered if Darlene snapped to the fact that the entire time they spent upstairs, she hadn't so much as cracked a file.

Several blocks from the PD, she curbed the vehicle, let the motor idle, and fished out the pictures.

The first was an angelic image. The round face, perfectly sculpted nose and large blue eyes, hinted intelligence. Fawn-colored hair parted in the middle, hung well below thin shoulders. Her fleshy lips curled in a provocative smile.

Attractive, in an earthy, folk singer sort of way.

She flipped the photo over and read.

Beth.

Her heart stalled. A shiver snaked up her arms.

She slipped the picture behind the other photos. Her heart picked up its pace. Breaths came in short, shallow waves. The hair in the next snapshot might be jet black and clipped short, and the makeup toned down, but the face belonged to Michelle Parker.

Cézanne shuddered. She found a smaller photo stuck to the back and carefully peeled them apart without tearing. The image staring back chilled her to the bone.

He had every reason to have the photo, Cézanne thought. They were on the same team. Through misguided instructions from The Brass, he was supposed to be helping her. But studying the snapshot, she couldn't shake the dread.

The unblinking stare of Carri Crane in her police cadet uniform held her transfixed.

Cézanne picked up the cell phone and dialed.

Chapter Twenty-Two

Even before they formally met, Cézanne expected she and Bobby Noah would lock horns. It wasn't that he insisted she make the thirty-five mile drive down to Cleburne before sundown that rankled her feathers; after all, she was the one asking the favor. It wasn't that he told her if she wanted the information she'd have to look it up herself, since the SO was short staffed, and Eunice spent her free time on a cigarette boat at Eagle Mountain Lake with a Mai Tai in one hand, and the other flipping through pages of the latest issue of *Cosmopolitan*. Either way, professional courtesy assured her the run of the place.

What really got her goat was the fact he insisted she pick him up at his farm in the sticks. He'd loaned his patrol car, he said, to a dipshit deputy who'd wrecked his, and he needed a lift into town.

To top it off, Sheriff Noah gave suck-dog directions. With the sun setting fast, she'd be searching the darkness for tin roof markers, log cabins with tacky pinwheel lawn ornaments and a paved road just past a gravel road leading to a weed-infested cemetery.

She spotted Johnson County's version of the Marlboro Man propped against a pipe gate, a real Wyatt Earp with his arms slung out along the top rail and one knee bent to catch a boot heel against a lower rung. She pulled onto the paved drive and hit the electric window gizmo long enough to slide it down a crack. The cowboy tipped his hat, nice and respectful. Gave her a down-home grin.

With a tractor rumbling in the adjacent field, she shouted to be heard. "I'm lost." She held up the scrawl of right angles, squinted into the last of the sunset and shielded her eyes with a hand. "I'm supposed to meet a guy named Bobby Noah. Am I anywhere near?"

"Close enough to chunk rocks at."

"He said he lived on a farm."

The cowboy thumbed at the John Deere inching along the fence line. "That's a farm."

"Is that Bobby Noah on that tractor-thingy?"

"Yep. But 'round here, we call it a combine."

Cézanne let out a string of profanity. By now, she figured she owed the cuss-kitty a hundred dollars.

"That sorry sack of shit was supposed to meet me, take me into town. Which isn't your fault but dammit, you people should have road signs, not just go telling people they should turn left at the third spotted cow."

"They're Holsteins."

"You can call them Oreo cookies for all I care. I'm lost, and I'm late. And after a bad first impression, I wanted this Bobby Noah to respect me."

"That's Bobby Noah, Sr."

Heat started at the pulse in her throat and flamed past her cheeks with such ferocity she thought her hair would catch fire.

"You're him. You're the sheriff." She rubbed her eyes. Sneaked a peek. "I ought to strangle you, giving me such a bad time on the phone."

"I've been waiting ten years to pull that scam. You seemed like the type who could handle it."

"I was rude. I wouldn't blame you for calling it off, especially since I'm practically holding you at gunpoint. But you wouldn't believe the kind of pressure I'm under to solve this case."

"I never welsh on a deal. Don't expect you to, either."

He strolled around to the passenger side, opened the door, pitched his gray Stetson into the back and climbed into the seat.

"Mind if I push this back?" He didn't wait for an answer, just accommodated his long legs. "Watch out you don't hit the ditch. Pop doesn't like towing people out with the tractor-thingy."

He didn't have a problem poking fun.

"Which way?"

"You're headed right."

"But I turned left."

"Which is right."

"Don't start." She tightened her grip on the steering wheel.

"I don't always have to be right," he said without guile. "It's just, I usually am."

"Are you always this cocky, or do you stockpile for visitors?"

"I'm nice to voters. I imagine a classy lady like yourself would call them constituents. But to me, they're bread and butter on the table or more importantly, veterinary supplies."

"I'm a voter."

"Not in this county."

They rode the next few miles in silence. Which was just as well. Privately, she thanked her lucky stars she didn't live in a hick town where people voted for the likes of Bobby Noah. In the distance, the road forked.

"Where to?"

"Just drive. I'll say when to turn. Mind if I smoke?"

"Yes."

"Then I expect it's a good thing I don't."

"Why do you do that?" she asked. "Set me up that way? Like yesterday."

"Just havin' fun. Don'tcha know how to have fun?" His grin mocked her.

"Look, Sheriff—"

"Bobby."

"Sheriff. Truth of the matter is, I rather enjoy being miserable. It ensures people keep their distance."

"So what's a city slicker like you do for fun?"

"I don't advertise my personal life. There're already too many people interested as it is."

"I get it. You're CIA." He punctuated the statement with a nod of confidence. "No? Witness Protection Program? Mysterious past?"

She saw no reason to swap histories. After all, once she got what she wanted from this one-horse town they'd never again have to cross paths. Trouble was, he smelled good. Delicious, really. That perfect combination of leather, soap and woodsy aftershave. She could almost imagine a day's growth of whiskers grazing her jawline.

The thought brought a shiver.

"Cold?"

"I've been accused of that, too."

A few miles down the farm-to-market road, she found herself wanting to talk. After all, they didn't even know each other. Didn't travel in the same social circles. Hell, this yokel probably didn't even leave No-Culture, Texas more than once or twice a year. It wasn't as if they'd run into each other at the Jewel Charity Ball and she'd be embarrassed to have him approach her. She took a deep breath and relented.

"My partner's on the meathook for a murder he didn't

commit. I'm the only one in his camp. For God's sake, his own mother's an Alzheimer patient in an old folks home, and she thinks he's good for it. And yesterday I got some information, made me rethink his innocence. Then, this morning something happened, makes me ashamed I ever doubted it."

"Always go with your gut."

"My gut's flip-flopping."

"First impression, then."

"If I did that I wouldn't be here with you." She cut her eyes in his direction and saw she amused him. "I don't like what I've become since this whole mess started. All I ever wanted was to be a lawyer. Now I'm stuck at the PD because my partner's in a jam.

"My career's hanging by an eyelash, and I can't trust a soul. The Brass is trying to force this goldbricker on me and the creep's wife—who happens to hate my guts, by the way—is a magnet for sharp objects. Last time we crossed paths, she had a letter opener in one hand and my reflection in her eyes."

She powered the window down a crack, and the night air caressed her cheek.

"Have you ever known anybody with yellow eyes? Swear to God, half the time I feel like I'm being stalked by a tiger." She paused for a breath. "I think that about catches you up."

"You want friends, get a dog. Turn here. Dogs love you even when nobody else does."

The faint glow of a thumbnail moon cast enough light to silhouette his features. He fumbled along the door panel, and the electric window slid down several inches. Air rushed in, carrying with it the sweet fragrance of freshly plowed earth and country rain.

"You married?" he asked.

She answered with a snort.

"Ever try it?"

Stiffening against the seat, she defended her privacy.

"Roby Tyson, the guy who's in trouble? He's my best friend, and he doesn't even pry into my personal life."

"I always found if you talk about your troubles, you feel better." His voice emanated quiet strength.

She saw no point in spilling her guts about personal matters that didn't concern him, except that the sight of his profile, backlit by the moon, made her want to turn Catholic and click rosary beads together until they sounded like popcorn.

Forgive me Father, for I have sinned. It's been thirty-two years since my last confession.

Aw, what the hell?

"My first marriage lasted less than a year. The guy looked better in my clothes than I did. The second time made it three and a half days. We ran off to Cabo San Lucas while I was in the police academy." She anticipated his next question. "I don't even know if it was legal, not that it matters. He died in a scuba diving accident. I never told my classmates. Didn't want the pity."

She stared out the windshield. Try and get a body home from a foreign country, she wanted to say.

"You win the prize."

"It gets worse. A year later, I fell for one of my law professors. Keith. His father had pancreatic cancer, and Keith watched him suffer." Her gut knotted up the way it always did when she confronted her ghosts. "When the doctor diagnosed Keith with cancer, he took a fistful of Phenobarbital and checked out early. Did I mention I made a *C* in his class?

"But the real jewel in my crown is Detective Driskoll."

The sheriff stroked his chin. "Want to talk about it?"

"I think you have enough to work with."

"Kids?"

"I get along fine with kids. I don't like them, and they don't like me. That way, nobody pressures me to baby-sit."

Several moments passed before he sheared her concentration.

"You like horses?"

"One kicked me when I was seven. A year and a half later, I still had a hoofprint bruise on my hiney. How much farther?"

"Not too much. But you *do* like dogs."

"Long as they're attached to the arm of a burglar. Have you ever played *The Quiet Game*?"

His lips parted ever so slightly. "Cats?"

"If they're made out of chrome and leaping from the hood of an expensive car."

"Turn here."

They crested a hill and the lights of Cleburne twinkled in the distance. With the right person, the drive would've been romantic. She naturally gravitated to tall men, and this one smelled exceptionally yummy. And the voice she'd first pegged as a redneck's actually resonated with an unlikely combination of kindness and power.

She liked that he listened. And that he watched. Not that it mattered. After tonight, Sheriff Noah would be nothing but a memory until the next time she needed a police contact in Johnson County.

They drove through several small communities before he took another stab at conversation.

"A car like this wouldn't be much use on a farm."

"This one's not much good in the city, either. Anyway, I'm saving for a Mercedes."

His grin widened the crack in her resistance. "Money can't buy happiness."

"No, but it can buy a damned nice car to drive around while I look for it."

Her heart ached with an unexpected longing for Doug Driskoll. For the touch she never expected to feel again. She swallowed the lump forming in her throat and wished they were at the SO. Before she knew it, they were.

"Up yonder. Slow down, or you'll overshoot the parking lot. Pick your spot."

Inside the building, a sterile place put together with mud-colored bricks, he showed her back to his natural habitat. After offering her a chair, he disappeared through a side door. Except for an impressive wall display of police uniform patches representing different departments across the United States, the office pretty much resembled the inside of any other county building: dog-vomit-beige walls, gunmetal gray desk, swivel chairs on rollers, and a state-of-the-art computer.

A gold-framed sheepskin in veterinary medicine from Texas A&M University brought her close enough to fog the glass.

Bobby Noah wasn't a country bumpkin after all.

He returned with a stack of files and a friendly, "Be right back."

He showed up with two bottled Cokes and left one on the desk in front of her before settling in.

"You're a vet?"

He shook his head. "Nah, the gov'ment already started pulling troops out of Nam by the time my number came up."

"I meant, a doctor-vet."

"Occasionally. Let's see whatcha got that's important enough to bring you down to *Gnawbone* on a Sunday night."

She offered the *Glamour Shots*, and he studied each one with moderate interest. When he got to Carri Crane's academy photo, he said, "Don't recognize 'em," and handed them back. "These are all the unsolved homicides back to 1985," he said, tapping the stack, "but I've got an idea what you're wanting." He selected a thin file from the middle and held it out. "She lived just outside Burleson's city limit, but that's far enough out to make it an SO case," he said. "It's not a homicide, it's an accidental overdose. But I think you'll find it interesting, none the same."

"I'm looking for a gunshot wound, not an overdose."

"Just take a look."

Cézanne opened the file and the pictures spilled out. "Jesus." She devoured the contents like a smoked sirloin.

"The GSW to the head came from a twenty-two caliber," he said, moving around until he crouched over her shoulder.

"When the bullet entered her head—" He brushed aside a lock of her hair and touched the skin behind her ear to make his point. "—it was traveling at such a low velocity that when it struck bone, it zipped beneath the *sub-dura* like a thumbnail under an orange peel."

The way he drew his finger lightly through her hair left her skin dancing in chills.

The good kind.

"You think when the shot didn't kill her, she ingested something to speed up the process?"

"Oh she did dope, all right. Dropped a little acid, a rail of coke, popped a few pills. But what you really need to do is read the post mortem report," he said. "That's why, in this office, it's carried as unsolved."

The Tarrant County Medical Examiner's Office did the autopsy, and she flipped through the report until she reached *Cause of Death*. Bobby Noah was close enough for her to bury her nose in his neck and happily suffocate in his scent.

"The ME ruled it an accidental overdose?"

"That's what it says."

"What do you say?"

"I can tell you what it's not. It's not a jilted lover who got depressed and canceled her own ticket."

"What makes you so sure?"

"No weapon."

It was close to one in the morning before Cézanne left Cleburne, smitten. Bobby Noah made a charming host.

For one thing, he turned out to be more evolved on the Darwinian scale than she expected. For another, she warmed considerably to his rural humor. And when she dropped him off at the farm and he walked around to her side of the car and said, "Don't be a stranger," it was her mouth asking when it would be convenient to get together again, not his.

But the best thing of all was finding Glennis Pullin among Bobby Noah's dead files.

She left Cleburne dog-tired but with the knowledge it would take hours before the adrenaline rush subsided enough to put her mind to bed. By the time she reached Fort Worth, she talked herself into driving by Ali Baba's for a quick look.

Except for a few muscle cars, a couple of pickups and one old rattle trap parked next to a gold-toned Explorer at the rear of the club, the lot had pretty much emptied out. She parked in a grocery store parking lot across the street, beyond the peach glow of the sodium vapor street lamps, then reached under the seat for a pair of binoculars, cut the motor and waited. With Tiny standing guard, the dancers scampered to their vehicles and peeled off cleaner than a military aircraft formation.

Reno belonged to the clunker.

Cézanne shucked the field glasses, fired up the engine and left the lot churning up grit. At the first stop light, she pulled up even, tapped the horn and slid the window down halfway. Reno did the same.

"Hi," Cézanne shouted, brushing aside wind-ruffled bangs. "I'd like to talk to you. Can I buy you a cup of coffee?"

Reno laughed. "Lemme buy you one."

Cézanne followed the leader. The jaunt ended in a trailer park off the Jacksboro Highway not far from Downtown, where a dilapidated mobile home filled with low budget furnishings rested on cinderblocks.

Inside Reno's trailer, Cézanne initially refused an offer of food. But the stripper's hurt feelings and the aroma of fresh-baked cornbread sizzling in a cast-iron skillet made her reconsider. And when her hostess dished two bowls of homemade stew from a crock-pot and served it at a Formica and aluminum dinette straight from the fifties, she caved. Across the table, Reno sawed at a stick of cold butter until a chunk broke away and melted into the steaming cornbread wedge.

Hunkered over her plate with a knife in one hand and a soup spoon in the other, Reno ate as if someone was after her food. When she came up for air, she washed down her meal with a couple of swallows of slushy margarita she dipped out of a plastic tub in the freezer, and served in carnival ware. Beyond the flimsy curtains, a skyful of rhinestone stars flickered over Fort Worth. Nearby, Lake Worth glittered along its banks.

While Reno rummaged, half-buried, in the refrigerator searching for a lime, Cézanne's thoughts turned to Bobby Noah. The way he locked gazes and held her in an electric force field sent an unexpected current up the nape of her neck. The way his lips curled ever so slightly when she got carried away badmouthing The Brass stroked her ego. The way he said, "I'd rather listen to you," when she asked why he didn't have much to say, thawed the part of her heart that Doug Driskoll had iced over. Closing her eyes, she lifted the hand he squeezed good-bye to her nose and smelled the scent of aftershave.

"Wake up." Reno, back in her chair, licked her fingers. "So how long you been a cop?"

"Too long. How long've you been a dancer?"

"Since I was legal. Four—five years, maybe. How 'bout you? You ever think about it?" Reno gave her an appreciative look and stuck her tongue out to lick the salt from the rim of her glass. "You got the body."

"For dancing?" Cézanne snorted. "Line dancing, maybe."

"Line dancing's like masturbation. It may get the job done, but it's not the same as the real thing." Reno had a laugh like musical chimes.

"You like your job? All those pathetic old men ogling you?"

"I like the money."

"Wouldn't you rather do something else?"

"You mean with skills?" Reno tossed her head, and her waist-length red hair fell back over her shoulder. "I'm not talented, other than I can dance and men like me. Women, too."

Large, blue-gray eyes hinted of deep taboos.

"Sometimes people have to do things they don't want to, you know, so other people can have it easy. It's like . . . you'd probably rather be somewhere else right now if it wasn't for you want to help your partner, right?"

"I'm having a nice time," Cézanne fibbed. She drank from her glass thinking Reno went a little heavy on the tequila. "Tell me about Hollywood."

Reno scrunched her face as if she had just squirted lime juice in her eyes. "Hollywood's nuts."

"In what way?"

"I roomed with her a long time ago." She freshened her margarita at the sink, raised it with a flourish and lapped at the sweat building on the glass. "I worked out better than the others."

"How so?"

"For one thing, we weren't competing for the same lovers. For another, I'm still here." After a cheery, "Want seconds?", Reno cleared the table and stacked the dishes in the sink before ducking out on a crisp, " 'Scuse me."

When she didn't return after a few minutes, Cézanne called out.

"Everything all right?"

"C'mon back," came Reno's distant holler.

Intangible pressure ratcheted up.

Cézanne strolled past a bath, stopping halfway down the narrow hallway to breathe in the intertwining scents of violets and vanilla. What appeared to be the door to a bedroom stood ajar, with the unmistakable flicker of candlelight dancing in the shadows.

I'd do anything for Roby. But if I go through this door and she's in a silk kimono with 'I Touch Myself' by The Divinyls playing on the stereo, I'm outta here.

She rested her fingers against the knob and hesitated. Druidic music grew louder.

Relax. She probably has a couple of shot glasses, a bottle of tequila and her favorite TV show about to start.

Cézanne pushed the door enough to peek inside. She blinked her surroundings into focus. *The Divinyls* would've been beyond her wildest dreams compared to the visual assault rocking all five senses.

Black walls. A whip hanging by a nail. Bindings dangling from the bedposts. And except for a black lace merry-widow with the cups cut out to expose the tiny gold rings piercing her nipples, Reno lay naked on the bed. A studded collar glinted around her neck. Spiked leather bands encircled her slender wrists and a leather riding crop rested on a nearby night table. Reno wet a finger with her tongue. She slid her hand past her breasts, down to the gold loop piercing her

I'm outta here.

Cézanne's mouth went slack. That margarita she downed, coupled with the unexpected shot of adrenaline raging through her body, momentarily took the room out of focus.

Reno squirmed against the sheets, sultry and determined.

"C'mon in and close the door."

"You've got the wrong idea. I'm straight. I just came back to thank you for the chow and say g'bye."

In the time it took to blink, Reno produced a cat-o'-nine-tails. Dragging the leather strips against her thigh, she locked Cézanne in a lusty trance. In the creamy light of the flame, her glistening tongue slid across pontoon lips. She slapped the whip mightily against one bare buttock. Angry welts plumped up like slashes from a red ink pen.

Cézanne's feet turned to lead.

From behind, minty breath grazed the back of her neck. She jerked her head. Blocking the way out, was the club's wild-haired blonde. Alligator clips bit into her nipples and connected a triangle of silver chain from her breasts to her

Oh my God

and her mouth shimmered in an open pout. A bolt with a silver ball pierced her tongue.

"Let's get something straight, Sweet Pea," Reno said, her voice low and no-nonsense, her hand outstretched and holding a blindfold. "You want answers. I want somebody who's not afraid to discipline, or be disciplined. I think it's time we find out just how much you care about your old partner."

Chapter Twenty-Three

Monday morning, Darlene Driskoll was the talk of the PD. Unfortunately, in order to get that kind of attention she had to be officially classified as a missing person.

According to office scuttlebutt—and Three-fifty was humming like a tuning fork—Driskoll last saw his wife around nine o'clock the night before when she headed to HQ to pick up some credit card bills in her desk. The dual status of police employee and officer's wife meant Missing Persons stepped up to the plate a full twelve hours earlier than they would have for Joe Q. Citizen.

Carrying a styrofoam cupful of *menudo* to fend off a hangover, and trying to dismiss the psychic overload produced by Reno's lifestyle, Cézanne lacked the usual spring in her step. She bypassed taking the stairs in twos and headed for the elevator.

Up in Homicide, Greta pointed to Cézanne's haphazardly buttoned violet blouse and the silk rosette pinned, lopsided, at her collar and said, "What's with you?"

"I'm running on fumes." She set the container of soup on Greta's counter and re-fastened her shirt.

"Let me help you," Greta said when it came to securing the flower. "I thought maybe you had to wrestle your breakfast. And zip your skirt before I make a citizen's arrest. What'd you do, sleep in this stuff?"

"It's linen, okay? If it was good enough for Princess Diana, it's good enough for me. What the hell's going on around here?"

Beyond the earshot of nosey colleagues, she and Greta exchanged opinions.

"I think something bad's happened," Greta hissed, giving the heads-up warning with a cut of her eyes to indicate Driskoll sat nearby. "And if you haven't already noticed Doug trouncing around like it's business as usual, take a peek. He was on the cell phone when I got here—what's he, too good to use a land line like the rest of us *peons?* You ask me," she said knowingly, "he's got himself a sweet-patootie on the side."

"Maybe he figures his wife wanted to get away for awhile," Cézanne said, surprised charity came so easy.

But then she knew.

Thoughts of Bobby Noah put a smile on her face and cleared the muck from her head more than once since she returned home. She opened the lid to her voodoo potion, drank the Mexican hangover cure without chewing bits of flotsam she didn't care to have identified, and pronounced herself recovered.

"Darlene's not exactly what you'd call a free spirit, Shug." Greta fluttered her lashes. "You've seen the way she is. You practically have to sandblast her off him."

"She could be trying to make him jealous. If he can stay out all night, so can she. Equal rights."

Her eyes flickered to Detective Driskoll grinning into the cellular.

Schmuck.

"You ask me," Greta whispered conspiratorially, "it's mighty convenient for him she met with foul play."

Cézanne lifted a skeptical brow as Greta typed U-P-Y-O-U-R-S into the password block on the computer.

"Come off it, Shug, you know as well as I do he'd like

nothing better than to be rid of her. I hear she can't swim. Can you imagine a forty-seven-year old woman who can't swim? If you get a floater call today, I'm going with you."

Greta attached the earpieces of her rhinestone glasses to the loops of a thin, silk braid and wore them as a necklace while she banged out a series of keystrokes. Then she positioned the frames halfway down the bridge of her nose and glanced up, certain.

"It wouldn't surprise me, he killed her," she said, jutting her chin at Darlene's husband.

"This is a guy who runs eight miles an hour and gets eight miles to the gallon. He's no killer. Anyway, we're not even sure she's dead."

"Shug, you've worked here long enough to know: under the right circumstances, push the right buttons, anybody's capable of anything."

Cézanne glanced into the cubicle. Detective Driskoll still spoke in hushed tones. "You're right. He killed her."

Greta nodded, triumphant. "A couple of weeks ago, around three in the morning, he caught her standing at the foot of the bed, watching him. He said she told him she heard a noise, but it creeped me out just the same. You ask me, Mister Driskoll ought to sleep with one eye open."

Cézanne conjured up a visual of Darlene in the shadows hovering over her husband with a meat cleaver behind her back. She shuddered.

"Did you know Doug's missing a couple of grand?"

Cézanne frowned. "How do you find this stuff out?"

With a flip of the wrist, Greta sing-songed, "He told me some, she told me some. He'd been saving six months so he could take those bratty twins of his to Disney World. All of a sudden—" she snapped her fingers, "—gone. She said it was a break-in. But you want to know what's really weird?

A few days later he intercepted the mailman and found out the mortgage was behind. They've been at each other's jugulars ever since," she said, virtually hemorrhaging with ideas. "At first I thought he was pissed because they pulled him out of Narcotics and stuck him here." She shook her head. Leaned across her desk as if to pinpoint Doug's exact whereabouts. "When I point blank asked him, he admitted he twisted their arms to get this assignment."

The high voltage news gave Cézanne a jolt. Over the tightening of face muscles, she fought to keep her reaction flat. It took several swallows to wash down the lump in her throat.

"Coming to Homicide was Doug's idea?"

"According to him. He said he told the Chief how he and Carri were pals, and if the administration wanted to get to the bottom of this, he could help."

Only way you can help is if you knew her.

No mor'n anybody else.

Cézanne gritted her teeth hard enough to crack a filling.

The man had a picture of Hollywood.

And a dead girl named Beth.

Make that two dead girls, counting Carri Crane.

For somebody chomping at the bit to help, the lying bastard hadn't peed a drop.

Suddenly, Roby plummeted to distant second while Doug Driskoll—a virtual unknown in the Carri Crane murder investigation—rocketed to number one on her hit parade.

Undetermined.

That's how Carri's death certificate read.

"You can look at it, you can even take notes, but I can't

let you have a copy," said Marvin Krivnek, assistant to the Medical Examiner, about the autopsy report.

The fussy, hunchbacked little man who wore his lab coat as proudly as any coat of arms walked over to Cézanne with a jar of *Vick's Vap-O-Rub* and offered it up.

Pointing toward the back room, he said, "They're fixing to carve the turkey."

She gladly dipped her finger in and swabbed gel beneath her nostrils. Camphor fumes stung her eyes. She planted herself on a stainless steel stool with rollers on the feet, near Krivnek's desk.

"Why can't I have a copy? I'm working the case."

"They're not my rules, Detective. The edict came from your own department."

Crane.

"What? The victim's father calls, thinking he can put his thumb on this investigation?" The very idea made her want to ring up Channel Eighteen for an interview. "We'll see about that."

She headed for the nearest phone with Krivnek in tow, snatched up the receiver and stabbed at the number pad.

"What do you think you're doing, Detective?"

She covered the mouthpiece with her hand. "Calling Deputy Chief Rosen. I'll get it okayed through him."

Krivnek depressed the switch. "The decision came from Rosen."

Her lungs deflated.

"Just be grateful he only said not to release it." Krivnek grinned. "I don't think he wanted you reading it either, but he never specifically said, 'Don't let her read it, Marve.' What he said was, 'Release it to her, and I'll see to it your boss turns your balls into calf fries.' "

It was a man-thing, Cézanne thought, that Krivnek automatically grazed a hand against his crotch to make sure the family gemstones were still in the jewelry box.

It took almost an hour to make copious notes on a legal pad, but she recorded what she needed. And the more she read, the more nefarious the circumstances appeared to be.

First, the suspected weapon of choice was a long-barrel twenty-two caliber. Six inches, to be exact. Add another couple for the cylinder and frame—well, she couldn't be sure, but. . . .

She spun the stool around and faced Krivnek.

"The paraffin test on Carri Crane's hand didn't show any gunpowder," she said, "so why didn't you just rule it a homicide and be done with it?"

He lowered his rimless bifocals enough to peer over the top.

"Means nothing. A person can still kill themselves and not have a trace of gunpowder on their hands."

When she frowned, he launched into a scientific diatribe.

"Let me ask you this," she said. "Let's say there's no gunshot residue on her, but somebody else in the house has some on them. What would that tell you?"

"Nobody else did."

"What about her roommate's test?"

"What roommate?"

"That's exactly my point. Hypothetically speaking, wouldn't that alter your opinion?" she said, wincing at a row of organ-filled jars lined up on a bookshelf in a macabre display.

"Not necessarily." He must have found the long, dumb stare she gave him irritating. "You've got a theory, Detective. Why don't you just spit it out?"

Her breath went shallow. The noxious odor of chemicals, gases and God-knew-what coming from the next room

216

made her stomach backflip.

"Do you have any idea how hard it is to stick a six-inch gun barrel behind your ear and pull the trigger?"

"Something tells me *you* do." He narrowed his eyes and appraised her evenly.

She wanted to tell him it was inconvenient as hell using a two-inch barrel much less a six-inch, execution style. A person would need orangutan arms.

Instead, she said, "Carri Crane was petite with small hands. According to the firearms logs the PD keeps for qualifications, her off-duty weapon was a Lady Smith with modified grips. There's no evidence she ever owned a twenty-two caliber in her life. Why would she dust herself with some cheap, low grade weapon—we don't even know where it came from—that might turn her into a carrot instead of doing the job?"

"People do all sorts of foolish things. But, hey—what do I know? I'm just the Medical Examiner."

Krivnek got up from his microscope and charged across the room to the bookshelf. He reached for a black binder and flipped through it. Still reading, he meandered over to the copier, burned off a couple of pages, returned the binder to its proper place and sashayed over.

"Here." He shoved a handful of articles under her nose. "Read up on it in your spare time."

She rolled the papers into a cylinder and pushed them into her coat pocket. Krivnek slid onto his stool and went back to comparing slides.

She returned her attention to the autopsy report and allowed her eyes to soar over it. Unexpectedly, her hawk eyes scouted out the insignificant field mouse in the food chain. It was only one word, but it jumped off page four of the document. Such a tiny morsel waiting to be devoured. She swooped down and hooked it with a mental talon.

Fetus.

Carri Crane got knocked up.

Chapter Twenty-Four

By nine o'clock Tuesday morning, Cézanne had a *subpoena duces tecum* in her hand.

Instanter.

Meaning, if that lowlife, Tiny, from Ali Baba's didn't fork over a copy of Michelle Parker's work application, he'd be cooling his hocks in front of the Grand Jury by ten. What was the phrase? *The angel sits on the head of a pen?* Well the angel sitting on the head of the pen that signed the bad news was Old Judge Pittman.

She stepped inside an empty club. No wonder they kept the lights low. Beneath the fluorescents, the place had the dingy quality of an opium den. An Asian janitor pushing a broom in a far corner opened an exit long enough to let in a slice of daylight.

Cézanne smelled the bouncer before she saw him. She whipped around and came eye level to a pair of breasts straining the fabric of the Aloha shirt preventing their escape. Worse, the bouncer's were bigger than hers. He needed something in a fifty-two-long, bless his heart. Tattoos snaked down both forearms.

"We ain't open."

"You are now."

"You're trespassing." He reached out to take her elbow.

"And you're about to be sitting in the cage of a squad car, you don't produce the goods." She whipped out the subpoena and slapped it into his hand.

His eyes wandered over the page, settling on nothing. A dead giveaway. Her tension evaporated.

Knucklehead couldn't read.

"The owner ain't here."

"Who's in charge?"

The scofflaw braced his arms across his chest. "I am."

"Big dude like you runs the place when the boss's out? So we go to the office, you burn off a copy of Michelle Parker's application and I go away happy."

He let out a hearty laugh, exposing a mouthful of neglected teeth. Rancid breath, bad enough to choke a goat, surrounded her. Cézanne felt her gorge rise. She keyed the hand-held radio and gave her call sign over the air.

"Send a couple of units over to Ali Baba's. And a supervisor."

The dispatcher responded. "Whatcha got?"

"Stand by." She looked at the goon. "You gonna give me that app or do we do it the hard way?"

Carefully, she eased her thumb across the handy-talkie and hit the off switch. Holding his gaze, she raised the radio to her lips and keyed the dead mic.

"Send an ambulance. I've got a man down."

He said, "Whatcha gonna do? Take me on?"

"No, A-wipe, you're gonna take me on. Big difference."

"Eat shit."

He lumbered off with Cézanne hot on his heels. She switched on the radio and volumed it low. Kept her hand inside her purse, squeezed the Pachmeyer grips on the Smith, finger on the trigger.

Inside the boss's office, her adversary produced a stack of papers, complete with snapshots. He tossed them onto a desk already full of trash, half-eaten fast food and an ashtray that hadn't been emptied since the forties, and snarled,

"You find it. I got better things to do."

With Tiny out of earshot, she keyed the mic. "Disregard, it's Code Four out here," she said in a husky whisper, then turned her attention to the applications once the dispatcher acknowledged her transmission.

Lucky for her the bouncer couldn't read.

She leafed through each one quickly. But not so fast she'd miss names like Glennis or Bethany. Three-quarters through the stack, she spotted a résumé for Michelle Parker and deliberately passed it by. She'd pull it out, get him to copy it after she checked them all.

The shocking sight of the next to last application was enough to curl her lace-top thigh highs down around her ankles.

Sugar Cane.

With a snapshot of Carri Crane stapled to the top.

Back at Three-fifty, it took a little hip-shot chutzpah to try to ferret out the truth.

Rosen's secretary came up out of her chair like a pop-up target, but she wasn't fast enough to beat Cézanne to Rosen's door. Cézanne let herself in, forcing him to abort his telephone call and wipe the smile off his face.

"Detective, you can't—Chief, she can't just storm in—"

"It's okay, Ellen. Close the door behind you."

When the lock snapped, he said, "Next time you barge in here unannounced you're going to find yourself pounding a beat in Poly."

Cézanne ignored the threat and zeroed in. "What was her assignment?"

"Whose assignment?"

"You know whose assignment. Carri Crane's."

"You think I can tell you the beat of every commissioned

officer on this department? We don't pay much attention to rookies up here."

"She was in Vice, wasn't she? You *have* to know because only you or the Chief could approve an assignment like that. You took a rookie fresh out of the academy and stuck her undercover, didn't you?" She heard what she was saying and thought for a second her brain misfired. It didn't. A dangerous idea popped into her head. She clapped a hand to her mouth. "Ohmygod. You put her in Narcotics."

It started to make sense, the unlikely acquaintance of Carri Crane and Doug Driskoll. Rosen's eyelids fell to half-mast. She knew the look. She'd witnessed it on a lot of men. He was about to lie.

Her eyes burned, and she wanted to rage loud enough to raise the dead rookie and warn her about men like Driskoll. Instead, Rosen reduced her to hammering one of the wingbacks with her fist.

"Her own father didn't even know, did he? You demanded strict confidentiality. I bet you even made her swear secrecy and sign a release, didn't you?"

"Lower your voice."

"I want to see her file."

"Don't you have it?"

"Not my file, *your* file."

Rosen came around the desk and propped his well toned frame against the edge. With arms folding across his chest, he asked the inevitable. "Where are you going with this information?"

She thought hard and fast. She didn't want to end up like Carri Crane. "I made tapes. Anything happens to me, there's this Texas Ranger I know—"

Rosen's tan faded to gray. His shoulders slumped, making them the same height. "Zannie, you didn't. Good

God, say you didn't."

"Here," she snapped. She tossed a photocopy of the snapshots from Ali Baba's onto his blotter. "For your scrapbook. And don't worry about it being the only one. If you people give me any more shit, I'll rent a Cessna and have fifty-thousand copies snowing over Downtown before Three-to-Eleven shift conducts show-up."

Instead of taking the elevator from The Penthouse, Cézanne ducked down the stairwell to Homicide. With the echo of steps still resounding in her head, she entered the cubicle to find Detective Driskoll lounging in his chair with the phone growing out of his ear, massaging the cellophane wrapper containing a fortune cookie. He tore it open, snapped the cookie in half and pulled out the paper strip. It took all the willpower Cézanne could muster to keep from depressing the switch and bottle-rocketing into an interrogation.

"Whoever that is can wait."

He looked up, startled.

"Gotta go," he muttered, replacing the receiver in its cradle. With the force of a pilot pulling two Gs, he reclined against the seat back.

"Hey, Babe, you look like you just got laid. Want me to play connect-a-dot with my tongue?"

He licked his lips, but instead of the waistband of her pantyhose unraveling, she actually felt it tighten.

"You have some explaining to do," she said.

" 'You will always be on top'," he read from the cookie strip. "Gee, that's too bad. When it comes to sex I hate doing all the work."

Her jaw tightened just short of cracking tooth enamel. Driskoll could bring out the heretic in a nun.

"What's the news on your wife?"

"While I was home watching football, she drove down here to get the bills and didn't come back."

"Doesn't that strike you a bit unusual?"

He shrugged off the question. "Like a bad penny, I have every reason to believe the old ball and chain'll turn up. Darlene can't do *jack* without me."

She fought the urge to smack him, but a panicky yell from Greta stung in her ear.

"Doug, Sarge's on Northside." With her hand covering the mouthpiece, Greta stretched the telephone cord to peer over a waist-high wall divider. "Says to get out there right away. Your wife's been found."

Driskoll's arrogance evaporated. For a man who should've reacted with relief that his wife had been found, he wore the expression of a man who wished the old ball and chain hadn't.

During the drive out North Main, Detective Driskoll—Cézanne insisted on formalities—fixated on her refusal to part with the car keys.

"I'm *not* selfish," she said, checking the rearview mirror before switching lanes. "This unit belonged to Roby, first. Now it's mine. Besides, you're too upset to drive."

"No, I'm not. You've always got to be on top. That's your problem."

"On top? Me, on top?" She slapped the steering wheel to register her disgust. "That's so like you to make something up so you can shift the blame, make yourself feel better."

"That's right. That's your flaw. You always have to be on top whether it's work, personal or whatever."

"Frankly, I've pretty much tried to forget. But I'll say this much—and this goes double for that unfortunate weekend I must have been brain-damaged, traipsing off to Cancún with you—if I have to be on top, I feel quite sure it's because I don't like the way I'm getting screwed."

"I never heard any complaints."

"You were too damned busy worrying about your own self to hear much of anything."

"That's a crock, and you know it." His face flushed beet red. "I spent plenty of time on you. Didn't I always wait until you finished?"

"If you were half as good as you think you are, the women of this department would erect a life-size bronze in your honor."

"That's so typical, you bitching about stuff."

"Of course if I were you I certainly wouldn't want every damned thing done to scale."

"Let's hope nobody ever does a bust of you."

She didn't appreciate the way he ogled the curve of her breasts like he thought maybe there wouldn't be enough there to keep the sculpture from toppling over.

In unison, they pronounced each other's fate. "You'll never be happy."

Cézanne broke the frosty silence. "I want to know what you know about Carri Crane."

"There. Up ahead," he said, ignoring her. "Pull in."

At a corner convenience store, uniforms swarmed around an ambulance like somebody peed on an antbed. Cézanne bounced up the incline and braked hard, scattershooting pea gravel into the side of the sergeant's patrol car. Detective Driskoll unlatched the seatbelt. He bailed out of the car with her hot on his trail.

Cézanne filled her lungs with a deep breath. Someone in the 'hood had fajitas sizzling on a charcoal grill.

The sergeant's eyes grew wide. "Hey, aren't you two—"

225

He ground to a halt. "This is pretty brazen, you being seen together."

Driskoll sneered, "Such as it is, she's my partner."

The sergeant cocked his head, then slapped a good-ol'-boy arm around Driskoll's shoulder and steered him toward the ambulance.

"Your old lady's got a knot on her head the size of a grapefruit, and she's had a real bad night," he said with just the right touch of gloom, "but she's alive."

Detective Driskoll wore the expression of someone who had prepared himself for the worst, and then heard it. When he didn't bother to probe for details, Cézanne, following in their wake, did.

"She said she was leaving the station about midnight," the sergeant recounted, "and a Mexican bushwacked her. He forced her into her car and made her drive around 'til she finally escaped."

"How'd she manage that?" Cézanne's mind flashed on an array of sharp objects, and she felt a faint quiver of excitement that Darlene found someone else to target.

"She said he took her to a field to rape her, and she fought him for the gun."

Cézanne's shoulders tensed. "What gun?"

"The gun he used to rob her with."

"She wrestled his gun away?" Driskoll lingered somewhere between halfway impressed and completely disappointed no one got capped.

"That's the story."

The sergeant reached into his shirt pocket and tapped out a Camel. The wind blew out the first match, and he cupped his hand over the second as it hissed across the matchbook cover.

He took a couple of drags, blew smoke at them and said,

"She told us she fired two shots, and he took off across the field."

That Darlene couldn't shoot straight brought Cézanne a certain degree of comfort. She said, "Ask her the make and model."

Driskoll seemed baffled by the suggestion. "Darlene doesn't know diddly about firearms. She's petrified of them."

"I'll bet," Cézanne began, but Driskoll had started to speak so she kept quiet.

"The woman couldn't hit the side of a barn. Once, I offered to teach her to shoot and she started bawling. Said one gunslinger in the family was enough."

Marking time, listening to each other's food digest, wasn't doing anything to further the investigation and Cézanne didn't feel inclined to cut Driskoll's wife any slack.

She looked over at the sergeant. "When did she escape?"

"According to her, a few hours ago."

"Let me see if I get this straight," she said facetiously. "Our victim drove around until she found sanctuary in this God-forsaken place."

The sergeant flexed his jaw. "That strikes you odd?"

"Not at all." For effect, she let her gaze roam the graffiti-tagged building. "A Pakistani-owned convenience store would certainly be my refuge of choice."

Driskoll chimed in with a question of his own. "What'd the guy take?"

"Just her purse, I reckon."

"Any money?" Cézanne pressed. At the shake of the sergeant's head, she deadpanned, "Let me guess . . . *the only thing missing was the bills*."

This time it was Driskoll who tightened his jaw. He shot her a scalding look before angling over to the ambulance.

227

She took a deep breath and made a serious observation. "I imagine she had to gas up sometime during this ordeal, Sarge. Did she say how she paid for fuel?"

When half of the sergeant's face corkscrewed in confusion, she laid it out in simple terms.

"I'm willing to accept the possibility that there's a black market for unpaid bills. All I'm saying is, the guy took her purse so how'd she pay?"

Annoyance moved across the sergeant's face in squinty creases and plumped cheeks. Clearly, the question stumped him. While she waited for input, she dug for her field notebook. She clicked her pen and poised to write.

"Mexican National, or a Hispanic?" she asked.

"What's the difference?"

"If it's an alien abduction, I'm calling the tabloids."

A murderous scream pierced the calm.

"Holy shit." The sergeant gripped his baton and took off in the direction of the ambulance.

Cézanne sprinted in his tracks. They arrived to the sight of Darlene Driskoll with her hands raised, defensively shielding her face.

"Don't hurt me," she shrieked in bloody-murder, Jack-Nicholson-wielding-a-hatchet theatrics. "I'll do anything you say, just don't hurt me again."

Bug-eyed and cringing, her beloved recoiled.

A paramedic thumbed at Driskoll and shouted to no one in particular, "Get him out of here."

Cézanne backed away, too, but not before Darlene sneaked a peek through her well-manicured fingers.

In a dull tone, Driskoll's wife said, "She can stay."

For an instant, Cézanne thought she had an earwax problem.

"Who, me?"

"Stay here with me." Darlene squared the bizarre request with the paramedics. "I don't want to go to the hospital. She can take me home."

All eyes moved in a collective shift. People who had once treated her with disdain, now afforded her the kind of respect normally reserved for a potentate.

Cézanne balked. "Maybe you ought to let your husband—"

"No." Darlene gave a vehement shake of the head. "I feel safer with you."

With the snout of the police car pointed toward the freeway and the tail of the ambulance receding in Cézanne's side mirror, Darlene did some feverish clawing at her leg.

"What's wrong?"

"He must've stole my anklet. I had on the birthday anklet my Dougie gave me, with charms and birthstones for each of my kids." Her voice trailed off in a whimper.

"He'll buy you another one."

"You really think so?" Perking up.

"Sure, why not?"

"You think if I filed a claim with the insurance, they'd pay up?"

"It's worth a try."

Cézanne didn't say what she wanted to say. That a glass-eyed ape could see through the cheap ploy for attention. That nobody in their right mind would fall for such a yarn. She hit the electric window buttons and slid them down a crack for better ventilation. The car reeked of an unseemly combination of sweat and manure. She glanced over at her passenger and noted several curiosities.

For one thing, the left side of Darlene's head did seem seriously out of whack, owing in part to matted hair, caked with blood and stuck to a goose egg. But even more surprising was her clothing. The emerald green blouse showed grime and grass stains. Her tan leggings were snagged, and behind the vicious rip in one knee, her skin showed signs of road rash.

Never had she seen Darlene in a more conservative mode of dress.

"You look like a train wreck," Darlene said. She eyed Cézanne's Austrian shirt. "Is it high fashion to wear clothes that look slept in?"

"It's linen. It's supposed to be wrinkled."

"Didn't you ever hear of polyester?"

How Bohemian.

"Whatever was I thinking?" Cézanne mumbled.

"Where'd you buy it?"

"There's a drive-through up ahead. You thirsty? If you like, we can whip in and I'll buy you a soda."

Darlene declined with a shake of her head.

"You want to talk about it?"

Another headshake, bigger and slower.

For several miles, they rode in silence. Trying out bizarre scenarios in the privacy of her own skull, Cézanne settled on one she liked: the woman riding beside her gave devotion a bad name.

"Sarge said the kidnapper pulled a gun. What kind?"

"A cannon."

"No, really. What caliber?"

"Big enough to make this." Darlene reached up and gently grazed the goose egg beneath her hairline.

"Revolver or automatic?"

"When you're staring into a gun barrel, all you see is a great big tunnel to the end of the line."

"What happened to the weapon?"

Darlene rubbed her fingertips together until the blood

disappeared. "After he ran off, I flung it in the dirt."

She muttered something else, but the rest of her sentence drowned in the laughter inside Cézanne's head.

"I don't remember where you live, Darlene."

"You've been to my house."

"Only that once."

"You never came to my house besides that time I walked in and saw—?"

"Stop." Her molars scraped out a tiny squeak. "I'd tell you if I had."

"You don't respect me, do you?"

She didn't figure on disabusing Driskoll's wife of the notion. "Look, I realize it's unnatural as hell, Darlene, but I'd like us to get along."

"Really? You're not just making that up?"

"I'd never patronize you," she said, letting the whopper linger on her tongue. She conjured up what felt like an expression of innocence, then sweetened it with sincerity. "I never set out to hurt you. I'm sorry for the pain I caused. And I know it's silly, but I even feel guilty about this."

Darlene braced her feet against the floorboard, jammed a hand into her pocket and fished out a

hypodermic needle.

In terror, Cézanne stomped the brake. Tires screamed against the asphalt. The rear end of the cruiser slid into the curb. Cars with horns blaring swerved close enough to swap paint.

Darlene let out a shriek. "What's happening?"

With her eyes fixed on her passenger and her heart in her throat, Cézanne grappled for the door handle. When it didn't open, she fumbled for the electric lock button and kept focus on Darlene.

Darlene glanced at the syringe. Then back at Cézanne,

panting in her scramble to bail out.

"What? This? I'm diabetic."

Cézanne went limp. The adrenaline dump left her light-headed and drained. She watched, dumbfounded, as Darlene lifted her blouse and jabbed the needle into her stomach. In the time it took to blink, the injection was complete.

"Don't ever do that again," Darlene said, capping the needle, returning trappings of insulin to her pocket.

"Do what?"

"Scare me like that."

Chapter Twenty-Five

By late afternoon, Old Judge Pittman signed the evidentiary search warrant for the former residence Michelle Parker shared with Carri Crane, and Cézanne delivered it to Crime Scene. She left it with the bloodhound everybody called Slash, but the Grand Jury subpoena she procured for Reno, she kept for herself.

At sundown, an eerie tangerine glow pulsed above the horizon and the amber swatch of sky directly overhead fueled Cézanne's already foul mood.

With her luck, she'd tune into the six o'clock news to find Fort Worth under a tornado warning. When she saw what Devilrow did to her roof, she prayed for one.

She rolled into her driveway to the sight of a shirtless Leviticus Devilrow and another con-wise reprobate outfitted in overalls straddling the peak. On the porch, Levi lay propped up on his elbows, uncharacteristically decked out in starched denims and a cowboy shirt, studying a picture book.

Devilrow's new sidekick lurched down the ladder. He tossed the hammer onto the porch and turned around.

Roby.

"Ohmygod," she said, dropping her voice low enough for lip-reading. "Are you crazy? Get inside before you end up strapped to a gurney with a needle sticking out of your carotid."

She handed over the house key, stepped back out into

the yard and cupped her hands to her mouth.

"If you think I'm paying for this shit you've got another think coming," she shouted. "Don't think I don't know shoddy workmanship when I see it, Devilrow. I'm no roofer, but even I know not to start shingling at opposite ends of the house and meet in the middle."

"Yo' roof's near finished."

"So are you."

"It looks nize."

"It looks like a friggin' zipper. I want this screw-up fixed, but right now I want you gone."

She stormed inside the house, toggling the deadbolt behind her. In the kitchen, she found Roby's big denimed rump backing out of the refrigerator. He held up a couple of sodas, seated himself at the breakfast table and popped the tabs.

"You growin' penicillin?"

"It's roast beef. Where in the hell have you been? I've left messages. I've driven by your house."

"Been fishin'. Went to a little no-nothin' town on the Gulf a few days. And if I can sneak past those two dickweeds eyeballing my house, I'm headed up to Colorado to moose hunt a spell."

"Since when do they have moose in Colorado?"

"Shows how much you know." He slammed down his drink while she studied him in awe.

"Aren't you acting a bit cavalier, traipsing off on vacation? And how much did you tell Devilrow?"

"Devilrow's all right. For an ex-con. Forget what I said about firing him."

"You used to say there's no such thing as an ex-con. You said they're always convicts once they're convicted."

"He'll keep his yap zipped."

"I've never seen such a gross lack of concern, especially when the DA bumped up the charge to a capital offense."

Roby shrugged off the news, making her want to slap him to his senses.

"You're the most frustrating man I know." She sipped from her drink, pushed it aside and rested her hands on the table.

"I've been thinking about what you said the other night," she began, humble this time. "I'm willing to give you the benefit of the doubt."

"Mighty big of you. I'm not concerned whether you think I'm guilty or not. I just want you to find my girl's killer." He reached into his bib pocket and pulled out his smokes.

"I thought you quit. You'll ruin your health."

"Did you quit cussin'? You ought to have enough money socked away by now to pay cash for a limo."

"I'll get an ashtray."

She returned to the table with a saucer. Roby already lit up and blew a cloud of smoke in the direction of the light fixture. He reached across to fan the blue film away from her face, and the short-sleeved shirt rode up his elbow.

"What happened to your arm?" She squinted at the bruise in the crook.

"My doctor has a vampire masquerading as a nurse. I thought she was on an archaeological dig for a vein. Ain't nothin' to worry about. Happens every time I go for my annual."

Thoughts of Darlene Driskoll popped into mind and she shuddered.

"We don't have much time, Roby. And I'm never sure when I'll hear from you again, so I've got to ask questions. Some of them you won't like."

His eyes narrowed. "You asking as a cop or as my lawyer?"

"As your friend. I want to know why you weren't up front with me. Why you didn't tell me Carri was undercover."

"Undercover?" Roby's face grayed. "She wasn't undercover. She worked day shift."

"Did you ever see her working day shift?"

"She told me not to bother her at work."

"You didn't think that was strange?"

"She was eat up with her job."

"You called her *Sugar,* the morning we found her. I heard you."

"She made me call her that ever since she first hit the streets. Said she preferred it. She said, 'Don't ever call me Carri. To you, I'm Sugar. I'll always be your Sugar.' "

His eyes instantly rimmed red and she knew by his expression they were feeling the same thing. Remembering that awful Friday left her tasting bad Greek food from lunch, and he wasn't feeling so hot himself.

"Undercover," he whispered. Then the real heartbreak dawned on him. "She didn't trust me."

"I want you to tell me about your relationship with Carri."

He cocked his head. "What's to tell? We met when I taught Search-and-Seizure at the police academy. We hit it off, Capt'n pitched a walleyed fit, we kept our distance awhile and got going again once the commotion died down and the gossips lost interest."

She didn't want to tip her hand with details of the autopsy.

"When did Carri dump the firefighter?"

Roby scrunched his lip. "I've got no idea. Far as I'm

concerned, he was just a cover story to throw off her old man."

"How long had you been intimate this last time?"

"You sure do pry." He polished off the last of his cola, crushing the can in his fist. "I'd been back in her good graces, oh, say, two-three weeks."

"Contraceptives?"

"I assume you have a damned good reason for asking."

"Humor me."

"I shoot blanks."

She found the disclosure chilling. If Roby was telling the truth, he couldn't have fathered Carri's baby.

But she had an idea who could.

Around ten o'clock that night, long after Roby tucked the cashier's check under the crumpled soda can and sneaked out the back door and into the bed of Devilrow's rattle-trap, Cézanne slipped into a black silk teddy, *sans brassier,* her shortest suede skirt and sheer black pantyhose. With the bathroom illuminated in a blitzkrieg of lights, she slathered on makeup and shadowed her eyes as if auditioning for "Cats".

This time, she strutted into Ali Baba's with the command of a fifty-one percent shareholder. She glimpsed Tiny having it out with a drunk trying to climb up onstage, where the frizzy-headed blonde seemed to be trying out for the part of "Rubber-Woman" by contorting hairpin curves into unnatural positions that looked more grotesque than arousing. At a cocktail table surrounded by blue-collar workers, Reno glanced over, moistened her lips and winked.

Cézanne sidled up next to her.

"What's up, Sweet Pea? Change your mind?" Reno asked, undeniably interested.

"I've put a lot of thought into what you said the other night," Cézanne gushed as erotically as she could in a dive where customers' shoe soles stuck to the floor, "and you're right. There's nothing I wouldn't do for Roby."

"Really?" The dancer's voice came alive with excitement. With her eyes electrically charged, she touched her fingertips to the back of Cézanne's knee, sliding them halfway up her skirt. "What'd you have in mind?"

"A cozy get together, where you're the guest of honor."

"I knew it." Breasts heaving. Nipples, rock-hard. "Just the two of us?"

"I hope you don't mind. I'm really no good by myself, and the group thing rather intrigues me."

"Kinky." Obviously pleased. "So, are we partying at your place or mine?"

"Definitely mine."

Cézanne removed Reno's hand before she could spelunker through the pantyhose, lifting it waist high in her own. Her free hand snaked around to the small of her back for the Grand Jury subpoena riding in her waistband.

"Here's your invitation. Be there at nine in the morning or plan on eating warm baloney and green bread for the next few weeks. *Ciao*."

She left Reno quaking in her skin.

Cézanne scanned the place for Hollywood before heading for the dressing room.

Backstage, a naked Hollywood jammed her little finger up one nostril and vacuumed in a deep breath. Flecks of white dotted her upper lip. Someone had done an admirable job using colored eye pencils to turn a large bruise on her left breast into a tarantula. Cézanne slid onto the vanity stool, glanced at the rail of snowflakes still left on the hand mirror and waited for Hollywood's glazed eyes to focus.

"It's you," said the dancer, swiping the underside of her nose with the back of her hand. Her tongue darted out. Traces of powder disappeared. She blinked and her eyelids drooped like shimmery painted curtains. "You gonna 'rest me?"

"Maybe. Maybe not." Cézanne fixed her with a hard stare.

The woman had misted her entire body with glitter.

"Want I should put on clothes?"

"I don't give a flip one way or the other."

"Then I pass," Hollywood said, rubbing sparkles from the bend in one arm. "This shit itches bad enough as it is."

Cézanne fished in her purse for a stack of photos. Some Hollywood should know. Others she wouldn't.

"Tell me whether you recognize any of these people."

Instead of checking out the pictures, a devious smile angled up one side of the dancer's face. "Reno said she had you for dinner."

"What the hell's that supposed to mean?"

"Reno's a pip. I think she's got the hots for you. What did you think of The Scene?"

"The what?"

"Reno's into BDSM."

"I don't know what you're talking about." Indignant.

"Bondage. Dominance. Sado-masochism. Reno said—"

"Reno's mistaken. Focus your attention." Flipping a picture over with the grace of a Vegas cardsharp, Cézanne presented the first of ten.

"You know this guy?"

Hollywood blinked, then shook her head.

Not that Cézanne expected her to recognize Captain Crane. It wouldn't surprise her to learn Crane had never been inside a strip joint. He was more the type to loathe

Hollywood and her ilk from afar. And when the time came, Hollywood shouldn't recognize Lieutenant Binswanger and the sergeant, either. Nor Rosen. Nor Greta. The rest, Cézanne wasn't so certain.

"Take a look at this one."

Another headshake. "I don' think so."

Cézanne held up a recent photo of Roby. Hollywood blinked, then leaned in for a closer look.

"That's Needle-Dick." She settled back with a look of great accomplishment riding on her face. "Now there's an ugly futher-mucker."

"You said he and Carri got into a fight at the apartment the night she died."

"No, I didn't."

"Yes, you did."

Hollywood's jaw went slack. Her eyes swirled in her head like unweighted floats.

"Not Needle-Dick. Needle-Dick treated her like royalty. Wuzza other dude. Five-O."

"They're not the same person?"

"Nope."

"Who's Five-O?"

"Beast me."

Cézanne mentally processed the information. Then she dealt the next photo.

"That's Pin-Dick."

"You know this guy?"

Hollywood stared at the snapshot of Doug Driskoll. She gave a hearty nod.

"Sure do. He gave me this." After running an iridescent nail across the spider, she picked up the hand mirror and slimed the last of the powder off with her tongue. "Doug's tough. Brutal. But I like it that way sometimes. When he bites me, it's a totally dif'rent kind of thrill."

Something Hollywood said jogged Cézanne's memory. A sick rush of adrenaline swirled through her body. The day she sat looking at Carri Crane's autopsy photos with a magnifying glass came back. The crescent shaped bruise on her neck was a bite mark. Had to be.

"I'm going to ask you something and I expect the truth."

"Want me to party? 'Cause if you ask right now—"

"No, you're doing a bang-up job all by yourself."

"—you look delicious. I could do you good—"

"I want to know if Doug and Carri Crane were lovers." Her heart ratcheted up its tempo. The dressing room didn't have enough oxygen for the both of them.

"Lovers?" Hollywood laughed bitterly. "Not long."

"Until when?"

" 'Til I took up the slack."

"Have you ever seen this person before?" Cézanne gritted her teeth until they hurt.

Hollywood took the photo and held it inches from her nose. She seemed to not trust her eyes. "Where'd you get a picture of Bethany?"

"Never mind." She'd pared the pack down to the last two. "What about this one?"

"Can't say. I may've seen her around, but I don't 'member where. Maybe the grocery store, but I'm not much of a cook, ya know?"

Cézanne exchanged the file photo of Darlene Driskoll for the last one. Showing it was merely a formality, so nobody could accuse her of slapping together a lousy composite.

"And this?"

Hollywood stiffened. "That's him. That's Five-O."

Shock racked Cézanne's body as sure as if someone fired

a hollow-point through her chest. Internal panic set in. Her heart's RPMs revved into the red zone.

"You're telling me this is the cop Carri Crane had the fight with the night she died?"

Hollywood stared through glazed eyes, then nodded.

"Check again," Cézanne said. "Are you sure?"

"Yep. That's Five-O."

She gripped the stripper's shoulder and gave it a violent shake. Enormous breasts didn't so much as jiggle.

"Are you absolutely, positively, stake-your-life-on-it sure?"

"Stick-a-needle-in-my-eye. That's old Five-O, hisself."

Cézanne's jaw dropped. The rush of fear turned to dread. The man in the picture wouldn't be smiling back if he knew she knew what she knew.

Rosen.

No matter how twisted her family was, Cézanne thought, they were still family. But Rosen wielded their secrets like a sword of Damocles, and she'd been so busy protecting herself, she never even thought he might be harboring a few new ones of his own.

She dialed the phone and listened to it ring. Eventually Roby's answering machine engaged.

Hi. Leave a message.

"Roby, it's Zan. Pick up the phone."

He must have sensed the urgency in her tone.

"Didja catch him yet? Remember what that old gas bag says: a really *good* detective would get locks on the case in under two weeks."

"I have to ask you something."

He took a deep, bored breath. "Yes, Carri liked the sex. Said I was the best she ever had."

"She was twenty-two. How many could there have been?"

"I'm just telling you what she said."

"Women lie."

That shut him up a few seconds. When he recovered, he made an announcement.

"I'm being sued. Remember that Mexican from the crime scene I locked up?"

"Yeah?"

"Seems he went to the Justice Department. I'm staring down the barrel of a civil suit for false imprisonment," he said grimly. "A private process server jammed the papers between the screen and my front door. Says on the back copy he personally served me at high noon. I was out buying me a new rifle. Stupid bastard ought to know it's illegal to fudge on these things."

"I'm sorry."

"The Mexican wants two million from the city and he's suing me, individually. Can you believe that shit?"

"That's not why I called. Listen carefully. Did Carri ever want you to bite her?"

"Bite her?" She could almost see him yanking the phone from his ear. "That's sick. Why would I bite her? I loved her."

"You never sank your teeth into her neck?"

"What do I look like? Count Dracula?"

"If I asked nicely, would you give me an impression of your teeth?"

The silence grew cavernous.

"Tell you what, Duchess," he said with ingratiating calm, "why don't I just leave them in a glass next to the bed and you can pick 'em up next time you're over?"

The *click* of a dead connection resounded in her ear.

★ ★ ★ ★ ★

The Jack Black was supposed to make her sleep.

In the sanctuary of her bedroom, Cézanne ransacked the nightstand until her fingers located the cold surface of the sterling picture frame. She pulled it to her, turned on the night light and studied the face. In many respects, she still favored the girl with periwinkle eyes so shockingly beautiful they jumped off the photo paper. A hint of omnipotence in their twinkle, and a strong jaw radiated the kind of character that normally came from the old and sage.

Fresh tears blurred the image.

"How can you forgive me, Monet," she said through a sniffle, "when I can't forgive myself?"

It took hours enveloped in darkness, consumed with sorrow and listening to herself breathe beneath the eiderdown covers, before Cézanne drifted off.

She stood on the back porch, scanning the lawn for Kitty-Kitty and the babies.

Momma, gardening in the far corner of the yard. A tow sack off to one side, dropped into the pit. Dirt scraped over in a vengeance and pounded level with the flat of her spade.

Momma, have you seen Kitty-Kitty?

Then she knew. Bolted to save them, but a nail from the banister caught her pinafore and held her in place.

Bernice's eyes icy with hate, coming toward her, speaking in that frightful Germanic hiss.

Dere are too many. Too damned many.

Chapter Twenty-Six

From the time she dragged her fatigue-wracked frame into a tepid shower and began what promised to be a full Wednesday, Cézanne thought of Bobby Noah. For someone she initially thought of as a crack-pot, Johnson County's sheriff had morphed into the sanest person she knew.

Having thoroughly mined the Homicide unit for allies willing to stick their necks on the chopping block without tattling to Crane or Rosen, she came up empty. So it seemed only natural to make a stop at Three-fifty's Narcotics unit before reporting for duty. Narcs kept secrets better than anyone. Probably since most of them were paranoid.

If anyone could tell her about Carri Crane, those guys could.

She badged her way past the secretary and headed for the file cabinet housing the unit's production statistics. Tracing a finger down a clip chart hanging by a string, she selected a departmental underachiever she went to rookie school with, spotted him across the room with his back to her, and sidled up to link arms.

His name was Paul Snelling, and he had both wrists set in plaster casts.

"Banged up in a raid?" she asked.

"I wish. Went hunting at the lease this weekend and fell through the stinking deer blind. Now I'm stuck on light duty."

"That's awful. Do you remember me from the academy?"

"Sure. You told me to go fuck myself when I asked you to the Christmas party."

"Oh." A weak smile. "That was ugly of me. Sorry."

"Water under the bridge. So what brings you here? You down to seeds and stems finding people to pal around with?"

"I hardly recognized you at Carri Crane's funeral," she said in an attempt to shine up to him, "without your glasses and all." She'd expected to find a steroid-munching, iron-pumper like some of the other rookie school graduates. So, it made perfect sense to see him in Narcotics, passing for a hype when he wasn't clean-shaven, wearing freshly laundered clothes. "I thought maybe you might have dinner with me some night."

"I'm married." He held up his left hand and showed her the band of shiny white skin where a ring should have been.

"I knew that," she lied. "I meant you-plural. Your wife's invited, too."

"Sure, why not? I just sit around while the other fellows make buys and arrest bad guys." He looked longingly at his bum hands, barely able to flex his swollen fingers. "I guess I'm lucky. It could've been a lot worse."

"Right, you could've been a deer," she mumbled.

A few narcs milled around the coffee pot nearby, and Cézanne talked Snelling into moving to an anteroom with a conference table. She seated herself across from him, cupped her hands around his casts and tried to be charming.

Not that charm always worked around the PD. If she'd learned anything the past three years, it was that charm lasted fifteen minutes, tops. After that, nothing short of big dicks or huge tits worked absolute miracles.

In bright light, Paul Snelling had a face like a weasel. But he seemed quick to forgive, and before she knew it, the magnetic pull of marvelous brown eyes had her invading his body space to see where the irises ended and the pupils began.

He didn't shy away.

"I saw you by the door at the funeral," she said.

That extinguished any smoldering glimmer on his part.

"Since I'm here, I'd like to ask a couple of questions."

"I can't talk to you about her. None of us can. Sarge says he'll bust us back to foot patrol if we so much as utter her name. Orders from above."

Rosen.

Son of a bitch got to them. Got to everyone.

"I can talk to you about drugs," he said. "I can talk to you about raids. I just can't talk to you about the other."

But he wanted to. Of that she was certain.

"Then let's talk about narcotics. This is your lucky day," she said. "You've had a little slump in activity lately. I'd hate to see you get transferred out especially since you seem to like it here."

He blinked, and a set of thick lashes dropped and rose like an encore after the final curtain.

"We need people like you." Palsy-walsy. "You could pick up your stats if you had a credible CI. That's where I can help you. For the next couple of days, your confidential informant's going to be me. But it's our secret or no deal. What say?"

"Is that legal?"

"I have a law license. Would I ask you to cut corners?"

His head oscillated as if he were checking the room for bugging devices.

She said, "Here's what you do. Go over to District Court and find Judge Pittman. Don't go to any of the other judges, only him. Tell him you've got a credible CI and that she's worked with the police before. That's not really a lie.

"Tell him your CI's qualified to testify in court. Also, the truth. Then swear out an evidentiary search warrant for Ali Baba's, specifically, Michelle Parker's dressing room. There's cocaine in a little vial with her cosmetics, but you can still toss the room like a Caesar salad. You'll like that."

He dug a clumsy finger under a pocket flap for his field notepad, but she stopped him with an umpire's *safe* move.

"Don't write it down. I'll be back tonight. Remember what I said: nobody knows about this."

"What about my lieutenant? Shouldn't he approve it?"

"Honey, this is so classified it had to be cleared by Deputy Chief Rosen."

"I don't get it, Martin. Why don't you just swear out the warrant yourself?"

She put it in a context he could understand. "I'm undercover."

By God, one way or another, like it or not, she'd see to it Hollywood appeared before the Grand Jury. If it took exerting leverage with a dope charge, tough titty.

She spent the rest of the morning down at City Hall jawjacking with the Code Inspector until she bartered down the fine for Devilrow's little short-cut and wrote out a check to cover the cost of the remodeling permit. When he suggested they catch a movie sometime, she said, "I'm seeing a fellow from Johnson County."

It wasn't exactly a lie.

Mid-afternoon, the cold front the Channel Eighteen weatherman predicted stalled at the Panhandle and left the

Metroplex mercury setting a record winter heatwave. Back in Homicide, Cézanne became aware of the vapors of Captain Crane's aftershave bearing down on her even before he rounded the corner.

He had lost ten pounds in his face, alone.

"Sue-zanne."

She slapped the Crane file shut and stood protectively in front of it. "Hi, Captain."

"Have you cleared all your cases?" Snide.

"I've made a great deal of headway."

"A *real* Homicide ace could close a case in under two weeks."

Beyond the confines of her cubicle, the Crime Scene sergeant appeared in the doorway, accompanied by a dignified looking man wearing an expensive suit. They motioned Crane over, and after what appeared to be a grave exchange of conversation, the captain returned with his face ghastly pale.

He looked like a man who survived a glancing blow from a speeding car. His speech came out thick and in a monotone. "Your Grand Jury witness failed to show. The Assistant DA wants to know if you want an arrest warrant issued."

"He walked across the street just to ask that?"

"No," said the captain with just enough retribution to raise the hair on her arms. "They also informed me Crime Scene served your search warrant and presented their evidence this morning."

She held her arrested breath.

"It seems you got the right house. They luminoled the rooms and found high-velocity blood spatter on the walls. And smeared patches on the carpet where somebody tried to clean up."

Which meant Carri Crane was killed at home. And her body dumped in that flea bag on Hemphill.

"How'd you find out where my daughter lived?"

"Off a job application her roommate filled out."

"Good." In a hoarse whisper.

She sensed he could use a chair, and she rolled one close in case his knees buckled. He rested his hand on the upholstered back.

"Captain, sit down. I'll get you some water."

"No need. It's been almost two weeks since I've felt halfway decent. I just came back over to say, 'Nice going.' "

He was hallucinating. Or she was.

Gradually, the color returned to his face, and he no longer needed to steady himself.

"They also found an empty pack of Marlboros on Hemphill. Tyson's prints were all over it. And an ashtray full of cigarette butts at my daughter's house, with his DNA on the filters. So any way you cut it up, Sue-zanne, that places him at the scene."

More than anything, Cézanne needed someone to listen. Someone with more experience. Someone not from the PD. Someone with rural cunning.

When she learned Detective Driskoll had commandeered her squad car without permission, she made the short jaunt to Cleburne in a borrowed cruiser, low on Freon.

She arrived, perspiring, in the doorway of Bobby Noah's office. In the middle of a shared laugh with what appeared to be a field hand, the sheriff cut his eyes in her direction.

"What took you, City Slicker? Drag up a chair."

The room seemed to brighten with his smile. He dropped his gaze and gave her aqua silk blouse and matching suede skirt and jacket a look of approval.

"I'd like you to meet the Fire Chief. Benny, this is Miz Martin."

"Pleasure, Ma'am," the burly man said. He offered a calloused paw thick with hair.

"I was in the area and thought I'd drop by. Say, 'Howdy' or however it is you people greet each other. Be sociable."

"I didn't peg you for the neighborly type."

It wasn't as if she wanted to be here, for God's sake.

She realized her mistake, coming. He saw through her clothes, through her skin, through her head. The road to his land was probably paved with tear-away lingerie from previous victims.

His grin liquefied her bones to the point she needed a chair. Her heart skidded in her chest. Probably tachycardia. Probably about to stroke out. Seven minutes of oxygen deprivation meant brain death, and since there seemed to be a shortage of O2 in the room, she figured she was well on her way. Cleburne probably never heard of a trauma center. Maybe even still used midwives. Or, vets.

Threading her clammy fingers together provided imagined support. "If you're busy I can leave."

"You're not putting me out dropping in without an invite, if that's what you mean. I was just setting Benny here straight. You know how sparkys are."

She had an idea he was fixing to tell her.

"There we were, trying to preserve the crime scene, when Benny's pyro-eaters axe down an unlocked door like they're on some kind of search-and-destroy. I never understood 'em," he went on, taking a second to gnaw his bottom lip. "I expect it's that twenty-four on, forty-eight off rigmarole. And now Benny's got himself a female smoky. Some of my deputies are taking bets how long it'll be before there's a little firefighter on the way."

Carri had a cadet in the making.

Cézanne 'fessed up while she still had the nerve. "I need your professional opinion."

"That a fact?" Except for his jaw muscle tensing ever so slightly, the Sheriff kept a poker face on.

She glanced over the cramped quarters. Eyed a grandmotherly woman near the front counter where a desk plaque read Eunice Bailey, Office Manager and decided the processed blonde in support hose must be Eunice.

"Do you suppose we could go someplace more private?"

This time he beamed.

"Benny," he said, offering a handshake, "good to see you."

With the fire chief out of the way, the sheriff snatched his cowboy hat off a wall peg and adjusted the brim against his forehead.

"Been wantin' to show you something ever since we met. After you."

Eunice trailed them to the door with a suspicious glint. At the patrol car, Bobby echoed Cézanne's thoughts. That before quittin' time, the whole town would know their sheriff skipped out early with the city slicker.

With the windows down and a fresh breeze blowing through her hair, they rode down a county road, ribboned at the edges in winter rye. When the police radio's blaring chatter got to be too much, Bobby leaned over and volumed down the squelch.

"You like cows?" he asked.

"Medium-rare."

"I'm talking about dairy cows."

"Only if they give chocolate milk."

"Picture shows?"

"A waste of time. You won't find out your blind date's a

serial killer if you're sitting with him at the movies."

"So, what do you do?"

"Brood, mostly."

"What if you wanted to celebrate? Let's say you solve your case—"

"I may not."

"—and you wanted to kick up your heels."

"I'd probably swallow a Valium and go to bed. Or read a Bridge book on how to bid. Bidding irritates the hell out of me. Hang-gliding—I'd like to learn to do that. Jumping off a mountain with a kite strapped to my back scares the B-Jesus out of me. Or take flying lessons. Flying makes me sick."

"Then why do it?"

"To make me more interesting to me."

"Don't you like anything?"

"Not at the moment."

"What about me?"

"Especially you. You're like hang-gliding."

This time, it was Bobby Noah who pulled off the road and braked inches from a cattleguard. He jammed the gear shift into park and killed the motor. The set of his jaw suggested he wasn't to be tangled with.

"This shows a lot of cheek, driving out of your way to pick a fight."

"I don't think of it as a fight. We're having a lively discussion."

"Save your wind. I can smell an agenda a mile away. What's so all-fired important you'd look up a bumpkin-lightweight?"

"Your words, not mine."

"Lady, every time we talk you're drawn, aimed and cocked."

Pride had a way of sticking in her throat. She found an apology in something Roby once said to her after the laundromat fiasco—when The Brass partnered them together.

"I misjudged you."

"Is that a fact?"

"You have to understand. My whole life, I've had to run faster, make better grades, work twice as hard. I almost didn't get into law school. I admit I'm not half the investigator Roby Tyson is. And he's counting on me to save him. I can't go to The Blue for help, so please don't make it worse."

Asking for help choked her up. She swallowed the golf ball in her throat and said, "I think I've jumped off a mountain here, and I don't know if I'm falling five thousand feet without my hang-glider. Please . . . help me."

She unfurled the articles Krivnek made on his copier. The ones published in major law enforcement journals. The ones by John Robert Noah, Jr., DVM. She held them up for him to see.

"What'd you do? Get back to Cowtown and research me on your computer?"

"You studied forensics." She ticked off the topics. "Blood spatter patterns. Stab wounds. Gunshot wounds. Questioned deaths."

He leaned his head against the head rest. "So that's what gives. You've been bending Krivnek's ear at the ME's."

"Why didn't you tell me you toy with forensics when you're not playing Sheriff?"

"Out," he said.

"What?"

She couldn't believe he'd leave her in the geometric center of nowhere with no way back to town. Snakes came out to feed at night. Eighteen wheelers splattered deer without even feeling a thud. And if that wasn't bad enough, there was always death by exposure. A norther was expected around midnight.

He pulled the keys from the ignition, popped open his door and slung out a leg. The guy meant business. He was fixing to drag her out and ditch her. She should apologize.

And she would as soon as he finished stalking past the hood. She swallowed enough to moisten her throat.

The passenger door came open with a yank. Her mouth went slack when Bobby Noah gave her arm a firm pull. She came out of the car, where they stood toe to toe. Son of a bitch was going to—

—kiss her.

The adrenaline rollercoaster she hadn't felt since high-speed patrol chases surged through her extremities. Her hearing faded. Her vision tunneled. Jell-O kneed, she melted into his embrace. Closed her eyes. Savored his lips. Drew in the lingering scent of wintergreen breath, hot against her ears. His nose grazed her neck, sending shockwaves through her arms. In one smooth move, the memory of Doug Driskoll disintegrated as sure as a flash-bang tossed into a meth lab.

Chillbumps remained on her skin long after he stopped. The crystal blue left his eyes, replaced by huge, dark pupils ringed in the green of a gusty sea.

He spoke first. "Know what your problem is?"

She could barely conjure up enough reserve energy to breathe. Speaking was out of the question.

"Your problem is you've gotta be a cop twenty-four hours a day. You don't go home, take off your cop hat or your lawyer hat and put on your cowgirl hat. Take me for instance—"

She could.

Right here and now.

He'd never know what hit him.

Probably wouldn't even worry about pea gravel digging into his raw flesh. . . .

She didn't trust herself to finish the thought.

"—I get up in the mornin', go to work, come home at the end of the day and take care of my animals. Weekends, I go to the *Stagecoach*. Trouble is, I've been lookin' for somebody that never showed up. So how come is it you're able to live in Fort Worth your whole life and you never went two-steppin' at the Stagecoach?"

He answered for her.

"Because you never take a day off. You're young, but you're ever bit as hard-boiled as these old burnouts you work with."

He grabbed her wrist. Pulled her toward a gate posted with a NO TRESPASSING sign.

"Let's go." He tugged a keychain from his pocket. Opened the lock.

"If you think I'm tromping out in somebody's pasture in heels, you're nuts."

Wordlessly, he flung her over one shoulder easy as a burlap sack and for her, uncomfortable as all get-out. He trudged through dead grass until they reached a line of volunteer pecan trees. The low rumble of a spring fed brook filled her senses with the freshness of morning rain. A few steps more, and he unceremoniously slipped off her shoes, dropped them on the ground and deposited her at the creekbed.

"Ever go skinny dippin'?"

"It's the dead of winter."

He peeled off his shirt, then slipped off his wrist watch and added it to the pile. She kept busy staring at his taut muscles and tawny shoulders.

Whatshisname never ever looked this good.

"You're not seriously considering—I mean you left the patrol car on the side of the road, for God's sake. People'll come looking."

Off came his belt. It hit the ground with a *clunk,* and she averted her eyes, but the sound of a metal zipper running along its track redirected her attention. She tried to focus on his face but her gaze kept dipping to his

JESA.

"How long you expect it'll take those clothes to dry out?"

She took a backward step. Penises might be in short supply lately, but the high cost of repaying student loans made designer clothes even rarer. Tree bark crunched underfoot, its woodsy fragrance tweaking her nostrils.

"No, see, you don't understand. This cost a fortune."

"I'll buy you another. Or take it off. Your choice."

The sun hung low in the sky, resting in a hammock of peppermint clouds. In minutes, its apricot glow would be a memory.

"You don't strike me as the type to take advantage of someone in a vulnerable situation."

"It's Texas. It's winter. It got up to eighty degrees today. Aren't you hot?"

A suntanned hand reached up and unhooked the silk bow at her collar. He stripped it away where it became part of the heap.

"Is this the way country folk get acquainted?"

"Anybody ever tell you you talk too much?"

Shards of light filtering through the trees disappeared, replaced by a veil of shadows. She raised her hand and tentatively touched her collar.

"I can't swim." A lie to save the clothes she bought. The ones she planned to wear when Judge Pittman swore her in.

An amused crinkle thinned Bobby Noah's eyes. He helped her one-handed, as if he minored in buttons at Texas A&M.

"Seriously. I'm scared to death of water. I can't swim a stroke."

"Lady, you ain't scared of the Devil himself."

He sounded like Roby with a lean, hungry look to match.

"I'll drown."

"I'll save you."

"I'll bet."

Something told her he already had.

Images came in snippets. Roby, bullying his way into the evidence room. Ignoring the sign-in log.

Outta the way, Kid. I know the drill.

Finding a twenty-two caliber. Concealing it beneath his jacket. The plan? Return it later, and no one would ever know.

Hunting down his cheating girl. The fiery outline of Roby's hand imprinted on her face.

Whose baby?

Pulling the gun. A blast from the muzzle. Lady Godiva, face down on the floor of the flop-house.

But where Roby's head should've been, two spheres enveloped in vapor took shape. Ember eyes narrowed. Fog dissipated. The face that stared back in demonic glee belonged to—

Cézanne lashed out a defensive arm. "You're under arrest." Her eyes refused to open.

"Who's under arrest, Darlin'?"

Strong arms slid over her sweat-drenched body and tugged her close. Bobby. She'd gored him with an elbow.

"I'm sorry. I had a bad dream."

"Go back to sleep," he whispered. "Everything's Code Four."

He tightened his squeeze and a comforting warmth spread through her. He nuzzled her neck, and she rolled into his protective embrace. Drifted back into quieter slumber.

Then dreamed again of Bernice.

Chapter Twenty-Seven

Sometime before sunrise, snuggled deep beneath the covers, Cézanne noticed the hollow in the other side of the feather bed.

The faint smell of bacon frying in a skillet filled her senses. She opened her eyes and blinked the room into focus. The furniture had the kind of rich patina that could only come from age and linseed oil. And not a thing out of place. No shirts draped over the chair, no Wranglers piled up in a heap. Not even her suede suit. With Pops at the far end of the house, the situation became lightning clear.

The Sheriff hid her clothes.

Newspapers wrote about crazy people all the time. Father-son teams living in the wild, kidnapping joggers. Capturing them for indentured servants. Or worse, wives.

Cézanne Martin-Noah. Cézanne Noah.

She realized she was trying out Bobby Noah's name. And no matter how she said it, it always came out *No way.* She checked the bedside clock.

Five-thirty.

About the time she propped herself up on elbows with the thought of ransacking the place for her clothes, the sheriff strolled in carrying a box. He emptied it onto the bed.

Five, no, seven puppies swarmed over her, licking her skin. She took safety beneath an ancient, wedding ring quilt while Bobby settled his trim frame onto the mattress.

"Time for breakfast," he said with unequaled tenderness.

"I don't cook." Puppies rooted all around her.

"I'm inviting you to breakfast. I hung your clothes in the closet."

She peeked out from under the patchwork. From the mischief in his eyes, they read each other's minds. She'd have to parade stark naked to retrieve them.

"Get these mutts out of here."

"They're purebred coon hounds. Anyway, I thought we finally settled on an animal you liked."

"In the cage of a squad car."

He rounded them up, put them back in the box. They yipped ferociously and banged against the cardboard sides in a concerted effort to escape.

"I don't know what to think of you," she blurted, ticking off his accomplishments. "You're a lawman, a vet, some forensics expert Krivnek worships as a demi-god, a farmer—"

"Pop's the farmer."

"—a cattleman—" She clutched the covers tight against her chin. There was that gleam again, the one that landed her in the water. "A madman—"

"You forgot one."

She raised a quizzical eyebrow. He rose and reached around the far side of an ancient chest of drawers she suspected had been brought to Texas in a covered wagon by one of his ancestral captives—some refined New Englander shanghaied by the Noah clan. He pulled out an old violin and bow.

"You play the violin."

"Fiddle. 'A fiddle on the middle is just a fiddle, but a fiddle on the chin is a violin.' "

He tweaked the strings. Adjusted the tension on one and

drew the bow across. The same fingers that caressed every inch of surface area below her earlobes last evening, now moved effortlessly across a wooden neck of invisible frets with the same amazing dexterity. No wonder she found him fabulous. All he had to do was rosin up the old bow and let his fingers play *Westphalia Waltz* across her bare skin.

The fiddle mewed only slightly louder than she had.

She recognized *Bonaparte's Retreat*. Which made sense.

She should get her clothes and get the hell out.

Before dragging a nice guy like Bobby Noah into the muck.

She launched out of bed, embarrassed and determined. Pawed through the closet and found her shirt. The toe-tapping musician settled down on the bed with his back to her and started his own rendition of *Orange Blossom Special*. Her instinct to bail increased with each frenzied measure. By the time she dressed and the tune reached its most feverish pitch, she remembered she wasn't going anywhere with the unmarked cruiser parked back at the SO.

She stood in front of the Marlboro Man prototype. He lay the fiddle aside and patted a spot next to him.

Cézanne shook her head.

She couldn't afford to linger. To chance the feel of the warm hand electrifying her skin again. A man like this could jolt her back among the living.

"You're an amazing man, Bobby Noah."

"You dream." His expression free from recrimination.

"I hear your father rustling around in the other room." She ducked her chin and studied the grain of a plank in the flooring. "I should leave. I have to get to work."

"Pop's blind."

"What?"

She glanced through the open doorway past a sprawling living area with a center rock fireplace, into an enormous rustic kitchen. A feeble old gent ran his hand along a tiled countertop until it contacted squarely with the handle of the coffee pot.

"This is the same man I saw plowing a field?"

"I reckon you didn't notice that section of fence down yonder." He pointed out the window. "Smashed it to smithereens. But you till the same soil for more than fifty years, you know your boundaries."

Then it hit her.

Boundaries.

It all boiled down to knowing her limits.

Now she understood why relationships went sour. She picked emotionally unavailable men because they were free from the ability to commit. And the last thing—the very last thing she wanted or needed—was a perfect match like Bobby Noah cluttering up her life.

"I can't be late."

"Pop's not a problem."

She stood close enough to see her reflection in his eyes. A stirring in her chest warned her off.

"It's not your dad. It has nothing to do with you. It's me. It's always been me."

She resisted the magnetic pull of his eyes and of his hand.

"You need me," he said, emphatically. "To help solve your case." He plucked his Stetson off a bentwood hat tree. "After you."

The smell of fresh coffee wafted across the room like a genie, released. She tiptoed towards the fortress's massive exit.

"I'm off, Pop," Bobby called out. The door swung open and Cézanne stepped into the crisp dawn. "The pups are in my room. Would you set 'em back out in the barn for me?"

"Sure 'nuff, Sonny. Take care, now. And mind your manners. Your mama'd want you to treat the ladies nice and respectful."

Through the hinged slit, Cézanne watched the old man, propped against the counter, sipping from a steaming cup.

"Like the gal you toted home last night," he said, with the beginning of an ethereal smile on his lips. "Can smell that expensive perfume from here."

Back at the SO, Cézanne was all business.

Bobby joined her at the car as she climbed in and slotted the key into the ignition.

"I don't know how that cigarette wrapper got there, but Roby didn't do it. You should've seen his face when he talked about her. He loved her."

"Oldest reason in the world. 'If I can't have her, neither can you.' "

"What do you know about bite marks?"

"Your girl's got a bite mark?"

"I'm not sure. The ME didn't address it, but I was looking at one of the autopsy photos with a magnifying glass and there was a mark on her neck."

"Ted Bundy was a biter." He seemed simultaneously repelled and excited. "If it *is* a bite mark that's one good way to narrow your field of suspects."

"At first it didn't occur to me that's what it was. For one thing, it was behind the ear, disappearing into the hairline in what could be a couple of misshapen crescents. For another, even with long hair, Carri Crane couldn't very well show up around her parents with fang marks. Then I got to thinking maybe it wasn't consensual. Maybe it wasn't one of those rough sex deals that got out of hand."

"Sounds sexual. One thing for certain, if it is a bite and

your killer made it, the teeth marks'll do him in. It's as good as a fingerprint. Now all you've got to do is get some impressions to compare it to."

"How do I do that?"

"Apples or cheese," he said wickedly.

"What are you suggesting? That I carry around a hunk of cheddar with a 'Bite-me' sticker on it?"

He stepped back from the unmarked car as if he were about to leave.

"Do me a favor?" she said in an excited rush. "Let me see Glennis Pullin's crime scene photos again?"

He grinned in a way that made her think he must have figured she couldn't get enough of him. In his office, they pored over the glossies. Down to the last three, she found what she was looking for.

"Look." She pointed out a spot on the dead girl's neck. "Does that look like a bite to you?"

He leaned in close enough for her to throw him down and go for it, right there on the carpet.

"It's discolored, all right," he said using the magnifying glass Eunice kept by her telephone book. "Could be from shooting up, though."

"In her neck?"

"The autopsy report indicated her arms had collapsed veins," he reminded her. "She was a hype, remember? I've seen marks in crazier places. In the webs between the toes. On the labia. You name it and people have tried it."

Chills ran the length of Cézanne's torso and her face scrunched into a grimace.

"Run it by Krivnek," Bobby said.

"I'd like copies. Am I going to have any trouble getting them?"

"I can round up exposures of the Polaroids. The autopsy

pictures are duplicates. Krivnek's got the negatives." His eyes turned shrewd. "I know where you're going with this, and I can tell you right now, if you expect to tie this case in with yours and you don't have a bullet match or finger-prints, you'll need dental impressions. Ask your suspect to do it voluntarily. If he won't, you'll need a court order."

With a sniff and an eyeroll, she said, "You must have somehow gotten the misimpression that people I work with aren't stonewalling this investigation. Dental impressions? That ought to be about as easy as shaving a cat."

"Easier than it'll be getting a judge to sign an order ex-huming the body."

Chapter Twenty-Eight

One thing for certain—and Cézanne was willing to stake her reputation on it—if the Cranes hated having to bury their daughter, they'd loathe the idea of digging her up even more.

She left Narcotics thankful Paul Snelling had the presence of mind to leave the evidentiary search warrant for Hollywood's dressing room in a sealed envelope with C.R. MARTIN scrawled across it. And she didn't blame the guy for not sticking around, especially when she came to pick it up almost a day late.

Upstairs in Homicide, Detective Driskoll appeared to be AWOL. Greta, with her face carefully blank, stabbed out his home number with a pencil eraser-tip. After a few unanswered rings, she pronounced him shacked-up, and lost interest trying to find him. While Cézanne stood nearby dialing Forensics and digesting the news, Captain Crane appeared out of nowhere, his eyes flat and dead.

"Sue-zanne."

" 'Morning, Captain."

"I want that file closed out and in my office before noon."

"There's one more lead I want to check—"

"Noon."

"—before I—"

"Are you contradicting my order?"

"Captain, I think this—"

"Insubordination's a firing offense."

She cowed to his brusque demeanor and slipped out before she singed his feathers more than she already had, by breathing the same air. She made herself a promise to take up matters of bite marks and ballistics with him as soon as she returned from Ali Baba's. Hollywood could tell her who had access to that apartment. Reno may have skipped out on her, but by the time she got through with Hollywood, the platinum tease would by God sing like a rock star.

With search warrant in hand, Cézanne rolled into the strip club parking lot. There by the rear exit was Michelle Parker's muscle car, a late model Firebird, black with flame decals on the hood. She keyed the mic and announced her call signal over the radio.

"Hold me out at Ali Baba's."

"Ten-Four," came the dispatcher's disembodied reply.

The cold front still hadn't blown into Cowtown, and she momentarily considered shedding her jacket. Before she reached the building, the airways unexpectedly came alive with activity.

A brother officer wrecked out in a vehicle chase. Three miles away, an off-duty officer called in a hold-up at a convenience store, with MedStar responding. As soon as the troop completed the suspect's description, a motor jock radioed in pursuit.

In an unflappable monotone, the dispatcher pronounced the frequency closed to non-emergency communications.

At the door, Cézanne weighed her options.

A golf ball sized rock wedged at the threshold of Ali Baba's raised her hackles. But sneaking a peek inside the dismal den and seeing not so much as a piece of lint floating in the darkness, set off lights and sirens in her head.

Over the Westside frequency, an officer called for *Air*

One. The suspect in the wreck bailed out, last seen on foot; the patrolman needed the police chopper, fast.

Seconds passed, waiting for dead airtime. She keyed the mic and gave her call sign.

"Channel closed," the dispatcher said flatly.

"Start me an assist."

"Everyone's tied up." Irritated. "I'll check Southside."

Running Code Three, the closest South unit was five miles and ten minutes away, give or take a few traffic signals.

"Disregard. I'll handle it."

"Stand by, Detective." Somewhat relenting. "I'll see if I can pull somebody off a call."

"Negative."

Everything she learned in rookie school told her to wait for back up, but guilt got the best of her. If she'd met Paul Snelling in Narcotics like she planned instead of going undercover with Bobby Noah, she wouldn't be in this predicament in the first place.

Besides, the bouncer probably dashed around the corner to pick up some smokes. As long as she got inside before he returned, she could handle Hollywood without an assist.

She slid a hand under the flap of her shoulder bag and gripped the Smith. Nudging the rock aside with the toe of her shoe, she opened the door enough to slip through. A wad of alabaster latex on the floor ten feet away caught her scanning eye. In the time it took to bend down and inspect it, the door snapped shut.

But not before her mind registered it as a surgeon's glove.

The kind Homicide detectives kept in their supply cabinets.

Channel closed or not, lessons in survival told her to radio Communications and start the Southside unit rolling.

But if the street officers heard her—if they *knew* she needed back-up—they wouldn't need somebody telling them to break away.

They'd come on their own.

In the pitch black room, she twisted the radio knob to change frequencies and lifted the hand-held until she felt it graze her lips. An audible rustle from the direction of the hall leading to the dancer's dressing room silenced her.

Could be rats.

She held her breath and listened.

Maybe not.

Disoriented, she flattened against the wall and waited for her eyes to adjust.

Doug Driskoll hadn't checked in at work.

Her heart picked up the tempo.

Rosen's car wasn't in its reserved parking space.

Time crawled as shapes within the abyss became recognizable forms.

Rats would be good. Rats would be great.

Breaths came in shallow gulps.

Rats didn't shuffle. They skittered.

She didn't dare close her eyes, not even to blink.

If Driskoll was in it with Hollywood—

It wasn't the room's meat locker temperature that iced the blood in her veins, but the trickle of sweat tracking the curve of her spine—

—and that smell—

—that metallic whiff that tweaked her nose and caused her stomach to wrench.

Disoriented, she eased to the left, cautiously sidestepping her way toward what she believed to be the office—the only room in the place where the windows weren't blacked out with paint. She didn't get far.

Her foot made contact with a fleshy, inert
mass about the size of a bouncer, street-proned.
The air thinned and her throat closed.
Should've insisted on back-up.
The thought echoed in her head like a modiolus drip.
A shudder rippled through her body and the grips of the
Smith felt clammy against her hand.

*Rosen wouldn't kill. It wasn't his style when he could make
life so miserable people wished they were dead. But Doug? History was ripe with cops dealing drugs. And Doug needed money.*

An unexpected rumble from the building's air condi-
tioner sent shock waves through her chest. Still, her armpits
ringed with sweat. Whiffing her own fear, she came to a
stark realization.

She didn't want to die.

Not here. Not now. And not at the hand of a fellow officer.

She felt for the panic button on top of the handie-talkie.
They could track her location in Communications. In minutes, any squad car within a five-mile radius could arrive in
time to save her bacon.

Or not.

It didn't take much to figure out the lummox at her feet
wasn't exactly sleeping it off. Gingerly, she stepped over
what she believed to be Tiny's head and continued inching
her way toward the office.

"Stay where you are."

Hollywood.

Her ears were playing tricks. She thought she heard the
squelch of another hand-held, volumed down low.

A laser beam dotted her chest with a red pinpoint.

Doug's .40 calibre Glock had a laser sight.

Her chest thundered. A surreal, disconcerting buzz filled
her ears. She knew in an instant she was hearing her own

blood sloshing within the confines of her veins.

They were in it together, up to their gizzards. And to think, ever since Hollywood identified Five-O, she'd suspected Rosen.

"I can see you, you know." The cool in Hollywood's voice turned strident. "It won't do any good to run. Say something."

Cézanne got lock jaw.

They couldn't see her.

Of that, she was sure. The stripper was trying to hone in on her location so Driskoll could target the kill-zone.

Cézanne shrank a few inches until the laser dot appeared on the wall before she knew for certain. Carefully, she lowered herself to the floor. She wondered how many minutes had passed since she hit the panic button, and whether she could up-end a cocktail table before taking a bullet.

She wondered if she'd ever see Bobby again.

"C'mon, Cézanne, there's a light switch to your left. Hit it."

Her ears alerted like a canine.

Something in the way Hollywood said her name.

The faint echo of a siren wailed in the distance. And overhead, the distinct *whuppa-whuppa-whuppa* of Air One's rotor blades.

"What are you waiting for?"

She swallowed hard, stretched out her free hand and ran it along the floor to test for clearance before inching forward.

Another siren yelped in disharmony. But to Cézanne, clashing whoops were ear candy.

"Hurry up, Sister," Hollywood said, her voice tinged with desperation.

Cézanne touched the table stand.

Thank God. A shield.

She eased the bistro table onto its side. It scraped the concrete, and the eerie screech worsened the stench of fear already oozing from her pores.

"Don't make it any harder on yourself." A tremble in Hollywood's voice. Then she broke into sobs.

An unearthly groan filtered over from the floor.

Tiny.

Sirens screamed out their frenzied pitch.

In quick order, an explosion rocked the room. Hollywood delivered a guts-out scream. A deafening volley of shots pinged off metal, eclipsed only by flashes from the gun's muzzle.

Jesus-God. Doug would kill over drugs?

Behind her barricade, Cézanne returned fire—one-two-three.

Goddam revolvers. Should've learned on an automatic. With an extra magazine holding seventeen rounds.

She cranked off two wild shots and keyed the mic. "Shots fired, Officer Needs Assistance. Inside Ali Baba's."

Never should've listened to Roby when he said a good shooter didn't need extra clips, just make the first shot count. Son of a bitch never got in a gunbattle in the dark.

Gunfire echoed in her head.

She cranked off shot number six, melted against the makeshift barrier and groped through her purse, desperate to feel the cylindrical speedloader.

Footfalls receded, leaving only silence and the smell of cordite in her nose.

With the hand-held balanced on her lap, she emptied the cylinder one-handed, and coaxed the bullets in with the other.

Five seconds, max.

She snapped the cylinder shut. Crouched into position.

Took aim at nothing.

A dull rumble came from outside. Somebody got on the bullhorn; damned if she could make out the words.

A black-washed window shattered. A fist-sized hole opened up like the white tunnel to Heaven. Smoke billowed in and noxious fumes filled the room. She pulled her scarf to her nose and tried to breathe. The front door splintered open and the battering ram disappeared into the light. A powerful suction swirled the smoky haze.

Blindly, she groped for her badge.

Somebody set fire to her eyes.

She crawled toward the gaping mouth with her badge in one hand and her gun hand pressing the scarf to her face. Every breath seared her nose until she was sure her throat would close and she would strangle on her own spit. She bumped into Tiny's huge feet and stifled a shriek.

With the last of her strength, she pushed herself up on all fours and flung herself through the opening in a pall of smoke. Before collapsing in fresh air, she raised the panther shield and cried out.

"POLICE—Hold your fire."

It would be so like a rookie to gut shoot her.

Chapter Twenty-Nine

"Sip?"

To Cézanne's ringing ears, the voice came from off to one side and slightly behind.

Seated half in, half out of the driver's seat of a K-9 car with a plastic nosepiece pressed against her face and sucking in pure O2, she regained her senses. The wet nose of a well fed Belgian Malinois slimed against the cage and wheezed into her ear. His handler held out a bottle.

"Want a drink?" he asked again.

She answered with the stunned monotone of somebody who had just been pulled, alive, from a fiery crash.

"Make it a double."

A chuckle. "I'm afraid it's just water."

With heat radiating up from the blacktop, she drank with lusty enthusiasm. Having abated her thirst, she rested her shoulder against the seat and surveyed the scene. Uniforms fanned out across the parking lot. An ambulance full of animated attendants waited nearby while a second rolled up and cut its emergency strobes.

"I'm all right," she said to the officer, "but they ought to check out that guy inside. And we need to put a BOLO out on the dancer. She's Ten-Zero so be careful. She has a gun, and she's not afraid to use it."

Absent-mindedly, she inspected a tear in her jacket and tried to recall Michelle Parker's DOB and the license number of her Firebird.

"They already took the big fellow. It's the gal they're here for, though I don't expect they'll be able to do her much good."

"Hollywood's still inside?"

"Is that her real name?" He glanced over at a group of uniforms and beckoned with his arm. "Hey, Sarge. Come here."

A lanky, middle-aged officer with gold chevrons on his shirt sleeves sauntered over with a cheekful of tobacco and a pouch of Red Man sticking up out of one pocket. She couldn't recall his name but she recognized him.

The motor jock who cited her for the headlight violation.

He raised a bushy eyebrow as if he knew her too, and knew she was still driving the BMW around, unrepaired.

"She knew her, Sarge," the K-9 officer said. "Says her name's Hollywood."

"Michelle Parker." Cézanne poured the last of the water into her hand and splashed it over her face. "Did y'all arrest her?"

He didn't answer. Just towered over her with his arms braced across his chest and tried to menace her with a glare.

"What happened to her?"

The sergeant drew himself up tall. He arced a wad of amber spit at the front tire.

"You ought to know, Detective," he said flatly.

He pointed a crooked finger to a station wagon with the Medical Examiner emblem on it. It was parked next to the Crime Scene van, blocking the area where she had last seen Hollywood's car. An ME investigator unloaded a gurney from the tailgate. He ratcheted it up waist-high and rolled it, clacking, through the door.

"Follow me," the sergeant said with authority.

The K-9 officer offered a hand, but she refused it. The

shabby treatment gave her a pretty good idea how Roby must have felt when the brothers turned on him. With trepidation, she angled over to the ME's car and waited. Ten minutes later, with the mid-morning heat beating down on her head, Cézanne watched the gurney roll out, body bag and all.

In the glare of the vehicle window, she watched her features freeze in a trance and felt the guilt begin to devour her like flesh-eating bacteria.

When she recovered enough to speak, Cézanne said, "She fired on me, Sarge."

The sergeant nodded knowingly. One of the MEs unzipped the bag.

Cézanne blinked. Her mind refused to process the gravity of Hollywood's wound, and she blinked again. Slowly, her brain assimilated the sight, applying the knowledge of a Homicide ace. Hollywood stared back with the unresponsive eyes of a doll. The pinpoint pupils that were so obvious during their last encounter widened like an open camera shutter, unreactive to the noon-day sun burning through spotty cloud cover.

But the wound—

Cézanne stared in disbelief. A hole the color of Devilrow's eyes opened up Hollywood's abdomen just to the left of her navel.

Cézanne's eyes grew wide.

Her mouth gaped open and rounded into an *O*.

"What the. . . ? This is an exit wound."

The sergeant fixed her with an unyielding glare.

She knew from the cigarette pack-sized bulge in his breast pocket that he carried a micro-cassette recorder and that it had probably been activated the moment the K-9 officer called him over. And even if it hadn't, she didn't have to be reminded that inside his head, he was taking down every word.

Like the fine craftsmanship of a Swiss watch, every cog meshed into place.

The reason for the panic in Hollywood's voice.

The fact that Cézanne had never given the woman her first name, much less pronounced it for her. PD business cards carried her name as C.R. MARTIN.

But Doug Driskoll knew how to say it.

And Doug Driskoll had a laser site.

And the hole in Hollywood's stomach was about the size .40 caliber Glocks made at close range.

She looked away from the carnage and saw the back door to Ali Baba's fly open. Slash came out carrying an evidence bag. And she could tell by the way he carefully cupped his hand beneath it, he was feeling the heft of a handgun.

That reminded her. She patted down her purse.

"Where's my gun?" she asked dully.

"Evidence."

"You can't take my weapon, sergeant," she said, knowing good and damned well he could. And did. But it gave her something to say and bought her a little more time to think about how she needed to find Doug Driskoll and make him account for the bloodshed before he found her first.

"We durned-sure can take your piece," drawled the sergeant. "After all, you're the one shot her in the back."

She might have gone down arguing if she hadn't glanced inside the ME's car and seen a copy of the *Fort Worth Star-Telegram* on the front seat with the headline in a type-size normally reserved for political assassinations and alien invasions.

Homicide Detective Indicted for Capital Murder.

Chapter Thirty

Back at Three-fifty, the grapevine took on a life of its own.

Captain Crane wore his contempt like medals on the breast of his dress blues but it was Greta, the office *yente,* who rushed into Cézanne's cubicle chattering faster than a Vietnamese peddler.

"They say you shot some lady in the back. Did you? They say Internal Affairs is gunning for you. I hear the DA has the case right now, and they're going to prosecute you."

Cézanne bristled. "Whatever happened to good old-fashioned police work? When people investigated things before they started running off at the mouth? And who's the lead investigator on the case, anyway?"

Greta's eyes flickered to the furnishings. "Captain Crane's working it himself. But don't worry, Shug, he'll treat you fair."

Fair as in fair? Or, fair as in fair game?

"Tell me what happened, Cézanne. I won't say anything, I promise. Just tell me how it felt to kill that woman." Her eyes glittered with excitement. "Were you scared? I would have wet my pants. But tell the truth. Didn't it feel just a little bit *good?*"

For a brief moment, she thought she might vomit all over Greta's pointy-toed shoes.

Her mind wrestled with dozens of scenarios, but only one of them made it to the top and stayed there. The latest fad in the Texas Penal Code was the hate crime. And the

DA would probably want to file it as one, for the enhanced penalty.

Not that they could kill her twice.

An unidentified shout carried over the cubicles. "Yo, Martin. You're wanted in IA."

Cézanne picked up an empty purse and snorted at the irony. Her badge and ID had already been removed.

Chapter Thirty-One

By seven o'clock that evening on the hands-down worst Thursday of her life, Cézanne left Internal Affairs with a bad case of amnesia, a temporary suspension, no Smith & Wesson until Forensics finished ballistics, and no badge and ID until her short-term memory loss lifted and IA had her statement on file.

Not that she gave a rat. Krivnek would vouch for Hollywood's lethal injuries. And she hardly expected to retain custody of her building keys and key card as long as she was in the penalty box. But she would have liked to have had the gun, badge and ID returned to her, seeing as how Doug Driskoll hadn't so much as made a dent in his chair. For all she knew, he'd taken the department's drug-buy money and whatever he'd made running coke out of Ali Baba's, and high-tailed it to some country where extradition was a myth.

Either that or he was laying low, waiting to kill her.

As for Driskoll's motive for murdering the captain's daughter, the DA could use her theory or think of one on his own.

Whichever, she'd solved the Carri Crane murder in under two weeks' time and that should have counted as a good lick by anyone's standards.

Under orders from The Brass, one of Rosen's henchmen, a gray-headed fellow seasoned enough to be one of Roby's contemporaries, accompanied her back to Homicide to retrieve her personal belongings.

Twenty feet from the door, he pulled out a key card. "You're the one they call The Brain, ain'tcha?" When she didn't answer, he said, "Yeah, you are."

"If I'm so smart, how'd I get in this mess?"

"Chin up, Detective." He swatted her hard enough to dislocate a shoulder. "A couple of us made book you'll be reinstated by Monday."

"You know something I don't?"

"Crime Scene tagged a twenty-two caliber they recovered at the scene. It's being tested right now."

"With my luck, they'll say I planted a throwdown. Or charge *me* with killing Carri Crane."

"Don't think so. Got a hundred riding on it."

"I appreciate the confidence."

With an amused twinkle, he said, "Has nothing to do with it. Frankly, none of us figured you're sharp enough to pull off anything that complicated."

"Thanks . . . I think."

He swiped the key card across the wall plate mounted outside Homicide and said, "I'll wait here. Don't take all night."

Dejected, she made the walk down the dimly lit corridor with all the enthusiasm of a Death Row convict, wondering if Roby had heard the news.

At the entrance to her cubicle, her brain's startle reflex engaged, and she flinched. For someone who ducked in just long enough to fetch her address book and the cuss-kitty, the last thing she expected to see in her office was—

—Darlene Driskoll—

—grinning out from a color, eight-by-ten photograph in a silver frame on her husband's desk.

She slumped into her chair, picked up the telephone and

punched out Roby's home number on the keypad. He should know about Doug. And about her suspension. Maybe they could even get together later and polish off a bottle of Jack Black.

The fourth ring activated the dulcet tone of a pre-recorded message. While she listened to the canned recording, her eyes cut to the photo of Darlene. A new *Glamour Shot* of Driskoll's wife, dressed in a conservative brown suit and pumps. With a turquoise scarf knotted loosely around her neck.

Copycat.

Hair prickled her neck.

Her eyes locked on the pattern. On the splashes of orange, purple and blue in the cloth. In a gut-cramping moment, her stomach went hollow. She grabbed the photograph off the desk and stiffened. Her heart went dead.

At the other end of the line, an electronic tone gave her the go-ahead to speak.

"Roby, pick up the phone. I know you're there. I know who the killer is. Meet me at Doug Driskoll's house."

It wasn't about selling drugs to pay bills.

It wasn't about public scandal.

It was the oldest reason in the book.

Her ears alerted to silence. On a strained hope, she imagined him listening, wondering if he should pick up.

Words tumbled out in a hyperventilating rush. "I just figured it out. Ohmygod, Roby, you're not going to believe this. It was the fabric. It's the same material Carri wore in the picture on the Cranes' mantle. I came in to get my stuff and it all fell into place. Carri wore that Hawaiian print the night you went out, didn't she? Birds-of-paradise."

She drew in air that felt thick and unbreathable.

"PICK UP THE PHONE, DAMMIT. I know what happened to the dress. Only it isn't a dress anymore, it's a scarf. Come on, Partner. LET'S CALL FOR BACK-UP AND MAKE AN ARREST. It's not Doug Driskoll. It's—" A shadow caught past her rolling eye.

"Hang up the phone."

"—his wife."

Darlene stepped into view. Pointed the .40 calibre Glock.

Cézanne exhaled a ragged breath. The red pindot from Doug's laser site hovered between her breasts.

"I said, hang up, Say-Zonne." Darlene reached across her husband's desk, switched on a banker's lamp and flooded the area with light. Instead of dressing in the festive colors of a cheap piñata, Driskoll's wife wore all black.

Cézanne's throat tightened. She glanced away long enough to replace the receiver.

Only she didn't.

Driskoll had returned her pencil sharpener to its place near the phone, and she palmed it. The little square of plastic fit nicely into the cradle space and kept the prongs from depressing under the receiver's weight.

She said, "Where's Doug?"

Glassy-eyed, Darlene answered in a dispassionate voice. "He doesn't love you, you know. He didn't love any of those skanky whores."

"Of course not. It's always been you."

Darlene racked the Glock's slide back, chambering a round. The air thinned.

Images from childhood flashed, rapid-fire, through Cézanne's mind like motion picture out-takes that ended up on the cutting floor. Carnal panic set in. "Is that the plan? To kill me?"

"You killed *me*."

"That's how you want to be remembered? As a murderer?"

With lethal calm, Darlene said, "But I'm not a murderer. You're going to commit suicide."

Cézanne didn't get it. And Driskoll's wife must have read the confusion in her face. She stepped inside the cubicle and pulled Doug's chair to her. Blocking the entry, she slid into the seat with her back to the corridor.

"You think you can keep secrets," she said. "Sure, you're young and pretty, there's no getting around that. But something's wrong with your head. Everyone in this department knows about you, about how you tried to OD on Valium back when you were in the police academy. How your mother cracked up and they locked her in the nuthouse; that she's crazier than an outhouse rat."

Only one way she could know that.

Rosen.

Blood pounded in Cézanne's ears. "Ohmygod. Please tell me I'm wrong, how you got this job."

"It's almost like incest, isn't it? You had a fling with Doug; I had a one night stand with Rosen. In a way, it's almost like *we* had sex, isn't it?" A cruel smile danced at the corners of her mouth. "Was it good for you?"

A distant sliver of light swept the ceiling and disappeared. Her escort must've heard the crack of the slide when Darlene chambered the bullet.

"Poor Say-Zonne. Now you've gone and lost your job. The stress got to be too much. You found Doug's gun and ended it."

Stay cool. Keep talking.

Cézanne raised her voice. "You plan to kill everyone your husband meets?"

"Only the ones he sleeps with."

"It was you firing on me at Ali Baba's, wasn't it? Why didn't you just cap me right there? You had the perfect opportunity."

"I went to confront that tramp. You happened to get in the way."

"Why kill Hollywood?"

"She wanted Doug for keeps."

Cézanne's eyes throbbed. "So did I."

"You were the only one who acted sorry for what you did."

The escorting officer came into view, the top of his head barely visible above the cubicles. She imagined his hand meshing with the holster; his silhouette moving stealthily, his arms outstretched in an FBI gun-stance.

Her eyes flickered back to Darlene. "Why Carri Crane?"

"We had enough money troubles without my Dougie paying child support."

Cézanne's thoughts flashed to Rosen. "How can you be so sure Doug knocked her up?"

"I picked up the extension the night she phoned the house."

"She admitted it was his kid?"

"No," Darlene said almost wistfully, "but I knew." She rocked in her seat as if keeping time to an inaudible lullaby in her head. "Dougie told her, 'Remember two things, Sugar Cane: all men are assholes and married men never leave their wives.' "

Including Rosen.

"You would've let Roby Tyson take a fall for capital murder."

"How was I to know that cheap little trick was really an

undercover officer? I thought she was just another stripper like the others."

It was an admission.

"What others?"

Realizing her mistake, Darlene gasped. "You tricked me into saying that."

Cézanne's heart fluttered with the fragile beat of hummingbird wings. Where in God's name was that officer?

Her ears buzzed. Her voice warbled with the effort of speech. "You killed Bethany Faust. And that other girl, Glennis."

"The ME said it was an overdose. I didn't realize insulin would do that to a healthy person, or I could've done them all that way."

Cézanne swallowed hard. Her heart beat double-time, and then died in her chest. "Did you kill Doug?"

"Of course not." Darlene wagged her head. "I love him."

"He never showed for work. No one answered the phone at home."

Darlene narrowed her eyes. "You've been calling my house?"

"Greta did. That's her job."

"My Dougie's sick."

Cézanne's lips quivered. Licks of fear chilled her to the core. "Did he get a shot of insulin, too?"

Darlene raised the gun. A lightheaded rush filled Cézanne's head. Her life depended on how long she could keep the madwoman from pulling the trigger.

"Please. Before you kill me, answer one question. Why didn't you plug me at Ali Baba's? You already got away with murder."

"I didn't go looking for you. But once you showed up and things got out of control, I had no choice."

"You could've shot us both and been out of there."

"No," Darlene said angrily, "*you* could have shot her, and we could've *both* been out of there. I stuck the gun in her back and whispered what to say. You were supposed to shoot her for me and rid me of her for good." She glared accusingly. "You let me down."

The uniform materialized six feet away, beyond Darlene's line of vision. A tiny neon pinpoint shined through the weave of his shirt. Sonofagun audiotaped her, probably from the time they left IA.

Cézanne squared her shoulders. By now, he had heard enough to clear her and Roby, both. She said, "Listen to me, Darlene. It's not too late. Put down the gun, and we'll get you in to see Whitelark."

"Whitelark's a fool."

Even in the critical moment, Cézanne found the observation mildly amusing. "What'm I saying? You're absolutely right. Whitelark's an asshole. You don't want to talk to him."

"You think I'm crazy, don't you?"

"Not at all." It was mostly the truth. "You said, yourself, you didn't want to hurt me."

Darlene rolled her eyes and scoffed. "I said I didn't want to kill you. There's a difference." Her chin tilted in defiance. "That's all changed. I heard they kept your gun. Guess I'll have to leave this one with you."

"They found the twenty-two caliber lying next to Hollywood. Your prints are all over it."

"Liar."

"It's true."

"Latex gloves." Smirking, Darlene flexed her fingers.

A grating, staccato pitch pierced the conversation. Startled, Darlene cut her eyes to the blaring phone.

The laser danced.

Time ran out.

Cézanne dived to the floor.

The blast shattered the computer monitor, showering glass and piercing the wall. She bounced against the floor hard enough to knock out her wind. A crushing weight fell on top of her, driving the rest of her breath from her lungs and pinning her legs in place.

A stampede of officers, uniformed and plainclothes, materialized. Someone removed the suffocating bulk, and a plainclothes officer halfway to hyperventilating pulled her to her feet. It took a few seconds for her lungs to reinflate, but she recovered in time to see a beat cop haul Darlene Driskoll, bleeding from the head, up on tiptoes and hustle her out in handcuffs.

"You all right?"

That voice.

She turned to see Jinx Porter with a toothpick sticking out between his teeth, and slowly released her breath.

"What're you doing here?"

"Dispatch got a panic button and put out an Officer Needs Assistance broadcast. I was cutting through the building on my way to see the Justice of the Peace when one of your guys snagged me."

Her eyes shifted to the telephone. Someone had replaced it in its cradle. No matter. Her partner's machine caught the whole confession.

"Roby didn't kill Carri Crane," she told Jinx.

"Never figured he did."

"I need to tell him."

"You don't think he already knows?"

She ducked the constable's piercing gaze. "I have to tell him I'm sorry."

Jinx offered to come along. "But we're taking my patrol car."

Cézanne permitted herself a chuckle. "Roby'll get a kick out of that. He'll say it's high time I let the man drive."

Chapter Thirty-Two

The last of the sun pulsed in the sky like a blast from the muzzle of Darlene Driskoll's gun. Jinx wheeled the car into Roby's driveway and cut the motor.

Cézanne knew in a glance something was wrong.

For one thing, Roby burned the porch light twenty-four hours a day once the last Sunday in October rolled around and the state adopted Daylight Savings Time for the winter. That way, he didn't have to fumble in the dark when he returned from work in the evenings. And two days' worth of newspapers on the front lawn and mail bulging from the box—another bad sign. Worst of all, Mother Goose was parked in the drive with a cover over it.

Jinx popped open the car door and emptied a mouthful of snuff onto the dead St. Augustine. He looked over warily.

"Coming?"

"There's a note." She pointed to the screen door.

The tension in her neck moved up the back of her head and settled behind both eyes. As far as she was concerned, a note tacked to the door had about as much appeal as a certified letter.

Nothing good ever came of either.

They approached the porch in silence, but when the bold, squared-off handwriting of her partner jumped off the envelope in the shape of her own name, she clutched the constable's sleeve.

"Something bad's happened," she announced with a tremble.

From the look on his face he knew it, too.

"Do you feel it? Ohmygod, I'm going to be sick." When he reached for the doorbell she grabbed his wrist and held on. "Fingerprints," she said. "Crime Scene might need to take some."

Jinx pulled the envelope from the screen and handed it over. A lance of fear pierced her aorta.

Hi, Zannie,

Every valve in her heart seemed to tighten. Her eyes swam over the page.

I figured you'd show up sooner or later.

The constable's voice rumbled fuzzy and distant. "Whatsitsay?"

Truck keys in ice cube tray in freezer. Don't let battery on Mother Goose run down.

Her world stopped rotating on its axis. Time stood still. A low moan brewed in her chest.

And Zannie, clear my name. You know I didn't kill her.

P.S. Don't come in.

Call 911 and find my dog a good home.

It wasn't until Jinx Porter gave her shoulders a violent shake that she recognized the primal, guts-out scream filling her head as her own.

Chapter Thirty-Three

At Bobby's hounding, the emotionally detached Krivnek let Cézanne see a copy of Roby's autopsy. Unofficially, of course. Krivnek didn't stretch his scrawny neck across the political chopping block for anybody.

Suicide.

"I busted my ass." Like a rudderless ship, her eyes drifted over the sea of words. "I did things. . . ."

She stopped short of incriminating herself.

"I risked my reputation, self-respect, my life, and for what? So he could cancel his own ticket?"

Krivnek's hand grazed her shoulder with a touch so tenuous it startled her. "He was sick."

"Sick? What do you mean, 'sick'?"

"Cancer."

She shook her head. "You're mistaken. Roby didn't have cancer. I'd have known about it."

"It's not all that uncommon, not telling your friends. From what you've said, he sounds like a proud man. He probably didn't want anyone's pity."

"I don't buy it. Crane probably held that gun to his head and forced him to write that note. I want a complete investigation." Her voice climbed an octave. "I have this friend who's a Texas Ranger—"

"Don't be dramatic."

They sat on opposite stools, locked in each other's unwavering glares.

It was Krivnek who broke the silence.

"Suicide's more common than you might think. Sometimes, even sane people reach their level of tolerance."

He tilted his head back. She suspected he did so to scrutinize her reaction through his bifocals. "The cancer metastasized. I'm sure the prospect of spending his last days in jail was more than a little daunting. He was a goner and he knew it. If you'd seen all the medicine in the pantry. . . ." The rest of the thought went unspoken.

Krivnek made sense.

Deep-sea fishing while prosecutors scrambled to beef up their case? Whoever heard of moose hunting in Colorado?

Over the nauseating odor of chemicals, Cézanne made a tentative request.

"Jinx Porter said they found another note beside the bed. He said it was addressed to me. I'd like to read it."

Krivnek's eyes narrowed. Before he could bow up good and proper, she appealed to him for a thread of compassion.

"He was my best friend."

Krivnek's jaw tightened. By the way his brow furrowed into deep ruts, she knew he'd already made up his mind.

"Sometimes when people aren't thinking straight they say things they don't mean, Detective."

"We were best friends. Nothing Roby could say would ever change that."

"No?"

After a long, dedicated moment, the Assistant ME responded with a look that would make brakes fail.

"Take it from me, you don't want to know."

Chapter Thirty-Four

Around three in the morning, the remnants of Roby's Jack Black wore off, and Cézanne sat bolt upright in her bed.

Disoriented, she wondered why she forgot to wear clothes to her algebra final, and whether the other kids noticed her naked, with pencil shavings all over her lap; then snapped awake understanding she was all grown up now, with a Juris Doctor degree, and didn't need to know math now that she had an accountant. But especially, most definitely, realizing that she wouldn't have pulled that damned *F* in the first place if Monet had been alive.

She rarely thought of Monet in the daytime; her disciplined mind wouldn't allow it. But in moments of slumber or binge-drinking, demons took over. Kidnapped her from her mental gladiator and took her to the theater. Made her watch black and white snippets of a childhood only men like Hitchcock or Poe could have appreciated.

More than anything, she didn't want to attend Bernice's commitment hearing, mid-morning. In her head, she rehearsed her testimony, wondering when the time came and they asked her when Bernice went off the deep end, whether she'd tell them.

If they put her under oath, she'd have to.

For the longest time, she lay awake listening to the clock tick, seeking solace in cradling Monet's picture, face down, against her breasts. She didn't want Monet looking at her. Didn't want her twelve-year-old eyes to remind her how it all boiled down to drawing straws.

They'd selected broom bristles from Bernice's fist, the fair way, of course; their mother didn't play favorites.

Cézanne won the bed next to the only window. From there, she could do homework and peer outside at lush foliage springing up or watch the neighbors pass by on evening walks. In three out of four seasons, the bed by the window was a prize possession.

But in the winter of their twelfth birthday, they'd taken pneumonia. First her, then Monet.

Henri, deep into his James Dean phase, turned sixteen that Thanksgiving. Rebel without a car, since he wrecked the family's only transportation his first time out without permission. When Bob Martin took a second job working swing shift to make ends meet, Bernice's tirades worsened.

Cézanne remembered their last night together.

Henri declared he would no longer be known as Matisse. Said it was a stupid name. That it made the other kids call him a faggot. And that Bernice was the stupid bitch who ruined his life.

Then came the smack of a wielded hand.

Lots of yelling in the far part of the house. Bernice's voice, increasingly abrasive, hurling another volley of insults. If he wasn't a pansy, then what was he doing locked in his room with the boy down the street?

Never before had they heard their daddy lose his temper.

"I've had it up to here with your diatribes, Bernice. You made the boy this way. Deal with him. The girls, too."

Then, Henri untethered the statement that ended the family.

He knew about her and the cantor from the shul. Even the Rabbi knew. Everyone in the synagogue was gossiping about her fling with the soloist. And if Dad didn't do anything about it, then they could all get shtupped.

All hell broke loose.

The front door slammed, shearing Cézanne's delirium.

"Monet? I can't breathe."

"Shhh, Zannie."

"Get Daddy, quick." She lifted a feeble hand. "The draft's made it worse."

"Daddy left. Momma's on a tear. Take my bed. I'll take the window."

"But you're sick as me." Monet's shallow breath told her so.

"It'll be okay."

Monet clutched her bear. Exchanged places. Pulled the covers taut against her chin. Cézanne heard her teeth chatter.

"Golly, Zannie, it's awful over here."

"Mmmmm."

With lungs aching, Cézanne faded out. It took china shattering against the dining room wall to bring her around.

A slew of curses, then Bernice to Henri: "Out of da house."

"Make me."

"Dere will be no memory left but your picture on da Whirlitzer, you do not leave dis instant."

The door banged open. A shot exploded glass.

And then, the haunting words.

"I cannot raise dese children alone."

"Monet?"

Cézanne reached out a hand and drew a weak finger across her sister's blazing cheek. She barely stirred.

"Monet, can you hear me?"

Nothing. Nothing but the terrifying anticipation of foot-falls approaching.

"Monet, something awful's happened. Get up. We have to hide."

Her sister's lungs rattled with each labored breath.

Filled with terror, Cézanne waited.

She never heard the door open, so sly was Bernice. But she felt her mother's presence within the shadows and experienced the rotten stench of her own fear. When she made out Bernice's ominous silhouette through barely cracked eyelids, it was as tangible and frightening as anything her mind could comprehend.

Bernice held a gun.

A shard of light from a corner street lamp cut through the Venetian blinds and glinted off the barrel. Cézanne's heart galloped with the fury of a thousand stallions. Within arm's reach, Monet wheezed, each breath worse than the last.

Bernice placed the pistol on the dresser. She glided past the foot of Monet's Jenny Lind bed, to Cézanne's by the window. She reached for a throw pillow.

Lifted it up.

Covered Monet's face.

"Momma?" Cézanne's voice came out in a pathetic squeak.

"Quiet. We do not want you should wake Cézanne. She needs to sleep. She is . . . very . . . ill."

"But, Momma—"

"Shush. She will be better off."

"Momma, I'm not. . . ." Her plea faded into thought.

Monet.

"Shush."

The last image imprinted on the mental negative before Cézanne awakened in the ambulance was Monet's final, pitiful shudder.

And when the doctor pulled the oxygen mask away from her face, Cézanne's first memory when she came to in the hospital was him asking if she knew where she was . . .

. . . if she could tell him her name.

And Bernice's hellish shriek when she answered.

Cézanne.

Chapter Thirty-Five

The Friday morning commitment hearing began promptly at nine in a makeshift courtroom the hospital set up for the convenience of the judge. Jeremy Hill was hanging around like a loose tooth, studying Bernice's chart while the Assistant District Attorney prosecuting the case reviewed his notes.

While the Judge swore in the witnesses, a uniformed deputy brought Bernice inside and seated her next to her court-appointed attorney. Cézanne assessed the lawyer's competence strictly on appearance—if the guy were dynamite, he wouldn't have enough primer to blow his nose.

She glanced over at the State's attorney and didn't like the way Dr. Hill leaned across in his chair and whispered into the prosecutor's ear.

With a somber nod, the Assistant DA called her to the stand.

"Would you state your full name for the record?"

"Cézanne Renoir Martin."

"And how are you related to the Proposed Patient?"

"She's my mother."

He went along, innocuously extracting details. About Cézanne's visit to the nursing home, three weeks before. When Bernice set fire to her mattress.

"Are you the one who swore out the complaint?"

She glanced at Bernice. Her hair stuck out from her head like weathered wood from a picket fence, and tears puddled along the rims of her eyes. When she folded her hands, prayerlike, and began to whisper quietly into her palms, Cézanne looked away.

"Yes, I did the affidavit. It was either me or a nursing home representative, and I figured it would be more accurate coming from me."

"Did your mother say anything when she lit the match?"

"Kush meer in tochus."

All eyes riveted on Bernice.

Cézanne rushed out an answer. "I don't recall."

Dr. Hill leaned in from behind, enough to bend the prosecutor's ear. Another grim nod.

"Did she call you by somebody else's name?"

"She may have. I don't remember."

"Kush meer in tochus." Louder.

"Mrs. Martin—" The judge, pissed off, wagged a finger at Bernice. "You'll get your turn."

With her head bowed, Cézanne's mother shrank in her chair. The deputy, seated nearby, pulled his chair within tackle range.

His Honor said, "Proceed, Counselor."

"Could she have called you 'Monet'?"

"It's possible."

"And who's Monet?"

"She was my sister."

"Kush meer in tochus."

Cézanne cut her eyes to Jeremy Hill getting his rocks off on her pain. She locked him in her unforgiving stare.

"Ms. Martin—"

"Yes?"

"—you know what the penalty for perjury is, don't you?"

"Yessir."

He rose. Stood at the table. Asked the judge for permission to approach the witness. Came within several feet of her.

"I'm going to ask you a question, Ms. Martin. Before you answer I want to remind you, you're under oath."

"Yessir."

"What, exactly, happened to Monet?"

Chapter Thirty-Six

According to Roby's obituary, the Reverend Willie Lee Washington would preside over the service and interment. Cézanne folded the newspaper shut and pondered what would make somebody of Roby's means pick, of all places, a black funeral parlor in the seediest part of town. Such an uncharacteristic move carried the same odds as Doug Driskoll ignoring the new female recruits.

It wasn't the money. Roby set aside plenty.

Except for the one time he razzed her back in her rookie days about how they ought to stick her out in the thick of the battle zone—see if she could make it off probation—they rarely talked about the rough sectors of East Fort Worth known as Poly and Stop Six.

After a few minutes of dedicated thought, she hit on the reason.

He had no one. No friend but her. A life wasted.

Saturday morning turned out frosty coming off the Panhandle blue norther. On the way out the door, she snatched a thin, ecru cashmere coat from its hanger and threw it over one arm. On the way to the mortuary, she programmed the car radio to classical music but after a few strains of Beethoven's Pastoral, her depression plummeted to new lows. She shut it off, preferring to listen to the belching-lion noises coming from under the BMW's hood.

On a whim, she took an unexpected detour by the PD and spied Rosen's Lexus parked in his reserved space. She swerved into the lot with such abandon the summons the City Marshal served her the previous week shot across the dashboard and landed on the passenger floor.

She had an idea.

She stuffed the court document into her coat pocket and headed up to Rosen's office. It might come in handy if he gave her any flack.

On the elevator ride, she surmised he had come in early to pay Darlene Driskoll a jail visit. They needed to get their stories straight. Heck-fire, Rosen probably wasn't even in the building; he'd be across the street sitting in a holdover tank with a telephone pressed to his ear, glaring at Driskoll's wife through the plexiglass and telling her how the cow ate the cabbage.

It surprised her to catch him in his office, dressed in a starched denim work shirt and khaki dockers, shredding files.

"Mine, Carri's or Darlene's?" His head jerked in her direction, where he wasn't exactly bowled over to see her framed in the doorway. "I came for my badge and gun."

"Of course."

He dug in his pocket for a set of keys, located the right one and unlocked the desk drawer. Before returning her shield, he huffed his breath on it, then shined it against his sleeve.

"Welcome back." He handed her the Smith by its barrel, with the cylinder flopped-out, unloaded.

She kept her face carefully blank.

"I heard what you did at the hearing yesterday," he said, seemingly unruffled. "The judge called right after you testified. The case on Monet is being reopened."

The shredder gobbled up another police report. She suspected the file had never been sent to microfiche for preservation, and that she was watching the last vestiges of that awful night, fragmenting into thin strips of confetti.

"Looks like you dug yourself a big hole."

She continued her unwavering stare, hoping if she possessed any telekinetic powers they might activate, and incinerate Rosen down to a pile of ashes where his Bally loafers had been.

He said, "Do you think it's smart making sure they lock your mother in an insane asylum the rest of her life?"

"Smarter than you covering up for her all these years."

He shoved too many sheets into the shredder, and it made a death rattle groan, binding up. The skin beneath his eye jumped. She knew as certain as she stood there, the file she was watching disintegrate was Monet's.

"You can shred all the papers you want, but you can't shred my memory."

"I want to make this up to you, and I think I can," he said. "I have a friend with a law firm who's willing to take you on as a briefing attorney."

"Crane needs to retire."

"What?"

He didn't get it. And the longer she stayed there waiting for her words to soak in, it pleased her to see the tic by his left eye become increasingly more pronounced. With his face all but convulsing, Rosen bristled.

"How dare you try to railroad me? You forget I have your resignation. Come June, you're out of here."

"By that time, you'll have so much on your plate to say grace over you won't care anything about me. Besides, the Chief may want me to testify at your hearing. It would be hard for him to get my cooperation when the time came if he vetoed my memorandum to withdraw that resignation, now wouldn't it? Or you could just shred it while I wait and save yourself the embarrassment."

"Cézanne, are you crazy?"

"Homicide."

"We're not going to put some snip of a kid with a detective rank in charge of a major crimes unit—"

"Of course not. You'd have to promote me first."

"—you can't just come in here like you own the *forcocked* place—"

"People get promoted all the time for heroic deeds. Look at yourself. One day you're a flatfoot, next you're a headhunter. Now look at you. Talk about a meteoric rise—"

"Those days are over. There are guys in this department who have a lot more grade and service than you, who would kill for that slot. Promotions come through the ranks. That's the way we do it."

"I know you think I'm sap-green—"

"That doesn't begin to cover it. I think your brain's taken a direct hit from a stun gun."

"That's why I'm putting in for FBI school. You can send me to Quantico. I know the law, I've acquired a few street-smarts. Anything else I need, I'll learn in their training academy."

Anger pinched the corners of his mouth. He squinted fiercely while listening in stricken silence.

"It wouldn't be that strange having a lawyer over a unit like Homicide," she said, carefully loading her piece with *Plus-P* hollowpoints. "You obviously need time to digest this. Why don't you take the rest of the morning? Get back to me after Roby's funeral."

She snapped the cylinder shut and tucked the gun in her bag.

Sweat broke out above his upper lip. "I could put you

over Vice. You'd like heading up Vice."

"Homicide."

"Zannie—"

"Don't ever call me that again, Uncle Daniel."

"Zan, listen to me. Some things I just can't do."

"Then all I can say is, Kiss mine and cover yours."

His eyes blazed fire.

She slipped a hand into her coat pocket. "Last week, Roby Tyson told me I didn't have to take his side, just come out for the truth. Because if I got at the truth, I'd end up on his side." Knowing Rosen stood too far away to read the fine print, she pulled out the code enforcement summons and waved it. "Come Monday, I'm serving these search warrants for dental impressions. Darlene's, Doug Driskoll's, and yours—get the whole truth out."

"Good God, Cézanne. Think about what you're doing." Red slashes streaked his face like she'd turned a blow torch on him. "Don't complicate things any worse than they already are."

"Homicide."

"You bitch."

Their eyes locked in a murderous bent.

Silence stretched between them.

He pulled her resignation from under lock and key, and with an outstretched arm, held it where she could see. "Even exchange."

"You first." Her eyes flickered to the shredder and back.

Rosen cleared the paper path and fed the sheet into the machine's jaws. The blades caught the letter and devoured it faster than a tramp on a baloney sandwich.

With a smile on her face, she flicked the summons on his

blotter and walked to the exit, pausing on the way out for effect.

"We need to change the way we do things here, Danny. And if you don't like it, I know this Texas Ranger. . . ."

Chapter Thirty-Seven

The BMW clunked across town and died as Cézanne made a sharp right into an empty parking lot next to Reverend Willie Lee Washington's Celestial House of the Dove. She checked the address in the newspaper folded on her lap against the one on the building. No more pretending she had the wrong place. She cranked the engine until it caught and moved the car into a lined space.

A frail, white-haired officer in formal uniform stepped outside a set of massive red doors beneath the mortuary's porte côchere. Soon, three decrepit clones joined him. In tandem, each removed a white glove and dug a finger into their pockets for smokes.

The Brass sent an honor guard made up of broken-down, ten-days-'til-retirement has-beens. Probably fellows from Roby's academy days. She measured them with a cautious eye and decided they could use a canister of oxygen.

She rummaged through her purse, found her makeup bag and checked her face while the last of the honor guard ducked inside. In the mirror's reflection, she spotted Jinx Porter walking up the sidewalk with a cane, his bald head deflecting rays like sun through a magnifying glass.

She bailed out of the car and hurried to catch up.

The cane turned out to be an umbrella.

"Did I miss something?" She searched a perfect sky for clouds. "Is it supposed to rain?"

"You've never been to a Negro funeral parlor, have you?"

"No."

"You'll likely want to stick with me, then."

A metallic purple van with lightning bolt decals zig-zagging out from the headlights screeched to the curb in a cloud of brown smoke. She caught sight of the driver's eyes in the rearview mirror and thought he looked familiar. When he walked around to open the side door, she saw the "National Rodeo Finals" logo on his jacket, and almost pitched over in shock.

The shuttle driver let out eight to ten homeless people, each clutching two boxes of generic cigarettes and a bottle of wine. He jumped inside the van, stuck his head beyond the open door and looked the length of the street. His head disappeared from view, and the door slammed. Peeling tires and smoking rubber, the driver sped off down the road in a cornucopia of toxic fumes.

"Ohmygod. Did Roby know these people?"

"Willie Lee always cruises the night shelter right before a big funeral, to get the wailers and keeners." Jinx punctuated his words with a crisp nod.

"THE WHAT?"

"Wailers and keeners. It's an old Irish custom. Round up a bunch of old ladies to kick and scream and caterwaul during the service. Makes it look like the dead'll be sorely missed."

She narrowed her eyes in suspicion.

A man of indeterminate age and origin, wearing a robe iridescent enough to rival the sheen on his forehead, stepped out the front doors not twenty feet away. He lingered beneath the overhang and surveyed the Heavens. Finally, he shifted his eyes to the miscreants from the purple van. One *thumbs up* from him and the tramps tuned-up crying.

When the only black woman in the pack dropped to her knees and screamed bloody murder, Cézanne turned to Jinx for support.

"This is outrageous. This should be a dignified service to memorialize a wonderful man, and these people are making a mockery of it. What's wrong with you? You're screwing up your face like I have spinach between my teeth."

"Settle down. People are looking at you funny."

"At me? You think people are looking at me?" For a moment, she thought the neurons in her brain misfired.

"That's Washington's wife," Jinx growled out of the side of his mouth. "Roby helped put their oldest through junior college. Her grief is sincere. They've still got four kids in high school."

"This has to stop." She took a step.

He settled a hand on her arm. "Relax."

"You want me to relax?"

"I wish you would. Don't you have any Valium?"

"I'm trying to cut back." Her irritation was undisguised. He fished in his pocket, pulled out a cellophaned caplet backed with foil and offered it up. "What's that? Rohypnol?"

"Just a little something to take the edge off. Doctor prescribed them after my hemorrhoid surgery."

"Forget it. I don't need my senses dulled."

Jinx corkscrewed one eyebrow. "You may change your mind once you get inside."

He wasn't kidding.

They walked up the stairs to the landing. He threw back the double doors, and her lungs deflated.

The whole place was standing room only. An occasional hat, feathered and festive, pierced the gloom.

If this were her funeral, she thought, who'd show? A few figureheads from the top and the obligatory wreath, but no friends. Yet, for a social failure and outcast like Roby, the whole East side turned out.

There was much to learn about Roby Tyson.

They made their way down the aisle to the front where an all-black choir dressed in violet satin robes with red and gold sashes draped over their shoulders rose from their folding chairs. They broke into "Swing Low, Sweet Chariot", singing slowly, mournfully, and in a minor chord.

She grabbed Jinx's elbow and dug in her fingers. "This is turning into a freak show."

"What?" He thumbed at the singers. "Them? That's the choir from the First Mount Zion Missionary Church of the Shooting Star."

"Whose Midas touch was that?"

"Roby's." Jinx cocked his head as if he made sense of the madness. "Believe it or not, the man actually had a life before he met you. He patrolled Poly and Stop Six for twenty years, when you were still playing dress-up in your mama's old clothes. And he made a lot of friends doing it."

Strong, melodious voices dragged out the hymn, stretching what should have been a thirty-second verse into a minute and a half. When it took on the haunting tones of a dirge, a hefty soprano let out a beanstalk-climbing note that ran up three octaves and threatened to shatter the stained glass windows. Without warning, both rows of fifteen choir members launched into second verse, major chord, rock-a-pella.

Like flying purple people eaters on acid.

While mourners swayed between pews and clapped hands jubilee-style, Jinx steered her to a corded-off seat on the second row.

She caught him by the wrist and dug in her nails.

"We're in the wrong place," she hissed. "This is somebody else's funeral. Look over there." She pointed to a second coffin. "These must be members of a family who died."

"Free booze," Jinx said under his breath. "Willie Lee iced down twenty-five cases of Schlitz Malt Liquor as part of the pre-paid funeral package."

"Beer? That's booze in there?" she shrieked in a werewolf's-attacking-me, we're-all-gonna-die-and-you're-next voice. "In a friggin' coffin?"

"I hear the insulation's supposed to be real good."

"This is beyond the pale." She gave him her best *When-will-it-all-end?* look.

"Why don't you settle in and take a load off?"

"There's got to be a law. It's probably a felony, having hooch in here. We're felons. I'll look awful in jail greens."

"What're you gonna to do, call TABC? Roby knew what he was doing. This community loved him." Jinx stifled a yawn. "There's a lot more coloreds here than cops, that's for sure. And the way I figure it, that's two beers apiece. What church folks don't swill down, the cops will. Now put a lid on it and study your program."

She squinted at a wilted wreath. "What in the cathair is that?"

"A little jest." Jinx chuckled. "A couple of guys from the old school swung by Rose Hill Cemetery and swiped some flowers."

"That's funny to you?"

"It's not mean-spirited. Roby used to bring flowers to the secretaries every morning when he patrolled that beat."

"This must be what tripping on PCP is like."

They may as well have dedicated an entire day; no one

313

seemed in a hurry to end the celebration of Roby's life. It took the rag-tag pallbearers ten minutes to shuffle the body from the funeral home to the horse-drawn caisson waiting at the rear of the mortuary, underneath a cloth awning.

"Look at these people," she said. "You'd think somebody threw a party."

"They did. Lots of people die before they ever really live. Not Roby. They're here to celebrate his life. A good life. A full life."

At the graveside, Jinx muscled his way through the mourners with Cézanne in tow. He took a stance in front of a row of folding chairs filled with The Brass, crossed his arms over his chest and glowered until a couple of high-ups relinquished their seats.

"I've never seen that done before," she whispered, sliding in beside him. "You'd have been pretty embarrassed if they stayed put."

"Understand something," he said. "Being at one of the Reverend Willie Lee Washington's extravaganzas is like being on the Reservation. Willie Lee's the head Indian in charge, and The Brass represents the white man. They had the option of moving on their own, or those two prizefighters dressed in canary yellow tuxedos over there would've picked them up by the lapels and pitched them across the parking lot."

"So, next to Roby, we're the guests of honor?"

"Pretty much."

"What about The Brass?"

He dismissed them with a flick of the wrist. "They're here for show. Not because they appreciated him."

Jinx was right. They all had places they'd rather be. It was evidenced by their dull eyes, inattentive gazes, and droopy posture. But the rest of the folks—the community—

they came because they loved the guy.

The Reverend stepped up to a makeshift podium, and mourners fell silent at the sweep of his gaze.

"Praise God," he boomed.

Followed by a resounding "Amen."

While The Reverend seized every opportunity to pat himself on the back, whenever he mentioned Roby's contributions they were met with a unanimous, "You know that's right," "Amen, Brother," or "Praise the Lord."

Incredulous, Cézanne bent Jinx's ear.

"Roby created a scholarship at Poly High School?"

"Aw, that's old hat. He started that years ago."

"I don't get it. Roby was tighter than Dick's hatband."

"Not when it came to his daughter."

"Roby had a daughter?"

"Killed in a car wreck when she was a senior. Some people say that's why he drank."

The Reverend continued to spellbind listeners with his storytelling. At intervals, people chimed, "Amen." The Reverend cut his eyes to the night shelter vagabonds, where several dropped on all fours and howled on cue.

"Mista Roby touched a lot of folk," said the Reverend.

A lieutenant duded up in dress blues leaned over and buttonholed the guy next to him.

"He sure did. We got more complaints on that skullbuster for unreasonable use of force than—"

"Shut up," Cézanne snapped.

Leviticus Devilrow materialized out of nowhere and leveled a double-barrel glower until the lieutenant abandoned his chair and disappeared into the crowd.

Jinx flashed an approving grin. He cupped a hand to his mouth. "Ain't it great?"

"And now," the Reverend said gravely, "we would like to

extend Miz See-Zannie Martin, Mista Roby's special frien'—"

Six pints of blood settled in her feet.

"—the op-por-too-nitty," his voice rollercoastered with each enunciated syllable, "to touch our hearts with her words."

"Ohmygod. Jinx Porter, did you know about this? I've got Roby's Glock in my purse, and I'm pretty sure when this is over, I should use it."

"Step up to the plate, Counselor. Don't keep 'em waiting."

She rose on wobbly knees.

Behind the podium, she scanned the audience for friendly faces and spotted Reno sandwiched between a couple of motor jocks, her fiery curls haloing around her head like rusty bed springs. They exchanged a look as guarded as a Masonic handshake. Dabbing a lace hankie at the corner of one eye, the dancer favored her with a devious grin and slithered her tongue over her lips.

Elsewhere, a sea of eyeballs swam in their tears.

Without meaning to, Cézanne found herself developing an affinity for Roby's people. Off to one side, a wailer let out an eviscerating howl. Before Cézanne could stop it, a giggle escaped. She covered her face with her hands, and when she peeked through her fingers, no one seemed to notice her shoulders racked with laughter. They thought she was crying and tuned up as well.

Roby would've loved it.

She leaned into the mic and the words came easy. By the time she finished, she'd said what she knew and then cried for real.

When the last "Amen, Sister," rang out and she stepped away from the dais, Jinx Porter's umbrella shot open. He grabbed her elbow and pulled her under its shade. Dozens of parasols exploded in pinwheels of color.

Nearby, the Reverend's assistants yanked cloths off ten chicken coops, releasing the lids with a flourish.

Five hundred pigeons took flight.

And the people who came to make sure Roby was really dead ended up running for cover.

She took a last glance at the fresh mound of earth and wondered where she'd ever find another friend as good as the one she'd just lost.

Jinx Porter was on his way to the beer bash when Cézanne ditched him and headed for the BMW. A rustle from behind got her attention, and she whipped around, startled.

"Bobby? What're you doing here?"

"Lookin' out for you. Seems that's what I do best lately. Whatcha gonna do with yourself now that your partner's gone?"

"I dunno. Depending on who you ask, I'm either a hero or the goat."

"Come again?"

"The DA says I should've read Darlene her Miranda rights before I started questioning her, but I still maintain once they suspended me, I no longer had departmental authority to take her into custody."

Bobby's eyes crinkled at the corners.

"Pretty crafty," he said in a voice thick with admiration. "If I know my girl like I think I do, I bet you'll figure out a way to prosecute her, even if you have to take the case before the Grand Jury all by yourself."

My girl. He said, My girl.

The man had a way of drawing the current out of her.

Like plugging a One-Ten into a Two-Twenty outlet.

"Krivnek spilled the beans, you know," she said. "He said Roby asked to be buried next to Carri." She searched his face for a comforting sign. "Sad, isn't it? If it hadn't been for me and Roby, the Cranes would still be floating through their days like zombies. But even with plenty of real estate on either side of the burial plot, Captain wouldn't stand for it."

She ducked her head and toed the ground with her shoe.

"What's that?" Bobby asked, pointing.

The Reverend's strongmen had shed their yellow jackets and were trying to give themselves hernias unloading a huge bronze without benefit of a dolly.

"That? It's a Valkyrie," Cézanne explained. "Carri Crane had a fine arts degree. Mrs. Crane said she made it in college. According to Norse mythology, the Valkyries carried slain warriors to Valhalla. Pretty apropos, don't you think?"

"Spooky."

While he regarded the impressive sight, she filled in the details.

"When The Brass put Carri in Narcotics, she made a will. She actually left a huge, winged Pegasus to Roby. Only, the Cranes house is zoned historical, and the horse is in an English garden in the back yard. It would have taken a court order to cut into their wrought-iron fence. So I practiced a little hostage negotiation technique. Showed up at their door last night with a blow torch and a compromise: *donate the smaller one or the fence gets it.*"

"You didn't."

"Even sensible people have a little guerilla warfare in them."

He wrapped his arms around her and pulled her close.

"How did all this happen, Bobby?"

"Life's about learning lessons," he said, whispering into her hair in a way that made her ankles start to dissolve. "You keep repeating your mistakes until you learn the lesson. When you learn all you're supposed to learn, you get to put your books down and go home."

"What did I learn?"

"The lesson's different for each of us."

Her sour mood got the best of her. Pulling the lapels of the cashmere coat tight against her chin, she snuggled into the soft wool and thought of the first time she and Roby met. Who would have guessed they'd end up the kind of friends who would take a bullet for each other? She took in a cleansing breath and smelled rain in the air.

When she looked up, Doug Driskoll was headed straight for her.

"Oh shit."

She unsnapped her purse, shoved Roby's Glock and four clips aside and dug for her wallet. By the time she finished inventorying her money, the scent of *Angel for Men* invaded her nostrils.

"Hey, Babe," Doug said, regarding Bobby propped up against the BMW as if he were nothing more than the latest in hood ornaments. "Looks like your old partner pulled off the ultimate *Fuck you*. Did you see The Brass? Wish I had a picture of them covered in pigeon shit."

"What do you want?"

"Let's go somewhere quiet and talk. There's a lot between us that's still unsaid, and I think if we pull together I can help you get through this."

With a slew of profanity hotwired to her tongue, she felt a devilish smile spread across her face. Her cheeks tightened until they hurt.

"You don't happen to have change for a hundred, do you Detective Driskoll? I didn't think so. Well don't worry, I can handle it. Wait over there by that tree, and I'll be along."

God love him, he had no idea he was fixing to get called everything but a white man.

Driskoll swaggered off, casting devious glances at a couple of unescorted ladies lingering near the curb. Reno chugged by in her clunker and flipped him a stiff middle finger.

Cézanne turned to Bobby. The sight of his strong jaw and the comfort of even stronger character propelled her to her tiptoes. She planted an impromptu kiss on his chin.

"Stay put, Sheriff. There're a few things I've been waiting for the right moment to say." She flashed Doug a smile and thought of a hungry cuss-kitty polishing off a whole Ben Franklin.

She started toward Driskoll, then whipped around. "Tell me something?"

"What's on your mind, City Slicker?"

"At the moment, I'm still on restricted duty. I'm not sure where I stand at the PD, but I know the DA thinks I'm a loose cannon. Since I can't very well be a prosecutor right now, I might as well fight tooth and toenail to stay in Homicide until I can rehabilitate my reputation."

He reached for her hand and examined it closely.

"Think you could learn to milk cows? I know a place, could sure use your company." He gave her an approving once over. "If that ain't your cup of tea, I've got this investigator position I've been trying to fill."

"Where?"

"At the SO, of course."

His smile sent a jolt straight down to her

Uh-oh.

"By the way, I inherited a dog," she said. "Butch. Don't look so excited. He stares at me while I'm dressing. And this morning, he bit me. He's a Scottie and I hate him."

"You'll have him eating out of your hand before you know it."

She sensed Bobby was right.

Roby's funeral had a way of making her tell things she never intended to breathe a word of, like the time at the laundromat when Roby knocked the last of the rookie mania out of her. But folks laughed and some cried and hundreds of people she didn't even know made her feel like one of the family, and she wove her own tales of a big man she hoped would be made even bigger.

And as for Bobby Noah, it was now or never.

Which meant now.

"Do you really think we've got much of a future together, Sheriff?"

"What do you think?"

She could hardly believe her chutzpah.

"When I come back, I'm going to tell you about a woman who spent her formative years in a concentration camp. And about a little girl named Monet, and what happened a few weeks shy of her thirteenth birthday. And if you still want me—"

She drew in a hopeful breath.

."I'm all yours."

Epilogue

Cézanne said good-bye to Bobby with a promise to meet him at the farm for a good old-fashioned barbeque cookout. The morning chill had numbed her bones, but when she drove past the PD and saw Rosen's car still in its parking slot, a white-hot heat that started in her toes raged to the hair follicles on top of her head and stayed there. She had no choice but to go inside.

She found Rosen hovering over the wastebasket, shoveling handfuls of shredded paper into a plastic garbage bag. When he saw her, his satisfaction turned to dread, and the skin below his left eye began to flutter.

He said, "Did you come back to rub it in?"

"I'm here to see whether you decided to push that promotion through."

"You could rake in tons of money, working at a law firm."

"I've given that a lot of thought. It won't be so bad trying to live within my means a few more years." She locked her knees together to keep from shaking. "This place is going to the dogs. We need honest people running this organization. I can always be an attorney somewhere down the road. At least this way, as long as I'm around, I can keep an eye out. . . ."

On you.

"All right, you get your promotion." When she didn't leave, he let out an exasperated, "Now, what?"

"I want carte blanche to transfer any backstabbers."

"A bit early to be throwing your weight around, don't you think?"

"I intend to surround myself with trustworthy people."

"Just don't get carried away. Those men have over a hundred years of combined experience."

He stuffed the last of the strips into the garbage bag and knotted the tie-ends. The skin under his eye was still jumping.

"Look, Zannie, I apologize for calling you a bitch earlier."

"No offense taken. That's what men always call women who shrivel their dicks down to tequila worms."

She glided to the door so fast she practically left a vapor trail on her way out.

Having tossed the trash bag into the dumpster and returned to his office to check out the latest batch of recruits from his window, Deputy Chief Daniel J. Rosen flopped into his big leather chair, popped a couple of antacid tabs in his mouth and crunched with a vengeance. The unscheduled return of that conniving, cutthroat, pain-in-the-ass niece he shared DNA with caused the knife fight in his stomach to go from aggravated assault-deadly weapon to attempted murder on the pain scale.

For someone with the power to bust him back to clerking for his father-in-law, the little blackmailer treated him with unaccustomed civility.

Rosen was staring at an invisible point in space, doing a slow burn, when Crane appeared, seemingly out of the ether.

"Charlie." His stomach flared. "Just the person I wanted to see."

Crane's faded workshirt and the threadbare sheen of his khakis made his clothes look as if they barely survived the rinse cycle. The prickle of yesterday's whiskers shined white against his red complexion, and he heightened the tension by doubling up his fist like he might be fixing to move the air in front of Rosen's nose.

In a growl almost lethal, Crane said, "I hate what Suezanne Martin did to my family. I want her gone before she drags my name and my career through the mud. I don't care for the way she does business; and as for you, I've been here too long to let some One-Star ass-wipe with a Napoleon complex ram anything else down my throat. The case is done."

"Simmer down, Chuck, before you have an aneurysm. This time, you and I are on the same side. I came up with an idea, but you'll have to go along for it to work."

Crane fixed him with a crazed stare.

"We'll move you out of Homicide—"

"The hell you say—"

"Calm down and listen to me."

The lamp's colored glass deflected its illumination into a rectangle of bright yellow and for a second, Rosen thought Crane might grab the light by its base and cave his skull in.

"We'll put her in charge of Homicide, just for awhile. Nobody'll think anything of it; she's a lawyer now, for Chrissake. In a day or so, we'll re-open that murder case from the upper West side . . . what did the press call it?"

That got his attention. "Surely, you're not talking about The Great Dane Murder?"

"Yeah . . . and assign it to her. Force her into a fishbowl. Believe me, she'll never know what hit her once she has to start dealing with the media."

Crane snapped, "That's a cold case. I worked it myself.

There's no way she can crack it."

"Exactly." Rosen's eyes exploded like tracers ricocheting through the room, moving at the same feverish pace as his thoughts. "We'll call a press conference and announce her promotion. We'll say we're starting a Cold Case Squad and we'll say that she's directly accountable for its success or failure. She'll crater under the pressure."

"She doesn't have the experience," Crane said, testing the idea. His tongue darted over his chapped lips in a way that looked like he was licking his chops. "She'll fold."

"She put in for FBI school."

"You're not planning to send her, are you?"

"Hell, no."

Crane seconded Rosen with a pensive, "So, you're going to let her fall flat on her face, huh?" He rubbed the sweat off his forehead, and his search for closure seemed to be over. "Joey Wehmeyer was my best investigator. He died working The Great Dane Murder. I still think what happened to him was no accident. That case poisoned everyone who ever touched it."

Rosen's eyes pinned him. "And that's how we get rid of her."